W9-CNM-735

A reckless promise, made in the glow of first love, now bound Lord Sebastian Benbury to the Lady Beatrice. But though her beauty still stirred his inner fires, nothing could burn away the far-off memory of her with another man!

* * *

"I do not hate you," he said.

"Liar," she said softly. Her mouth trembled as though she might start crying, but her eyes were cold, colder than he had ever seen them. Their chill bit through him.

"I do not hate you," he said again. He was angry with her, angrier than he had yet been, and he did not know why. "I despise you."

The words hung in the air—he could not snatch them back. She caught her breath and then nodded. "So." She opened her hand, and rose petals fell to the ground like snow. "We are good company after all. You cannot despise me as much as I despise myself."

Without curtsying, without asking for leave, she turned and walked away.

"Beatrice." He had not meant to say he despised her. That was too simple a name for what he felt...!

Praise for Katy Cooper's first book

PRINCE OF HEARTS

"With a rare magic and grace, Katy Cooper
creates a vivid world of history and passion that readers
are bound to adore. An unforgettable debut!"
—bestselling author Miranda Jarrett

"This is a powerful, captivating novel....
Ms. Cooper carves out a slice of history, mixes it with
matters of the heart, and emerges triumphant."
—*Rendezvous*

DON'T MISS THESE OTHER
TITLES AVAILABLE NOW:

#635 BOUNTY HUNTER'S BRIDE
Carol Finch

#636 BADLANDS HEART
Ruth Langan

#637 NORWYCK'S LADY
Margo Maguire

KATY COOPER

LORD SEBASTIAN'S WIFE

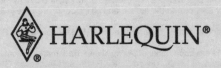

HARLEQUIN®

TORONTO • NEW YORK • LONDON
AMSTERDAM • PARIS • SYDNEY • HAMBURG
STOCKHOLM • ATHENS • TOKYO • MILAN • MADRID
PRAGUE • WARSAW • BUDAPEST • AUCKLAND

If you purchased this book without a cover you should be aware that this book is stolen property. It was reported as "unsold and destroyed" to the publisher, and neither the author nor the publisher has received any payment for this "stripped book."

ISBN 0-373-29238-4

LORD SEBASTIAN'S WIFE

Copyright © 2002 by Kathleen V. Cooper

All rights reserved. Except for use in any review, the reproduction or utilization of this work in whole or in part in any form by any electronic, mechanical or other means, now known or hereafter invented, including xerography, photocopying and recording, or in any information storage or retrieval system, is forbidden without the written permission of the publisher, Harlequin Enterprises Limited, 225 Duncan Mill Road, Don Mills, Ontario, Canada M3B 3K9.

All characters in this book have no existence outside the imagination of the author and have no relation whatsoever to anyone bearing the same name or names. They are not even distantly inspired by any individual known or unknown to the author, and all incidents are pure invention.

This edition published by arrangement with Harlequin Books S.A.

® and TM are trademarks of the publisher. Trademarks indicated with ® are registered in the United States Patent and Trademark Office, the Canadian Trade Marks Office and in other countries.

Visit us at www.eHarlequin.com

Printed in U.S.A.

Available from Harlequin Historicals and
KATY COOPER

Prince of Hearts #525
Lord Sebastian's Wife #638

Please address questions and book requests to:
Harlequin Reader Service
U.S.: 3010 Walden Ave., P.O. Box 1325, Buffalo, NY 14269
Canadian: P.O. Box 609, Fort Erie, Ont. L2A 5X3

To the Hussies, for prayers, hugs, CBs, warmth,
generosity and a place to hide
when it gets really rough out there.

Chapter One

London
July 1521

When Sebastian Benbury stepped onto the water stairs at the Earl of Wednesfield's London residence and began walking through the garden toward the riverside door, there was nothing about Coleville House to indicate that disaster lurked within its walls.

Golden in the July sunlight, the house appeared as it always had, its hundred windows glittering, its roofs reaching heavenward. As he walked the winding path through knots of herbs and flowers, as he crossed the threshold into a screens passage that was blind-dark after the brilliant light outside, Sebastian had no sense that his life was about to be irrevocably changed.

He paused in the passage, blinking his eyes to clear his vision. Out of the darkness an usher murmured, asking him if he wished to be announced. Sebastian shook his head and waved the usher away. Since giving up his post at Court, he had been a guest here, enjoying the Earl of Wednesfield's gracious hospitality. He did not need to be announced.

As Sebastian's vision cleared, a man spoke in the hall. "Why are you in black, Bea?"

The voice was strange yet recognition tickled on the edges of Sebastian's awareness, as if he knew the speaker. But how? He did not know anyone close enough to Beatrice Coleville Manners to call her by her pet name who was not also aware that she had recently been widowed.

"My husband died a fortnight ago. God rest his soul," Beatrice replied in her low, soft voice. The sound of it awoke tangled emotions in Sebastian's chest, pain and anger so mixed that he did not know how to separate them. Instead he swallowed them both, forcing them down beyond awareness with the skill of practice.

In the hall, there was a splatter, as if someone had spilled wine on the flagstone floor. The stranger said, "Then Sebastian Benbury is dead."

Dead? Who was this stranger who assumed that if Beatrice was a widow, Sebastian must be the husband she had lost? Crossing himself against the ill chance raised by the stranger's remark, Sebastian walked through the gap in the screens that led to the hall. "I am alive as anyone in this room. Who says I am dead?"

His glance flicked over Beatrice's sister, Cecilia, and the strange man and woman at her side before going to Beatrice, cool and distant in her widow's black. Beatrice, whom he had once loved.

"John does," Cecilia said.

Sebastian brought his gaze back to the strange man. His heart began to pound as if his body recognized the nearly familiar stranger before his eyes did, and then his eyes knew. The stranger was Beatrice's brother, John Coleville. He had left England five years ago, so long ago that he could not know of Beatrice's marriage to Thomas Manners. That was why he had made the mistake about Beatrice's late husband.

John is home. The impact of it struck him all at once and delighted laughter bubbled up, drowning everything but joy in its flood. John had been companion, friend, everything Sebastian had imagined a brother would be. Sebastian rushed forward to embrace him, to confirm the truth of this homecoming with the certainty of touch.

"Thank God! Thank God for it!" he cried, the words hardly serving to convey his pleasure.

His happiness was so intense that it took him a moment to realize that John was neither laughing nor returning his embrace. Sebastian's laughter died. He loosened his grip.

"You do not seem happy to see me, my friend. What ails you?"

"I am glad, more glad than you can know, to see you," John said grimly, reaching up to grasp Sebastian's wrists.

"You look it," Sebastian said, and pulled free of John's hands. "It cannot be grief for poor Thomas Manners that makes you look so black. You never knew the man. Come, tell me, tell us all. Why the long face?"

"Because Bea says she is the widow of a man she cannot have married."

Sebastian stared at him, the back of his neck prickling as if at the rumor of catastrophe. "I witnessed their marriage and Ceci attended her. Do you tell us we were not there, that it was all a dream?''

''No. I am sure there was a wedding. I am telling you that the marriage was invalid.''

''Invalid? On what grounds?''

''That she was promised to another man,'' John said. ''Promised in a binding betrothal.''

''Another man?'' he asked, disbelieving. His heart pounded, loud in his ears, hard against his breastbone. He had thought he knew the worst Beatrice could do. His sense of approaching disaster deepened. ''Are you saying she has known yet *another* man?''

''Another man? What are you babbling about?'' John asked, frowning, and shook his head. ''She is betrothed to you, Sebastian.''

''To me?'' The pounding of his heart was swallowed by a vast silence, a numbed stillness.

Beatrice cried, ''Are you mad? We are no more betrothed than…than… We are not betrothed. Do you think I could make such a mistake?''

''Or I?'' Sebastian demanded. ''This is not funny, John.''

''It is not jest, Sebastian, and I do not think it funny. Do you not remember that Twelfth Night when you and your family joined us at Wednesfield? I filched a ewer of mead and the three of us drank it in the old tower. You and Beatrice promised to marry when you were grown and then we all laughed and drank some more.''

''Oh, blessed Virgin,'' Beatrice said, closing her eyes.

''I do not re—'' But he did remember, no matter how he tried to forget. Details he had wanted to bury rose up from the depths of his mind. Words, the words of a vow… "Yes, now I do! What foolishness is this? We made no promises that bound." Promises to break, yes, not promises to bind.

"That is not what I remember, Sebastian. Think. Think what you said, the words you used. The promises you made bind you."

Beatrice clenched her hands into fists as if she might batter her way out of this. "You are no churchman. How can you know for certain?"

In a distant corner of his mind Sebastian wondered if perhaps he slept and John's appalling announcement was a part of a nightmare from which he would soon awaken. Surely this madness was the stuff of dreams. Otherwise his life had been disordered beyond recognition in the space of five minutes.

"Do you not remember? You promised to have Sebastian as your husband and he promised to have you as his wife. Both of you promised without conditions. You made a binding marriage between you," John said. "I have lived among churchmen for the last three years, Bea. Canon law fills the air in Rome. A man who has ears to hear cannot help learning a little."

Sebastian knew a little canon law, as well. Enough, he had thought, to keep himself from doing just what John claimed they had done. "We did not lie together. It cannot be binding."

"That does not matter in this case. If you never lie with her, she will still be your wife before God," John said gently.

"I cannot believe this," Beatrice said. She went to sit on one of the benches pushed against the wall and leaned her head back, her hands lying slack on her lap. For a moment Sebastian wanted to go sit beside her, companions in calamity. But he could not, not when she had betrayed him, not when she had abandoned honor as easily and thoughtlessly as she might discard a gown that no longer fit.

He had to do something, anything, to avert this disaster.

"I am betrothed to Cecilia," he said.

"You cannot be," John said.

At the same moment Cecilia said, "Do not lie, Sebastian. It will only confuse matters."

"We can pretend it never happened. If no one knows..."

His voice slowed. Truth was sinking into him, the awareness that he would not awaken from this nightmare slowly breaking over him. No matter how he might wish it otherwise, his betrothal to Beatrice was real, as unbreakable and real as marriage. He could behave like a fool and a child, and fight it for a time, but to what end? Damage to his soul, damage to his honor, and marriage to Beatrice at the end of it anyway.

But, God help him, he wished it were not true.

"You will know, Sebastian. And God will know. Can you take another woman to wife, knowing you make a concubine of her? And if you do not marry, who will your heirs be?" John asked.

"How do I get out of this?" Beatrice asked, her voice flat, bled of expression.

Sebastian glanced at her. Against the black of her hood and bodice, her pallor was stark, the color leached even from her down-turned mouth. She looked weary and sad, a woman alone despite the company of her kinsmen. Pity moved in him, pity she did not deserve, pity he refused to feel. Balling his hands into fists, he turned away and walked to the opposite side of the room. He leaned against the wall and pressed his forehead against its cool stone. Behind him, the others continued as if he were still in their midst, while slowly he tried to absorb the shocks of the afternoon— John's unexpected homecoming, his disastrous announcement.

"Ceci, why do they fight this? What has happened while I have been away?" John asked.

"I do not know, John. I do not now nor have I ever understood why they are at odds."

"It avails you nothing to do this!" Beatrice cried. "You will do most good by telling me how I may escape!"

"There is no way. You are married to Sebastian," John said.

"If I deny it? What then, O brother?"

"Sebastian can sue you to live with him."

"And how many witnesses will he need? Is one enough? And will you oppose me in this, my brother?" The fraying edge of Beatrice's temper rang clearly in the sharpness of her tone.

"It takes two witnesses to make a case, but if you marry another man, you will be committing bigamy and your children will be bastards," John said.

"I do not intend to marry again. Once was enough to last me a lifetime."

"Bea, you know you are married," Cecilia said.

"There are no witnesses!"

"I will be a witness to your admission of the promise," Cecilia said, her voice firm. "With John, that is two witnesses."

"A pox on you!" Beatrice's voice caught on the last word.

Sebastian lifted his head. The moment had come for

him to put an end to her bootless protests. He and Beatrice must face what they had done—it was past time to honor a promise that should not have been forgotten in the first place. This marriage was calamitous, but they had sown its seeds themselves. Who better to reap the bitter crop? He turned and crossed the hall, joining them by the hearth once more. He faced Beatrice, forced himself to confront her beauty, to meet her clear blue eyes steadily and to hold his simmering anger in check.

"I cannot marry another woman, knowing the marriage is a lie. I cannot let her risk her life to bear me a son, knowing that son is a bastard. You are my wife, as much as I wish it otherwise, Beatrice, and if you have a particle of honor left, you will come live with me as my wife."

"I will not. I will not be wife to a man who scorns me as you do," Beatrice said, glaring at him as if this garboil was entirely his fault, as if she had not made the same witless promises as he.

His anger flared. "I do not desire to be married to a woman so stupid with pride she will ruin herself rather than yield, but unfortunately, I am betrothed to one and have no choice. In law, Beatrice, you are already my wife and as such you owe me obedience."

"How dare you!"

John went to sit beside her and laid a hand over hers. "Beatrice, be sensible. You cannot win, not if Ceci and I both bear witness against you. Nor can you wish to spend the rest of your life in limbo, neither wife nor widow nor maid. I do not know what has happened to estrange you from Sebastian nor do I understand why the pair of you are behaving as if we were all back in the nursery, but surely neither of you is foolish enough to ruin your lives.''

Beatrice turned her head and stared at John for a long moment, her free hand gripping the front of the bench with such force her knuckles whitened. ''This means I am trapped.''

''We both are,'' Sebastian said. Stubborn jade, could she not see that?

''Yes, you are,'' John said gently, ''but only so long as you both see it so.''

Beatrice slipped her hand free of John's and pressed it to her temple. ''My head aches. I cannot listen to another moment of this. You will please excuse me.'' She stood, sketched a stiff curtsy at Sebastian, and left the hall without a backward glance.

Sebastian watched her go, his hands still fisted. Then he turned on John, resentment clenching into a hard knot in the middle of his chest, impossible to swallow or ignore. If John had remained in exile, painting pictures like a merchant's son... ''Why did you come back now? Why could you not stay in Rome?''

''I wanted to come home.'' John's voice was soft. He nodded toward his companion. ''I wanted to bring Lucia, my wife, home.''

Sebastian's face burned. If all his dreams and hopes were in ruins now, it was not because John had come home. It was because he had once been a fool for love.

John went on, his voice hard. ''I will not apologize for this, Sebastian. I had no way to know you and Beatrice were not married and raising a handful of yellow-headed babies.''

''I know, I know. Forgive me, I beg of you.'' He sighed and put his cap on. ''What an accursed garboil this is. I must go to my lawyer and I must find your father. There are contracts to amend.''

He crossed the hall to Cecilia. ''Ceci, I am sorry. What will become of you now?'' He had thought to marry her, clever and calm. Unlike her sister, she had been a sensible choice.

She took his hand and squeezed it. ''Dear Sebastian, do not worry about me. All will be well.''

''I cannot help worrying,'' he said. ''I have loved you for a long time.''

''As I love you and my sister. If you wish to do anything for me, mend this rift with Beatrice.''

''I cannot,'' he said, his voice low as if to conceal what he admitted. ''I cannot help thinking of her with Conyers and then I am so angry I cannot see anything.''

Her brows quirked together over her short nose. ''She does not love him, Sebastian.''

''Then it is worse than I thought.'' He sighed. ''Leave it be, Ceci. You cannot make it right.'' He kissed her forehead, and then stepped beyond her and embraced John. ''I am glad you are home, John. I could wish you had not had such news to bring with you, but I am glad you came before Ceci was utterly ruined. Your parents have kindly given me leave to stay here while I am in London, so I shall see you again later.'' He bowed to John's wife, still silent at his side, then turned and left the hall, walking behind the screen without a backward glance.

The ordeal of facing the earl awaited.

Only the busk in her pair-of-bodies kept Beatrice from hunching over to soothe the pain slashing across her abdomen. This could not be happening to her, not after everything else.

Pushing away from her bedchamber door, she crossed the room to kneel at the prie-dieu against the far wall. *What shall I pray for? Shall I pray for mercy, for aid? Or shall I pray for answers, answers that will not come?*

She could find no peace, no matter where she turned. Instead she found despair, as if her heart were under a cold, steady rain. Despair was a sin and she was weary of sin. Would it never end? Was this awful grayness clouding her heart never to be lifted, even if she did all her duty? She gripped the railing of the prie-dieu and leaned her forehead against her knotted hands.

She feared that she would spend her life struggling to do right, only to find that she had failed despite all her effort. She was weary, so tired of fighting for peace and a clean heart that sometimes she half wished the sweating sickness would swoop down and carry her away. But her wish was not much better than self-destruction, blackening her soul with yet another sin.

And now this. Trapped in another marriage, once more at the mercy of a man who would have none. Were her sins so terrible they warranted such punishment? She had done penance for the sins of the past year. Surely that had been enough…

Someone tapped on the door and opened it, the hinges creaking.

"Leave me be," Beatrice said without looking to see who it was. She could not bear company, did not have the strength to pretend a calm she did not feel.

"It is I, Beatrice," Cecilia said.

Beatrice lifted her head and stared at her across the

width of the room. Cecilia gasped at whatever she saw
in Beatrice's face, slipping into the room and closing
the door behind her.

"I do not want your pity," Beatrice said. Her voice,
in the quiet room, was harsh and unwelcoming. *Please
do not go, do not leave me.* "I said, leave me be. Do
as I bid you."

"I shall not." Cecilia sat down on the chest at the
end of the bed and folded her hands in her lap.

How obstinate they were as a family, how determined, each of them, to have his or her will. Beatrice
did not have the strength to fight her sister. Marriage
to Manners had stripped her of stubbornness, leaving
her as passive as a feeble-minded nun.

"I am trying to pray," she said.

"Only trying?"

Beatrice's breath caught. "I cannot pray if you
watch me."

"I worry about you," Cecilia said.

"Do not. There is no need." *I do not deserve it.*

"I do not like to see you and Sebastian at such odds.
And now that you are married—"

"Do not speak of it!" She could not talk about it,
not to anyone. "It would be better for everyone if he
married you—"

"Not for me, Beatrice, never for me," Cecilia said,
stiffening. "Do not think that."

"Why not? You have always been good friends,
much at ease with one another. You would deal well
together and both of you could do worse." It was easier to talk of Cecilia's problems and heart than of her
own.

"I cannot marry Sebastian. I was wrong to think I
could." Cecilia clamped her mouth shut.

What now? Beatrice rubbed the shelf. The kneeler had no cushion and was hard even through the layers of her petticoats. The window above the prie-dieu was open to the July afternoon. Below, in the garden, men murmured together and then laughed. The sound was loud in the silence between her and Cecilia and made her think of gardens and gardeners. Would Sebastian let her tend his gardens, or would he forbid it, as Thomas had done? *I will not think of it.* She dared not hope.

She opened her mouth to ask Cecilia to leave. "Do you ever pray and think God and the saints are not listening?" Tears came out of nowhere and filled her eyes; her heart felt as though the words had been torn out of it.

"No," Cecilia whispered. "Do you feel so alone?"

"Yes." Beatrice put her head down on her hands and wept.

Her sister was beside her in a moment, strong arms wrapped tightly around her as if she would hold all the demons at bay.

"Hush, my honey, hush. Hush, dearling."

Beatrice rested against her, sobs shaking her. She was weary of this, as well, the tears that brought no relief. Finally the weeping subsided, leaving her with swollen eyes and an aching head.

"I have no more strength left, Ceci," she murmured. "I have no strength to be married."

"You will not need strength, lovely," Cecilia replied, rubbing Beatrice's back with long, firm strokes. "Sebastian will care for you."

If only she could believe that. He had never harmed her, but she had never been in his power before. *I cannot endure any more. It will kill me.*

"Will he?" she mumbled. "He hates me."

"He loves you," Cecilia said. "Let me unlace you and then you lie down and rest. Anyone who thinks God does not listen when she prays is too weary to think clearly. You will be better for sleep, I promise you."

Beatrice straightened, laughing without amusement. "But I do not sleep, Ceci. I have not slept in years."

Cecilia stiffened, as if Beatrice had surprised her, then rose her feet. She took Beatrice's hands and pulled her up. "That does not mean you will not sleep now. Shall I play for you? It will only take a moment to bring my lute from the solar."

"No. I thank you, no. I shall lie down, as you bid me, but only if you leave me in peace."

Cecilia frowned. "Are you certain of this?"

"Yes. Grant me peace, I beg of you."

"Very well. I do not like it, but if that is what you want." She still frowned, eyes sharp with worry.

"It is. Go, Ceci. Please."

After unlacing Beatrice, Ceci left. Beatrice lifted the edge of her bodice and untied her busk lace. She pulled the busk out and laid it beside her on the bed. It was a good one, made of ivory and carved with saints and animals, flowers and plants. Thomas had given it to her; she hated it.

She rolled away from it and curled herself into a ball, letting the tears fall once more.

Chapter Two

The Earl and Countess of Wednesfield had left for Coleville House by the time Sebastian reached Westminster. Cursing his luck under his breath, he dropped a few coins into the usher's outstretched hand and returned to the water stairs. Please God the tide had not turned. Otherwise he would be trapped here for an hour or more, if not all night.

"My lord is in a great hurry," his gentleman, Ned, observed.

"Hold your tongue and find me a boatman," Sebastian said, frowning at him. The last thing he wanted or needed was a clack-tongued fool yammering in his ear.

Muttering, Ned shoved his way through the crowd at the bottom of the stairs. He disappeared for a moment and then reappeared, bounding like hound to Sebastian's side. "I have found the man, my lord. But it will cost you."

"Everything costs me," Sebastian said. "Lead on."

The tide was with them, lending speed to the return journey. Pulling his short gown around him, Sebastian slouched in his end of the boat, listening with half an ear to the boatman's shouts and curses, and to the abuse offered in reply. He hated London—hated the river, hated Court, hated the filthy, crowded streets. With the whole of his soul, he wanted to be home at Benbury, quietly filling his empty coffers by enlarging his flocks of sheep. But it was not the latent wealth of Benbury's fields he longed for; it was for the house itself, set behind its low walls, girdled by green gardens, a place of peace.

He scowled and the boatman rowed harder. There had never been peace where Beatrice was; Benbury would not be the sanctuary he had longed for.

The trip back to Coleville House was shorter than the trip away, and not only because he had been driven by the tide. He dreaded the coming interview with Lord Wednesfield, knowing that the earl would be displeased at the change in plans—if he was not outright angry. And what to tell him? That his elder daughter, in defiance of everything she had been taught, had made a marriage for herself the instant she crossed the threshold into womanhood? The earl would knock the teeth out of Sebastian's head for his presumption. And Sebastian would deserve it.

The boat pulled up at the landing by Coleville House. Climbing out, Sebastian mounted the steps that led into the garden, his thoughts still turning like a whirligig. Could he not simply say he preferred Beatrice to Cecilia? It had once been true enough.

The slap of Ned's shoes on the stone-flagged path disrupted Sebastian's thoughts. ''He took all my money, my lord. I shall need more,'' Ned said at his shoulder.

He did not turn to look at Ned. ''Not one penny more. You will not need it at Benbury.''

"Benbury, my lord? We are leaving London?"

"Tomorrow or the day after. Friday at the latest. You will need to make the arrangements."

"Aye, my lord. As you wish."

In the hall, the steward told Sebastian that the earl and countess had withdrawn to the solar above when they returned to Coleville House. Brushing off the man's offer to announce him, Sebastian crossed the hall to the stairs behind the dais that led to the solar. Though he dreaded the coming interview with the earl, he dreaded waiting for it more. He took the stairs two at a time. Once he set things in motion, they would be beyond his power to stop.

In the solar, the earl and countess sat side by side in the heavy chairs set beside open windows. The countess was busy with stitchery while the earl sat with his chin sunk on his breast and his hands folded on his stomach, apparently lost in thought and far from the room.

Sebastian bowed and said, "My lord, I should like to speak to you. For your ears alone."

The earl lifted his head and looked at Sebastian, his eyes narrowed suspiciously. His stare lasted only a moment, but it was long enough to make Sebastian feel as if the old man had seen into the dark depths of his soul. He repressed the urge to look away, the stronger urge to squirm like a boy. At the edge of his vision, the countess set down her needlework and frowned at him.

"Do you wish this audience now?" the earl asked, his hands still folded over his stomach.

Sebastian swallowed. "Yes, my lord, an it please you."

"This is in aid of what?"

"My betrothal to your daughter."

The earl's eyes opened at that, his face smoothing into the mask of amiable neutrality that he wore at Court. Did he suspect what was afoot? How could he? Yet he clearly thought something was odd.

"Walk with me." The earl stood and put his hand on Sebastian's shoulder, as full of vigor as he had been full of lassitude only a moment before. His fingers gripped Sebastian, the pressure uncomfortable through the thick layers of gown, doublet and shirt. Without the padding those fingers would have bruised him. Was the earl reminding him not to displease him? Or was this his ordinary response to dread? Sebastian had known the earl his whole life, but he could not answer his own questions.

He waited to speak until they were in the garden, filled to the tops of its walls with the long golden light of late afternoon. The gray shadows of oncoming dusk gathered softly under the plants that stood in solitary knots. None too soon, the endless day moved toward its close.

"What of your betrothal to my daughter?" the earl asked, releasing his shoulder.

Sebastian turned to face him. "I wish to marry your daughter Beatrice, not your daughter Cecilia."

The earl's brows lifted. "What is this?"

"I prefer Beatrice to Cecilia. Now that she is a widow, I am free to follow that preference."

Without so much as a flicker of change in his expression, the earl clouted Sebastian in the ear. Sebastian staggered, more from surprise than from the strength of the blow, though it still made his head ring.

"My lord?"

"That is for taking me for a fool."

Sebastian rubbed his ear. "I do not understand, my lord."

The earl cuffed him again, the harder blow knocking Sebastian back a step. Anger shot him forward, but he caught himself before he raised a hand against Wednesfield. Not only did the earl outrank him, but he had acted as a father to Sebastian for many years. He had earned the right to chastise Sebastian, even if it was with his hands.

"My lord! I have not deserved this."

"For lying to me, you deserve it. For telling me stupid lies, you deserve it more," the earl said, his mouth hard. "Now, tell me the truth and have done with this foolishness."

He should have known he would not escape without confessing the true story of the betrothal. "I beg of you, my lord, do not strike me again until you have heard the whole of it."

The earl nodded, his mouth a white-edged line, his brows pulled down over the bridge of his nose in a frown. He was not angry, not yet. Sebastian said a quick prayer for forgiveness, and then explained what had happened on that long ago Twelfth Night.

"Why do I only learn of this now?" the earl asked softly.

"My lord, when we made the promise, I did not think it a binding one. John has shown me it does bind us both." As it always had. But he could not say that to the earl. "When you betrothed Beatrice to Lord Manners, I knew it could not be." When Beatrice had told him Manners had offered for her, he had known the Twelfth Night promise had meant nothing to her. She would never have let a man go so far as to offer for her if she had considered herself promised. And he had also known that he meant nothing to her. "We were foolish children."

"Not children enough," the earl said shortly. He sighed. "Are you certain of this?"

"My lord, I am not certain of anything. But I now believe we made a binding promise and because of that, Beatrice is my wife in the eyes of canon law."

"What, then, do you need of me? She is your wife, with or without my blessing." The earl's voice was flat with displeasure.

"But not in the eyes of the world. I do not want to do anything that will shame either of us. For that, we must have a betrothal and a wedding, as if we are not married at all. And witnesses to our marriage will ease my mind."

"And if I have no care for the easiness of your mind? What will you do then?"

"I shall take Beatrice to live with me at Benbury, as my wife, with you or without you, my lord. She will have no dower rights nor will she have a jointure. Should I die before her, she will be left penniless, but so be it. I cannot fight you." He clamped his mouth shut, waiting for the storm to break over his head.

Sebastian met the earl's cold, black stare steadily, his stomach churning.

Wednesfield nodded, the confrontation of his gaze easing into thoughtfulness. "I shall tell you something I never told another man. If you speak of this, I will deny it." He looked past Sebastian, his mouth turning down at the corners. "I did not want to give Beatrice to Manners, but I could think of no reason to refuse him. When she asked for the marriage, I permitted it. After it was done and—I learned more truly what kind of man Manners was, I swore that I would never again allow a daughter of mine to marry a man I did not trust.'' His gaze sharpened and returned to Sebastian. ''You think me a softhearted fool for that, I doubt me not. Marriage is about alliances, you will say.''

''My lord, I have confessed that I pledged myself to your daughter for no better reason than affection. How shall I call you softhearted?''

''A neat answer,'' Wednesfield said, his grin flashing briefly. ''But think on this. Why should I trust a man as an ally when I will not trust him as a son-in-law? But that is not my point.'' He reached out and gripped the collar of Sebastian's short gown. ''I have known you from a pup, Benbury, but if you had not outfaced me as you did just now, I should not allow you to take Beatrice away. I should not think you man enough to marry her.'' He let go of Sebastian's gown.

And if Wednesfield had refused him, he would be free. *No,* the voice deep in his mind said with hard certainty. Regardless of what anyone said or did, he and Beatrice had yoked themselves together for life. In ignorance, he had abjured that promise once. He could not do it a second time.

The earl smiled, cold yielding to his customary warmth. ''However, I do not oppose you, so there is no need to pursue this. I give you my blessing right gladly. But I will not discuss the legalities tonight.'' His smile widened. ''See me tomorrow, before noon, and we will hammer out a contract to please us both.''

At some sodden point Beatrice's tears became sleep. Sleep led to dreams that made her jerk awake, sitting up in bed. Her hands were cold and shaking, but when she raised them to her face, she was sweating. The dream tried to return to her; she caught a glimpse of hands and thought she smelled cloves and decay. She crossed herself to ward off the nightmare and climbed down from the bed. Maybe the dream clung to the coverlet; maybe if she prayed, she would be safe.

She did not kneel. Even if prayer would wipe her mind clean of every memory of Thomas, she could not pray. Her heart turned to stone, her soul was as dry as the desert. She was lost, far beyond the reach of God's love, if not his wrath.

Besides, it grew late. Soon the family would come together to sup in the solar. If she wanted to eat before dawn, she must join them. Her eyes were gritty and swollen from her weeping. She needed to bathe them to ease the swelling and soothe the soreness. Evidence of tears would make her mother curious; curiosity would lead to sharp questions, though the questions would be meant kindly. Her heart and soul were too raw to endure much probing.

There was a ewer of water and a bowl on the table against the wall. Had Cecilia done this? Perhaps. Beatrice filled the bowl half-full of water and bent to rinse her face and eyes. The water, smelling faintly of lavender and roses, was cool on her hot skin and the scent, evoking memories of happier days in the garden at Wednesfield, eased her wounded soul. She dipped her hands into the water over and over again, splashing her face until she could smell nothing else.

Please, sweet Mary, let me be happy again. Blessed Jesú, grant me the strength to survive my trials and let me know peace.

The prayer was over before she recognized she was praying. She straightened slowly, waiting for the renewal of desolation that always followed her attempts to pray. Water dripped on her bosom, startling her. She felt no better for having prayed, but she felt no worse. Could that be an answer? She did not know and had no time to ponder the mystery. If she did not hurry she would be the last to arrive.

When she entered the solar, it appeared at first glance that her family had gathered around Sebastian. He sat near her father, watching John as he talked, the corners of his mouth quivering as if he were about to smile. Her heart hurt to see him so nearly happy, knowing that she could no longer bring him what had once been a simple gift. He would no longer smile when he saw her, for he despised her—rightfully so.

Cecilia rose from her corner to one side of the men and came forward. "Come sit with me," she said quietly. "I shall play for you."

For so long she had been unable to feel much more than pain and shame; other emotions had to force themselves past the darkness in her soul. Now the anxiety Cecilia hid behind her quiet solicitude pressed against Beatrice, demanding a response, crying out for reassurance she could not give. "I should like that," she said, taking her sister's hand. Cecilia squeezed her hand gently, her fingers firm and warm.

Crossing the room drew Sebastian's eyes to her. His shadow smile vanished as all the muscles in his face stiffened, his eyes as black in the candlelight as holes punched in a mask. John leaned close and said something in Sebastian's ear; Sebastian looked away, a muscle jumping in the angle of his jaw. Her heart pattered against her ribs like a trapped thing, suffocating her. She was alive today because she had learned in a hard school how to read a husband's tiniest flicker of expression, yet she could not interpret Sebastian's with any certainty. If she could not read him, how was she to survive?

A little voice in the back of her head whispered, *Sebastian has never harmed you.*

Sebastian had never had power over her. Thomas had been all that was kind and courteous before she'd married him; afterward— She flinched. She never remembered *afterward* if she could help it.

She settled herself on the bench beside Cecilia, arranging her skirts until she remembered that no one here would care if they were not just so. How long before she stopped trying to please Thomas? She folded her hands in her lap to still them and then, unable to prevent herself, she glanced out of the corner of her eye at Sebastian. He grinned at John. One corner of his mouth lifted higher than the other when he smiled; the unevenness made his smile mischievous. The pattering of her heart was submerged in a wave of longing and pain that made her breath hitch.

Smile at me the way you used to. While he still loved her, he had tempted her into more than one act of harmless folly with the wayward charm of that grin. She would have done anything for him.

I loved you so.

She swallowed and dropped her gaze to her hands, clenched in an angry, white-knuckled knot. She had thrown him away because she was a coward. Worse, because she had been a coward choked with vanity and pride.

"What shall I play for you, sister mine?" Ceci asked quietly.

"Can you play the songs Mistress Emma sang to us when we were children?" *Let me be a child again, if only in memory. Let me return to the time before I threw Sebastian away.*

"If you wish it, dearling, I can."

Out of the lute's strings flowed a simple round Mistress Emma had used to sing when she was mending and teaching Beatrice and Cecilia to mind their needles. Beatrice had loved needlework from her first stitch, while her sister had fought the cloth, needles and thread as if they were her mortal enemies. Insubstantial memories came on a wave of peace, as if the mellowness of innumerable afternoons mingled with the song flowing into the room. The tumult churning in Beatrice's breast slowed, smoothed and finally faded, ugly memory giving way to gentle recollection.

She remembered sitting beside Ceci on a bench in the old solar at Wednesfield, trying to smock a shirt for her father while Ceci, muttering curses and whining in frustration, wrestled with hemstitches that would not feather neatly. She could not recall a time when she and her sister had sewn together that did not feature an irritable, sweaty Ceci smudging her linen and knotting her thread.

The music shifted and changed to another of Mistress Emma's sewing songs, and Beatrice's recollections shifted with it. Now she was sewing alone, hiding in the old tower so no one might see the herons she stitched in elaborate blackwork on a linen shirt. Benbury herons…a shirt for Sebastian. How old had she been? Fourteen, perhaps? He had promised her he would always keep it.

"Play something else, Ceci," John said.

Cecilia looked at her, eyebrows raised in a question. *Shall I?*

Warmth stole over Beatrice. Growing up, John's

word had been law to Ceci, never questioned. Now her sister held him at bay for Beatrice. "Play what you wish," she said, the warmth overflowing in a smile.

The darkness inside her did not lift so much as it crumbled, like a wall collapsing after it had been undermined. Little things chipped away at it, from the thoughtfulness of lavender and roses in her washing water to the way her sister seemed determined to please her. Smiling seemed to damage the darkness still further. Could blessings, not blows, fall down on her?

Ceci grinned back at her. "I shall play to please myself then." She frowned thoughtfully. "I had just learned this for the queen when I left Court, so have patience. I am not well practiced."

She launched into a lively tune, playing with no missed note that Beatrice could hear. After playing the melody once, she began to sing in her silver-pure voice. The words of the song were a little bawdy, as Court songs usually were; the chorus was plain nonsense. "And a hey nonny, hey nonny nonny no!"

The third time Cecilia began to sing the chorus, John joined in, the darkness of his deeper voice shading the bright clarity of hers. Beatrice listened, wishing she did not croak like a rook and could join in, as well. The rollicking rhythm of the tune set her toes to tapping and when John began to clap his hands in time she joined in helplessly. Lucia, sitting on John's other side, followed suit, laughing as she did so. John had said she barely knew any English, but she seemed to understand English music well enough.

Her father joined Cecilia in singing the fourth verse. Here was the source of Ceci's music; her father's voice was as smooth and golden as honey in the comb. Beside him, her mother clapped her hands, her face shining in the candlelight. Her voice had no more beauty in it than Beatrice's but, like Beatrice, she loved music.

"And a hey nonny, hey nonny nonny no!"

Beatrice would have known Sebastian's voice if he sang with the choir at Westminster. Not as dark as John's nor as honeyed as her father's, it had the golden-brown clarity of water slipping over stones. Certain he would not be looking at her, she stole a glance at him.

She was wrong.

Even at this distance, the cornflower-blue of his eyes glowed. Surely those were the bluest eyes in England. She waited for his mask to clamp down, for the shifting, unreadable expression on his face to disappear, frozen into frightening stillness. Instead his expression coalesced into a scowl as he stared at her through narrowed eyes. An hour ago that frown would have unnerved her. Now, after Ceci's kindness and the joyous sound of "Hey nonny no!" she had a small store of courage to spend.

She lifted her chin and held his stare. It took every ounce of will not to look away; it had been far too long since she had tried to stare anyone down. A chill prickled her when she remembered that within weeks she would be entirely in his power, to use as he pleased, but a portion of Coleville obstinacy had come with the courage and she could not yield to him. She would have to have faith in the small voice that had said Sebastian would not harm her.

Sebastian looked away.

Beatrice sank back against the wall as if he had unhanded her. She had not outfaced anyone since marrying Thomas. How long had it been? Three years, four? She could not remember, not exactly, only that it seemed like a lifetime.

Her heart, which had lain quietly while she confronted Sebastian, took up a fierce battering against her breastbone, as if to register its protest, and she could not quite seem to catch her breath. How had she dared? Why had she been such a fool? He would be furious and rightly so. Worse, however much she hated and feared the knowledge, he was her husband, with the right to correct her with his hands. She ought to be terrified; surely the pounding of her heart was fear?

No, what she felt was not fear. Fear did not rush, sparkling, through her veins; fear did not make her sit straighter on the bench beside Ceci. The emotion driving her heart and catching her breath was excitement, excitement that was familiar and alien at once.

Why? Why was she excited when she should be afraid?

Through a supper of duck and goose, good English beef and capon, she puzzled over it. She knew her family spoke to her and she answered at random, absorbed in trying to penetrate the gray wall of empty knowledge. She could not remember why her act of daring felt familiar, nor understand why it did not leave her cold with terror. Could it be that Sebastian was not Thomas? She looked down the table at him, sitting just beyond John on her father's side. Candlelight glinted gold and honey-brown in his waving hair, limned the lean line of his cheek and glittered in the faint stubble of his beard. He seemed almost to have been washed in gold himself, even to the tawny orange of his short gown and brocaded doublet. Like a saint in a manuscript.

No, he was nothing like Thomas, least of all to look at.

Servants came to remove the cloths from the table and to lay out the cheese and fruit. Beatrice selected an apple and began cutting the peel off with her eating knife. She had always loved apples, especially when they were new, their flesh firm and full of juice. This one was particularly juicy; her hands were damp and sticky with it. She carved a sliver of apple and slid it into her mouth, nibbling it between her teeth.

She glanced at Sebastian. He stared at her, his mouth a thin, hard line, and then turned his head away from her, one more move in their dance of looking and looking away. How he must hate the thought of marrying her.

She could not blame him for wishing for another wife than she. What man would want a woman with a soul as black as hers, even if she had tried to clean the stains with confession and penance? She sighed and set the apple down. What either of them wanted had become meaningless. Without list or leave, they were married, bound together in the sight of God if not yet in the sight of man.

If she could not undo this madness, she could try to be the wife he must want. Meek, obedient, scrupulously honorable. How meek would he expect her to be? Would she need to be obedient only to spoken desires, or would she once again have to obey commands unspoken, and suffer the punishments for unwitting disobedience?

She glanced at Sebastian's end of the table again. Her father had claimed his attention. Sebastian frowned as he nodded while her father spoke, but he did not look angry, merely intent on her father. But anger did not matter, did it? A man might pretend to anger, so poorly she knew it for mummery, and still inflict bruises big and black as plums. A blow given with a cold heart hurt just as deeply as one given in heat.

She would drive herself mad if she stayed here, unable to keep from looking at Sebastian even when the sight of him sent her thoughts into places she did not want to go. He was a wound she could not help prodding. She would have time enough to prod it once she began to live with him as his wife, but not now.

She rose. All heads at the table swiveled to face her. Her mother looked irritated at this breach of manners, Ceci worried, John thoughtful. Sebastian's fist curled on the table as her father turned toward her, but that was all he revealed. His composure let nothing else escape.

Her father rose to his feet, as well. "Well, mistress?" he asked quietly.

"I beg your leave to retire, sir," she said softly.

He eyed her thoughtfully, the silence in the room stretching tightly. Her father could reprimand her, deny her permission to go, humiliate her before Sebastian and her family. She had acted without thinking.

He shoved his chair aside, creating space between his chair and her mother's. "Come here."

She went to him and knelt at his feet. Even if he shamed her, it would be nothing to her other humiliations. She had endured so much already; she could surely endure a little more. He surprised her by laying his hand on her forehead in a blessing, then, when she rose, saying, "Come closer, puss." She stepped closer, her forehead still warm where his hand had been. He kissed her cheek, patting the other with a gentle hand at the same time. He had kissed her that way when she was a tiny girl. She pressed her cheek against his rough one.

I wish I were the woman you raised me to be.

"You have my leave to go."

Her mother said in a very soft voice, "My lord."

Her father put his hand on her mother's shoulder. "No, Pippa."

Her mother sat back. They never quarreled in public nor before their children. Whether they quarreled at all had been a favorite topic of speculation for their children while Beatrice was growing up.

"Go, child," her father said.

She took a candle to light her way to her bedchamber, but it cast more shadows than light, and the dark quivered as if full of demons. No, not demons; she saw the shadows cast by her jumbled, unruly thoughts.

She stopped outside the door of the bedchamber, unable to lift the latch. Today had been the one of longest days of her life but she was not weary. A fretful energy twitched in her limbs, the kind of energy she had used to absorb with riding and walking at Wednesfield. She could not go walking or riding now, in the dangerous, deadly dark. Nor could she be still. Where to go? Where might she find a haven, a sanctuary against her fears and the demons within?

Sanctuary...

Blowing out her candle, unwilling to be accompanied by its unsettling shadows, she turned on her heel and began walking to the chapel at the other end of the house.

Chapter Three

Shortly after Beatrice left the solar, Sebastian rose and made his bows to the earl and countess. With Beatrice gone, all who remained in the solar—John and his wife, the earl and countess, even Cecilia—reminded him of what he would never have: a sweet, serene married life. The reminder was more than he could endure.

From the solar, he went down to the great hall. Night had fallen and it was past time to go to bed, but he was too edgy to sleep. If he returned to his chamber, he would lie awake, unable to stop thinking about wool prices, his rents, income that covered less and less of his expenses...and Beatrice.

Around him the house was silent, as if all its occupants, even those he had just left, slept without dreams. He envied them. He remembered how heedless he had once been, assuming that because no harm had ever come to him or his, no harm ever would. If it had not been for his uncle's aid, he might well have lost everything. Since then, he had taken fear for Benbury's future to bed with him.

At the far end of the hall a white blur moved into

sight, gleaming faintly in the low light cast by the fire-place to one side. Sebastian stepped deeper into the shadows. Who was this creeping through the hall when most of the household had retired? And why did he only see the white oval of a face?

She came closer and firelight glittered on her jet ornaments, smoldered on the velvet of her skirts. Dressed in widow's black, she had melted into the shadows, barely discernible even to his sharp eyes.

Beatrice.

She passed him without seeing him—or at least without betraying that she had seen him—and slipped through the arch that led to the chapel stairs. He crept after her, wondering why she went to the chapel at this hour, and hesitated at the bottom of the stairs. She had to have gone to the chapel; there was nowhere else. But why? Of all her family, she was the least pious, not the kind of woman to pray in the middle of the night.

Intrigued, and more than willing to let curiosity distract him from the weary round of worry, he followed her up the stairs.

The chapel was located at the top of the stairs. Faint light from within the room revealed that the door was half open. Resting a hand on its panel, he paused to reconsider entering. If Beatrice was praying, he could only be an unwelcome intrusion—and no matter what she did within, he would have to speak to her if he joined her. He had nothing to say, nothing that he dared say.

He imagined himself turning and going back down the stairs, crossing the hall and seeking his bed. Rest would only aid him in his meeting with the earl; staying here with Beatrice was folly. The days when he could follow every impulse were long past.

He pushed the door open.

The chapel was dim, illuminated only by the sanctuary light, a brave, weak show against the blackness of night. Beatrice knelt in the middle of the chapel floor, her head bent over folded hands. The gabled hood she wore concealed her face, but even if he had not seen her climb the stairs, he would have known her by the graceful bend of her long neck. In truth, he would know her anywhere, under any circumstance. When he had discovered her with Conyers, he had recognized her even though she had been enveloped in Conyers's arms.

Tension tightened his shoulders, the too-vivid memory of Beatrice embracing George Conyers sparking fury as if he faced it anew. He fought both anger and memory, pushing them down, beyond reach, and swung the door shut. It slipped from his hand to bang softly against the frame, the latch rattling.

Beatrice jerked around, her mouth open, her hands flying up to her breastbone. Then she saw him and the expression left her face.

"My lord, you startled me," she murmured as she rose to her feet.

"I did not intend to." He moved deeper into the chapel, drawn unwillingly closer. Then, because he could not help himself, because he could not reconcile her apparent piety with what he knew of her, he asked, "Why are you here?"

She blinked as if the question surprised her. "I came to pray."

"At this hour? When the household sleeps?"

She lifted her chin, her eyes wide and wary as if

she did not know whether or not he mocked her. "Why does the hour matter?"

"I should have thought you would seek the comfort of your bed."

She was silent for so long he thought she would not reply. She lowered her chin. "Prayer is good for the soul. If I did not know it before, I know it now."

Because of your sins. Again anger rose in him; again he pushed it down. He had not followed her to abuse her about the unchangeable past. Or had he? Fool that he was, he did not know why he had followed her, except that he could not stop himself.

"Do you pray to be delivered from our marriage?" He spoke without thinking and immediately wished he had said nothing.

Her face shuttered. "There is no deliverance."

He had thought her furious refusal to accept the betrothal earlier in the day had been shock. The way she had looked at him again and again at supper had given him hope that she would not go into the marriage furious and cold. Her bleakness now withered that hope.

"How can you know?"

"Because you are not pleased. If we were delivered, you would be happy."

That surprised him. He had not thought she would interpret his behavior so. "Do you think I should be pleased to be delivered?"

A frown creased her brow. "How not? You would be free of me then, free to marry Cecilia."

He did not want to marry Cecilia. He might not trust Beatrice, but he would not choose her sister over her. The realization was another surprise, as were the words that spilled from his mouth.

"You are not a bad bargain, Beatrice."

Her frown deepened and she dropped her gaze from his. "You do not know that."

"I know."

She smoothed her hands over her skirt, talking to the floor. "You cannot."

She spoke so softly he had to move closer. He stopped when the hem of her skirt brushed the wide toe of his shoe. "You are wellborn, well dowered. And you have been a wife before. None of marriage will be strange to you."

She looked up at that, speculation in her eyes as they searched his face. He waited for her to find what she sought.

"I have not been your wife nor do I think my dead lord's ways are your ways."

Pain sparked at the reminder. Just as he did not want to remember her dalliance with Conyers, neither did he want to think of her life with Manners. "I am a man, as he was. How different can we be?"

Some bleak memory stirred; he could see its shadow in her face before she turned away. "Not all men are the same," she murmured.

As you well know, a voice whispered in the back of his mind. He clamped his mouth shut lest he speak the words aloud. Despite the anger that would not remain at bay, he would not fling accusations at her, chastising her for sins he imagined, all of them greater than the one he had witnessed.

When he did not reply, she turned back to him, the question in her expression fading as her gaze traveled over his face. Understanding flickered in her eyes as if she saw what he wished to hide and then it was only the candlelight gleaming in their blue-gray depths while her face smoothed to blankness. The hair on the back of his neck prickled. Beatrice had somehow vanished, leaving her body to face him.

Come back to me.

"Beatrice," he said softly.

"My lord?"

Do not hide from me and name me as if I am a stranger to you. You know I am not.

"Call me by my name."

Her eyes met his and in their depths he saw Beatrice return, the distance between them melting like spring snow. She searched his face as if she had never seen him before.

"What do you want of me, Sebastian?"

"Nothing," he said. He could not say what he wanted. All he knew was that she could not give it to him.

She folded her hands. "I do not believe you."

He crossed his arms. "Does it matter?"

"I wish to know what you desire, so I may prepare myself to provide it."

"Do you think I will ask anything you do not know how to give?"

"Yes, I do."

"Why? What have I ever done that you should think that?"

"You are a man. That is all you need."

"Do you think so ill of men?"

"Think ill of them? No, Sebastian, I do not. Men are what they are, not to be ill or well thought of for it. I only ask so I may be all you desire in a wife."

"It does not matter. You can never be all I desire in a wife." *You lost that ability when you let George Conyers into your bed.* He clamped his jaw shut before he could speak the words. Anger ached in his chest, burned in his throat. If he was not careful, he would begin to curse her and there would never be peace between them.

In a quiet voice she asked, "If I can never be the wife you desire, Sebastian, will you not tell me what I can do to make the best of this bad bargain?"

"Anything you do will be well enough." Anything she did would have to be enough. They were knotted, not to be parted in this life.

She sighed and lowered her eyes. "I do not believe you."

"We cannot undo the past, Beatrice. You cannot undo your dalliance with Conyers and I cannot undo what I have said about it. From now, all I need is your obedience, and I do not doubt I shall have it." That much, at least, was true. He would make certain of it.

"If we cannot undo the past, I at least am willing to let it rest." She looked up at him, her clear eyes catching the candlelight. "Can you say the same?"

He eased his gaze away from hers, unable to withstand her scrutiny. "I do not care about the past."

"Do you not? You cannot leave it behind. I have done penance for my sins and promised never to commit them again. For my immortal soul, I will not so dishonor myself. You can neither forget nor forgive. How shall we ever live together, Sebastian?"

"We will because we must," he said.

She walked away from him, toward the altar. He followed.

"What do you want of me, Beatrice?" he asked.

She crossed herself and knelt, folding her hands. He knelt beside her.

"Tell me what you want."

Looking at the rood screen, she said, "I want to be at peace."

"I cannot give that to you."

"I know. No man can."

No man? Memories danced before his mind's eye: Conyers with his hands on her, Conyers with his mouth on her. And Beatrice allowing it all.

"Did Conyers?" he asked, his voice harsh and flat in the silence.

She closed her eyes, her mouth flattening, and then said in a weary voice, "Sir George Conyers wanted nothing more than an hour or two of pleasure."

"And you gave it to him." He did not want to talk about Conyers, but he could not stop prodding her. What ailed him?

She shook her head and opened her eyes, staring up at the rood screen once more. "I do not think so."

"Are you saying I was mistaken in what I saw?"

"What did you see?"

"I saw him touch you where no man but your husband should." The muscles in his arms and shoulders tightened, and behind his anger was pain, so fierce it did not seem a memory but agony renewed.

She murmured something, her voice too low to be heard, then said, "You are not mistaken in what you saw."

"You speak in riddles, Beatrice. You deny you gave him pleasure yet you admit you lay with him."

"I admit nothing."

"Did you lie with him? Was I mistaken?" The echoes of his cry clanged against the walls of the chapel, his fury escaping into the open at last.

She turned to face him, her eyes wary. He had a brief, bitter memory of her as a girl, as easy to read as a primer. Now he could no more decipher her expressions than he could translate Greek.

"It does not matter whether I lay with him or not. I will be faithful to you. I would promise it if you asked it of me, but a promise does not matter. I will never betray you because I refuse to risk my immortal soul to give any man living a moment's ease."

She looked away and stood. "Let us talk no more, Sebastian. I am weary and say what I ought not. If you will excuse me, I shall retire now." She walked toward the door.

His anger died as if it could not survive her absence. He scrambled to his feet and followed her. "Do not go, Beatrice."

She turned to face him. "Why not? We only brangle whenever we meet. Perhaps, given time, we shall be able to live together without quarrel. But that time has not come."

He held out his hand, no longer clenched in a fist. "I do not want us to part like this."

She sighed. "Nor I, but I do not see how else we may part."

He moved closer to her, his hand still outstretched. "If I say I believe you…"

"Do not lie for so small a reason, Sebastian. It does not matter enough."

His hand dropped; the two feet that separated them might have been twenty. "You are changed."

Her chin went up. "Perhaps I was never who you thought I was. Perhaps what you see now is the truth."

"Is it?"

Her mouth curled in a bitter smile. "You cannot leave anything alone. I cannot answer that question, I cannot allay your fears. I can offer you no comfort.

This is what we suffer for our sins.'' She turned away from him and crossed the distance to the door. Opening it, she turned to face him. ''Good night and God be with you.'' She disappeared, shutting the door behind her.

Without her, the chapel walls crowded around him, the air chilly and damp. The light on the altar flickered and danced, spilling shadows and golden light against the dark stone walls. Sebastian returned to the altar and knelt, casting about in his empty mind for a prayer, any prayer.

If he could, he would release Beatrice from this marriage. Not because he wished to marry any woman but her, but because she was right when she said they did nothing but brangle when they met. He did not want a turbulent marriage. Like Beatrice, he wanted peace, but when he was with her he could not find it for himself nor would he leave her be to discover it for herself.

Yet however much he wished otherwise, he could not be free, nor could Beatrice. They were bound to one another, tied before God. Some men might, for expedience, discard their wives like outworn shoes, discovering a convenient precontract or fortuitously remembered consanguinity. Unlike them, Sebastian would not dishonor himself, even to undo this marriage. Whether he wished for it or not, in a way he would never have chosen or imagined, he must marry the woman he had loved since childhood.

God help them both.

Chapter Four

Beatrice closed the chapel door and leaned against its panels, waiting for her heart to still its riotous hammering. The encounter with Sebastian ought to have alarmed her, proving as it had that she would not find the peace she sought as Sebastian's wife, but instead of dismay, there was exhilaration. Against all sense and wisdom, the same rushing excitement that had surged through her when she had faced down Sebastian's stare drove her heart now. Why was that so? What ailed her that she did not fear to meet or to defy him?

She straightened. She could not linger here, outside the chapel, while she puzzled it out. She hurried through the dark house to her bedchamber. After the waiting maidservant had helped her out of her clothes and into her night rail, she dismissed the girl, unwilling to have company while her thoughts churned and bubbled as if her head were a cauldron. Alone, she paced the room, too restless to be still.

Something had changed this night. Before Sebastian disturbed her she had been praying, mere hours after telling Ceci she no longer could. How had that happened? What had opened the stops in her soul?

Growing up at Wednesfield, she had often imagined that in early spring she could feel the earth quicken to life long before the green shoots thrust into sight, as if the sap moving once more in the trees moved through her, as well. That tingling awareness flooded her now, the sensation of sleeping things stirring awake. Somehow that feeling had to do with Sebastian and this garboil she found herself in.

She shook her head. Fear stirred, murmuring, *If you trust this feeling it will be the worse for you.* Fear? Or plain sense? She had thought she could trust Thomas and he had proven her wrong. So, for that matter, had Sebastian and George Conyers. No, better she should keep her counsel and bend herself to being a perfectly submissive, perfectly obedient wife. Tonight was the last time she would come so close to quarreling with Sebastian.

The door creaked open. Beatrice turned her head in time to see Ceci, holding her lute, slip into the room and check on the threshold as she saw that Beatrice was alone.

"Where is Mary? Edith?" Ceci asked.

"Mary was not here. I dismissed Edith."

Ceci's eyes narrowed briefly, but all she said was, "Will you attend me then?"

"Gladly."

They did not speak while Beatrice helped Ceci as the maid had helped her, but she was aware of her sister watching her, those dark eyes no doubt seeing more than Ceci let show. Beatrice knew she was no fool, but when she compared her wit to her sister's cleverness, she felt like one.

While Ceci braided her hair and put on her nightcap, Beatrice sat down. She ought to plait her own hair, but she did not want to. Not yet.

Ceci tied the strings of her cap. "Are you going to go to bed like that? Your hair will be a tangle in the morning."

"I cannot seem to find the will," Beatrice confessed. "Today is a day I should want to leave behind, but I fear tomorrow will be worse."

"Let me."

Beatrice nodded and drew the stool away from the wall. Ceci picked up the comb from atop the bed where she had put it and went to stand behind Beatrice. Her fingers threaded through Beatrice's hair, their touch light. Pleasure, or the anticipation of pleasure, washed over Beatrice. She had always loved it when Ceci or Mistress Emma combed her hair; both had the kind of touch that soothed.

A waving strand of hair drifted over her shoulder, glittering gold in the candlelight as it moved into her line of sight. Ceci's hand, lute-string calluses on the pads of the fingertips, reached forward and drew the strand back.

"I always wished I had hair like yours," Ceci said, and drew the comb through Beatrice's hair from hairline to the ends brushing the small of Beatrice's back.

The touch of the comb loosened every remaining knot of tension in Beatrice's body. It took her a moment to form the words to reply.

"Because it is fair?"

"And curly."

"But you have hair like satin!" True, Ceci was dark, but her hair was heavy and glossy, cool and silky to the touch. "I always wanted hair like yours."

Ceci chuckled. "You cannot have wanted to be a sparrow like me."

"Papa has dark hair."

"Ah."

As Ceci had always been closer to their mother, so had Beatrice been the light of their father's eyes. Beatrice sighed, closing her eyes. Those days seemed now to have been lived by another woman.

The comb passed through her hair and passed again in a slow, drowsy rhythm. Into the silence Beatrice said, "I spoke to Sebastian."

The comb stroking her scalp paused. "When?"

Beatrice opened her eyes. "An hour ago, perhaps. After I left the solar."

The comb resumed its long caress. "What did you say to him?"

No words came back to her, only the memory of Sebastian's eyes, blue as flame as they stared into her own. He had been angry at one point, angry enough to make her flinch to see it, but she had not feared him. However wise fearing him might be, she could not seem to do it.

"Beatrice, what did you say to him?"

"I cannot remember." Her mind emptied of everything but brilliant blue eyes.

"What did he say to you?"

"He talked about Sir George." Talked? He had shouted at her. And still she had not feared him.

"And how did you reply?" Ceci's steady combing never faltered, her voice as calm as if they discussed the weather.

"I told him I will not sin for any man's pleasure." Or displeasure. Within days of Thomas's death, Sir George Conyers had sent her a note, entreating her to meet him. She had sent that note, and the others that followed, back to him, unanswered. She was done with him and everything he had meant in her life.

"What did he say to that?" Ceci asked as calmly as before, her voice betraying nothing other than a passionless interest. How easy it was to answer someone who seemed unlikely to be upset by anything one said.

Was that the secret of Ceci's skill as a listener? That nothing said disturbed or agitated her? Talking to her was like confession but without the burden of remorse or the price of penance. Everything Beatrice had kept to herself pressed against her, a heavy weight, so heavy she did not know how to begin unloading it. But Ceci would know, and Ceci would help her. She knew that as certainly as she knew the sun would rise in the morning, the first good thing she had trusted since her marriage.

"He said I was changed." She leaned forward, putting her face in her uplifted hands. Through her fingers, she said, "We shall be wed in no more than a month. How shall we learn not to quarrel in that time?"

"I think the wedding will not happen until Michaelmas, Beatrice," Ceci said.

Beatrice straightened. "The end of September? Why so long?" Despite knowing that she and Sebastian needed time to find a way to rub along comfortably, she did not want to have to wait at all, much less wait two months. She was not free, would never be free, and wanted no time to begin to imagine what it would like to be unmarried.

"You are newly widowed. Enough time must pass to show you are not with child."

Beatrice whirled on the stool to face Ceci. "You

know I am not with child," she said, her heart fluttering. It was hard to speak of her childlessness.

"I do—"

"And Sebastian will know as soon he lies with me." *If he lies with me.* She pushed the thought away, refusing it room in her mind.

"—but the world must know," Ceci said. "You know as well as I that the show of truth is more valuable than the truth itself." She gripped Beatrice's shoulders and shook her gently. "If the truth alone mattered, you could join Sebastian at Benbury tomorrow."

"I cannot wait so long," Beatrice whispered.

"Are you so eager?" Ceci asked, her eyebrows lifting.

"Eager? No, I am no more eager to be Sebastian's wife than a condemned man is for the hangman. But I would rather not wait, day in and day out, for the rope."

"It will not be so ill, Beatrice, I swear it."

"I cannot keep a still tongue in my head when I am with him! I carp and complain as no proper wife should ever do. He will lesson me, Ceci, if not with a switch, then with the flat of his hand, and I do not know that I can endure any more of it. What shall I do?"

"Be still, dearling, hush." Ceci knelt and, setting the comb aside, took Beatrice's hands in her own, squeezing them gently. "However angry Sebastian may be with you—and he is angry, though I think him a fool for it—he is also a good and kind man. He is not Thomas Manners and he will not use you as Manners did."

"How can you know that? How?"

"How can you not? Sebastian does not beat his horses or his hounds. Why should he beat his wife?"

There was truth in what Ceci said. Sebastian was not given to harming those in his care, more than could ever have been said of Thomas Manners. Seeing that was one thing, trusting it another. She could not take that step. She whispered, "I am sore afraid." As senseless as it seemed, she did not fear Sebastian himself. She only feared to marry him.

"I know, dearling, I know." Ceci let go of Beatrice's hands to wrap her arms around her. Beatrice rested her head on her sister's shoulder, while Ceci rubbed her back as Mistress Emma used to when they were small girls. Ceci's cleverness had not made her cold or uncaring, nor had she forgotten how to love. Beatrice felt strength flowing into her as if it came from her sister.

"I am so glad you will be with us at Wednesfield," she said.

The hands on her back stilled, but Ceci did not speak. Beatrice lifted her head to face her sister. Her mouth was turned down, her eyes shadowed by her lashes. Beatrice's heart chilled.

"You are not coming home." She did not need to ask, not when she already knew the answer.

Ceci's lashes lifted, revealing sadness and excitement mingled. "If the queen gives me leave, I shall return to my post as maid of honor."

"Why?" *Why do you go? Why do you leave me when I need you?* "For the family's benefit? We do not need it. For love of the life at Court? You do not love Court, I have seen it in your face." She was bereft, betrayed, wanting to hold Ceci to her with both hands and angry at the knowledge that nothing could hold her sister back.

Ceci released Beatrice and sat back on her heels. "No," she said softly. "I do not love Court." She sighed. "I do not want to leave you at all, but there are things…people…one man I must face before I do anything else."

"Who? Who must you see? And why?" *Who is so important you can abandon me?* Beatrice pushed the thought aside. *I will not feel sorry for myself.* Pity, from whatever source, was worthless.

Ceci swallowed. "I loved a man." She picked up the comb and ran her fingertip along its teeth, the faint rattle of her fingertip's passage loud. "I thought he loved me." She laid the comb in her lap. "I need to know the truth. I need to know how he feels."

"Who is he?" Rumors returned to her, tales half heard because no one would tell her outright. Disbelief spread silence through her mind. "Not the Duke of—"

"Do not say his name!" Ceci cried, reaching up to put her fingers over Beatrice's mouth. "I cannot listen to it."

"There were rumors—" Beatrice said against her sister's hand.

Ceci nodded. "There is some truth to them." Her hand dropped away. "If he does not love me, I must know. And the only way is to see him again."

Her sister's courage stole the breath from Beatrice's throat. To confront the man she loved simply to know with certainty that he no longer loved her. The one time circumstance had demanded like courage from Beatrice, she had fled behind the barrier of pride, afraid to risk a little wound, a little pain. Ceci's risk seemed so much greater.

"And if he does love you?" she asked. She had to know, as if the knowledge might answer some question she had not faced, resolve some dilemma she had not acknowledged. "You cannot marry him."

"I know I cannot marry him. But if he loves me, I will know all I have done has not been a mistake." Ceci's eyes were unfocused, as if she gazed on memory and no longer saw the narrow, candlelit bedchamber.

"What did you do?" What could her good, clever sister have done that the knowledge a man loved her would transmute mistakes?

Ceci's attention returned and as it did, something in her face closed. "Turn. Let me comb your hair."

Beatrice turned her back on her sister. Even if the look on Ceci's face had not warned her, she would never pry into another's secrets. Too many fingers had poked at hers.

Yellow candlelight and gray shadows bounced off the flaws in the wall before her. The patterns of illumination and obscurity shifted as the candle flame bobbed, jerked by the drafts creeping underneath the door. Almost speaking to the play of light and dark before her, Beatrice said, "It will not be the same at Wednesfield without you."

Common sense reminded her she had not needed Ceci in years, so it should not matter that her sister would not be at the castle. Yet the forlorn voice she thought she had quelled asked, *Who will be my companion now?*

"It was not the same when you left," Ceci replied.

She lifted Beatrice's hair off her neck a moment before the comb resumed its gentle tug. "I shall return when you marry Sebastian."

Beatrice nodded. *What shall I do until then?*

Chapter Five

"Michaelmas?" Sebastian asked, certain he had misheard the earl. Surely Lord Wednesfield could not expect him to wait almost two months to claim Beatrice. "I do not see the need to put the wedding off."

The earl's stare reminded Sebastian of the days of his boyhood when the earl had treated him almost as one of his own sons, teaching him how to be a gentleman and landowner even as he taught his sons Jasper and John. That same expression had been the earl's response to foolish questions; seeing it now, Sebastian frowned. What was wrong with what he had just said? There could be no reason to delay the wedding.

The earl shook his head, the stare turning to a look of disgust. "No, there is no need. It does not matter that when your son is born men will count on their fingers and say the boy is of Thomas Manners's getting. So long as you claim him, what does it matter that men call him bastard behind his back?"

The earl's quiet, thoughtful tone annoyed Sebastian, all the more so because he deserved the earl's scorn. He had made foolish assumptions. Still, two months?

''Why so long, my lord? Beatrice has been a widow for over a fortnight.''

''Are you so eager?'' the earl asked, his eyebrows lifting.

Something the dark depths of the earl's eyes made Sebastian wary, wary enough to hold his tongue. ''No, my lord, I am surprised. But I see your point. Michaelmas it is.''

The earl smiled. ''That was simple enough, lad.'' The smile deepened. ''I do not think the rest will pass so easily.'' He raised his mug of ale to his mouth and drank deeply.

The apprehension tightening Sebastian's muscles eased. The drink was an old trick of the earl's, meant to make the man on the other side of the table believe he was gathering his thoughts when, in truth, he had already carefully considered everything he meant to say. Affection and admiration, so much a part of his relationship with the earl he could not remember a time when he had not felt them, surged through Sebastian.

The earl lowered the mug and sighed, wiping his mouth on the back of his hand. ''It is not right of me to criticize the dead, nor should I speak ill of his father to any man.''

What had this to do with Beatrice and him, with their marriage? Sebastian said nothing, waiting for the earl's apparently idle remarks to become his opening move.

''I have told you this a hundred times—land is the only wealth.''

A hundred times? The earl had said that to him a thousand times. Every time his father had sold another farm, another parcel of acreage, he had heard the earl's words in his mind. And faced with what his father had left of Benbury, he had recalled the earl's words with bitter regret. If land was the only wealth, Lord Lionel Benbury had left his son nearly destitute. Thank God and the saints for his shrewd uncle Henry Isham.

"So when your father came to me to offer me the manor at Herron, I tried to persuade him not to sell it. He would not listen to me, Sebastian, so in the end I bought the land from him. I thought that if I had it, someday you might be able to buy it back from me."

"Perhaps, my lord."

He had been born at Herron, snug and sweet in the center of its fields; it had been the manor he had loved best, mourned the most when it was sold. Fat when his father had lost it, Herron had surely grown fatter with the earl's management, putting it far beyond the reach of his purse for some time to come.

"I do not think Herron was the only land your father sold. Forgive me, but your father was a fool."

He was, my lord. Sebastian could not say it, however true it might be.

"I cannot restore everything he sold, but this I can do. Herron is Beatrice's dowry."

"Herron, my lord?" Had he heard aright? His heart pounded heavily against his breastbone.

"There is one condition," the earl said, "and on that I will not yield. Herron will revert to me or my heirs if Beatrice dies childless."

"My lord, how is this? Your daughter may well be barren. It is certain she bore her late lord no children." God help him if she were—he could not afford a childless wife.

The earl scowled at him. "You married her out of

hand some years ago, Benbury. Do you dare to complain of her dowry now? I owe you nothing.''

Sebastian spread his hands. "Then give me nothing. At least then all I have shall be mine, not liable to be snatched away because my wife cannot bear a son.''

"I said Beatrice must bear you a child, not a son.'' The earl held his scowl for a moment more. "Blessed Jesú, Herron can be yours by midsummer next year if you do your work well.''

He wanted Herron more than he could say, yet he feared to take it. How could he hold it? How could he bear to let it go?

I would rather have half its worth in gold, my lord, or a quarter's worth, than have that land slip through my fingers once more.

He could not say that to the earl.

"Very well, my lord. Herron Manor is Beatrice's dowry. I think it a far too generous dowry, but I am not fool enough to quarrel with you. You have my gratitude.''

The earl snorted. "Never tell a man he has given you too much. He might believe you.'' He glanced at Sebastian. "Now, as to Beatrice's dower property, I think a jointure would be proper.''

Sebastian raised his eyebrows. Give control of Benbury into Beatrice's hands if she outlived him? "No, my lord.''

"No? After I have given Herron for her dowry?''

For a moment Sebastian was tempted to tell the earl to keep Herron if that was its price. Another idea occurred to him. "Let her have Herron for her dower. No less, since it is such a rich property. And no more, so that my son can manage his lands even as she lives.''

The earl opened his mouth as if to argue and then grinned. "Herron it is." He leaned forward, the grin deepening until he looked like a small boy contemplating a raid on the buttery. "Let us see if we can come to blows over the details."

Three hours later, wrung out from the effort of keeping his wits sharp enough to bargain with the wily earl and then to keep the lawyers from further entangling a tangled agreement, Sebastian signed his name to his marriage contract. The settlement was not as bad as it might have been, had the earl been inclined to take advantage of the situation Sebastian found himself in. If the terms did nothing to ease his worries, at least they did nothing to worsen them.

"All that remains are the banns and the wedding," the earl said in a satisfied voice. "Afterward—will you keep your post at Court? Shall I see what I may do to obtain some favors for Beatrice?"

Beatrice at Court, where she could attract admirers as venal as Conyers? No, Beatrice would spend the rest of her life safely locked away at Benbury, no matter how she wept and pled. As for him, if he never returned to Court he would die a happy man. His father had insisted the only way a man could make his fortune was to orbit the king as the sun orbited the earth. Perhaps that was true, but it was also true, that there were few swifter ways to lose a fortune. Had he loved the intrigue and glamour of Court, he would still leave it; he could not afford its demands.

"No, my lord. We shall live at Benbury."

"You will lose many chances at preferment," the earl said, his brows drawing together over his nose.

Sebastian looked down at his hands. The earl was right; Court was the only place to dip into the largesse that flowed from the king like a river. Perhaps with time, Beatrice...

...Beatrice, a honey pot that attracted the worst kind of flies.

He raised his head and met the earl's eyes. "Court life eats up everything my lands produce. I cannot afford it."

The earl's eyebrows rose. "Not even now, when you will have Herron..."

"Every year it costs more to live. You called my father a fool for selling his land. He sold his land because his expenses were greater than his income. I will not make the same mistake."

"So be it. For myself, I shall be glad to have a man of your good sense in the county." The earl rose. "And I have no doubt that my lady wife will be pleased to have Beatrice so close. Come, let us find them both and give them the happy news."

In the hall a servant told them the countess, her daughters and their women had gone into the garden to enjoy a break in the morning's rain. At the end of the passageway that led to the garden, the door stood open, a rectangle of blue-and-green light that dazzled after the dimness of the hall and passage. Following the earl, Sebastian passed under the lintel into the damp, bright garden.

The wet leaves glittered and the stones of the pathway steamed gently in the sunshine. The smell of earth, brown and rich, rose to his nostrils. To his left, Ceci walked arm-in-arm with her mother, their maids trailing behind. On his right, Beatrice walked alone, twirling a rose in her hands, her head bent. He wished he might turn toward Ceci; after last night's puzzling and difficult encounter with Beatrice, he was not sure he was ready to face her again.

He rolled his shoulders to loosen them and straightened his back. Only a coward would run from a woman and surely he could rein in his anger enough not to berate her again. He turned to the earl and asked leave to go to Beatrice. A wave of the earl's hand dismissed him. Moving quickly to outstrip his worries, he strode down the path toward Beatrice.

She looked up as he approached, the rose in her hand no longer spinning. He stopped five feet away from her, halted by her wary, somber look. Violet smudges underneath her eyes turned them gray, the marks dark against her pale skin. She looked like a woman who had not slept in a year.

His jaw tightened and unnamable emotion moved in his chest. Did she hate the thought of marrying him so much? He smoothed the furred collar of his gown. Her happiness with the match did not, could not, matter. They were married, and had no choice but to make the best of it.

He said, "It is done."

"How long?" she asked.

He frowned. "How long?" How long had it taken to come to an agreement? How long until they married? She could mean anything.

"How long until I must live with you as your wife?" she asked. In her hand, the rose shook and a petal dropped off, drifting against her skirt. He stepped closer.

"Two months. The wedding will be at Michaelmas."

She nodded. "Ceci said it would be so."

"She knew?"

"I do not believe she knew. I think she guessed or reasoned it out. I must show I do not bear Thomas Manners's child."

"Do you?" he asked. For the first time he wondered. What would befall them if she was with child?

"I carry no child, of that I am certain," she replied, staring past him. Her tone was flat, yet full of meaning, meaning he could not begin to interpret.

More than any other woman he knew, she was a mystery to him. "What do you mean?"

Her eyes met his, a question in their depths. He held his breath until she found her answer. He could see, as clearly as if she spoke the words aloud, the moment when she decided not to tell him what she knew.

"I know as any woman does. My courses have not failed me." She blushed as she spoke, but whether it was because she lied or because she was embarrassed to speak of such intimate matters to him, he could not tell. "But the truth does not matter. It is what men believe is the truth that counts."

He thought of what he had once believed of her, and what he had learned. Conyers's arms around her, Conyers's hands on her breast… In defiance of his good intentions, his mingled hurt and anger spoke. "So a woman may betray her promises and it counts for nothing if no one knows."

"Or a man," she said sharply, anger flashing like lightning. And, like lightning, it was gone almost more quickly than his eye could see. She sighed and lowered her head. "Is this how you intend to use me? To remind me at every turn of my sins?" Her voice was weary and her mouth, half hidden by the turn of her head, curled down at the corner.

"No," he said. "It is not what I intend."

"Can we not make peace between us, Sebastian?" She raised her head and looked into his eyes. "I do not want to quarrel with you."

"Nor I with you. But I do not see how we may avoid it." Not when she said things that provoked him to unkindness, provoked his unruly, cutting tongue to mischief.

She lifted the rose to her face, brushing its petals against the tip of her nose, but he did not think she smelled its sweetness, not with the distance in her eyes.

"Ceci has courage," she said.

"She does." He frowned. On the face of it, her remark had nothing to do with his statement, but he did not think them unrelated. He waited for Beatrice to reveal the connection.

"She dares to do things I never dreamed," she went on, "and in doing so, she fires my courage."

Courage to do what? He wanted to ask, but something, some angel or demon, held his tongue still.

She looked up at him, her eyes searching his face. Once again, he saw the thoughts moving in her eyes, calculating, weighing him. When she looked away, he knew she had once more chosen to hide her thoughts from him. The morning, the afternoon, the rest of his life darkened; there would always be silence, things unspoken, between them.

"Forgive me, Sebastian." Her voice was harsh, as if she forced the words out. His jaw clamped shut and his mouth tightened. What new game was this? What if it was not a game? He could not think, could not gauge her honesty. "Forgive me for Conyers and forgive me for betraying my husband by intention if not by action."

Her offenses were not against him and not for him

to pardon even if he could. The man who could pardon her lay in his tomb. "Do not ask this of me."

"You cannot forgive me?" she cried, crumpling the rose in her hand. Its scent, heavy and piercingly sweet, clogged the air.

He spoke through teeth that would not unclench. "I have nothing to forgive. You did me no harm."

"If I did you no harm, then why are you so angry with me? Why do you hate me so?" Her face between the dark folds of her hood was stark pale, whiter than it had been before, her lips colorless.

"I do not hate you," he said.

"Liar," she said softly. Her mouth trembled as though she might start crying, but her eyes were cold, colder than he had ever seen them. Their chill bit through him.

"I do not hate you," he said again. He was angry with her, angrier than he had yet been, and he did not know why. "I despise you."

The words hung in the air; he could not snatch them back. She caught her breath and then nodded. "So." She opened her hand and rose petals fell to the ground like snow. "We are good company, after all. You cannot despise me as much as I despise myself."

Without curtsying, without asking for leave, she turned and walked away.

"Beatrice." He had not meant to say he despised her; that was too simple a name for what he felt.

He did not know what had driven her attempted apology—did she try to cozen him, or had she simply wanted to have done with her past?—but in spurning it he had also refused the chance to alter their demeanor toward one another. And he had spurned it in the harshest manner he knew how.

If he had simply accepted her apology, could he have put an end to their endless quarreling? He did not know, but perhaps it was not too late.

There was only one way to find out. "Beatrice!"

Chapter Six

Hurrying down the path toward the river's edge, Beatrice clenched her fists, trying by force of will to stop trembling. She did not know if she shook with anger, fear or hurt; it was all the same to her. Emotion caught her up and carried her away, a flood smashing through the barriers she had built to protect her heart.

"Oh, God, what shall I do?" she whispered. Her hard-won control was gone.

She had tried to make peace between them, but Sebastian had wanted none of it, throwing her effort to ease his fury back in her face. If he would not make peace with her, she could see no help for them. They would live and die at odds.

When Thomas had died, she had felt as if the walls of her prison had fallen down, releasing her from darkness into the light of day. She had not cared how she would live the rest of her life, only glad she would never again wait with one ear cocked for the sound of his curses, one eye open for his oncoming fist. Then, just as she was ready to begin considering the rest of her life, John had come home and this new disaster had overtaken her.

"Beatrice!" Sebastian shouted.

She knew she ought to turn—no doubt he would be angry if she did not—but she could not make herself stop and face him. Not while she fought to calm her turbulent soul.

"Beatrice!"

A few of the men working in the beds along the riverbank straightened and stared. Behind her, she heard swift footsteps on the path. A hand grabbed her arm and swung her around.

"Beatrice, did—"

She flinched, head jerking back, muscles tensing as she braced herself, arm flying up to protect her face. It happened so quickly, she did not have time to stop herself.

Sebastian's fingers on her arm loosened but did not let go. "Beatrice!"

She lowered her arm, her cheeks hot. Why had she reacted so? She knew Thomas was dead, his senseless blows in the grave with him. She had nothing to fear while in her father's house, so why had she revealed so much to Sebastian?

"Did you think I would strike you?"

Her heart slammed against her ribs, her breath shallow. She could not speak of this, not to Sebastian. *I will master myself.*

"No, I did not," she gasped, unable to catch her breath. All the air in England, sweet and foul alike, would not be enough to fill her.

"I do not believe you," he said, drawing his brows together.

Her head spun.

"You flinched. I saw it," he said gently.

Darkness swirled before her eyes. In the dimness she

saw Sebastian's lips move and heard his voice, but she understood nothing. *I am going to swoon,* she thought, and grabbed Sebastian's sleeve to slow her fall.

Serpent-quick, his free arm shot around her waist, dragging her against him to support her weight. "Breathe slowly," he said.

She rested against his strength, aware of his forearm pressing against the small of her back, his legs and hips pushing her skirt and underskirt against her. The feel of him ought to dismay her. Instead her breath calmed, the whirling blackness in her head cleared; her heart quieted. And all her tumult settled into something warm and dark.

For a moment she rested against him.

"Beatrice." Sebastian's voice was low, soft against her ears like the touch of velvet.

She looked up and met his eyes. The garden around her, the murmuring river at its edge, the chatter of the workmen, her father's booming laugh all faded, obscured by the darkened blue of Sebastian's eyes. His arm shifted, pulling her more tightly against him. Surely he could feel her tremble. Curiously she did not mind.

"Why did you flinch?"

"I—" Her voice deserted her and she could not catch her breath. How could she have forgotten how long and curly his eyelashes were or how gold their ends? "I did—" She could not tell him she had not heard him. Through her stiff skirts the strength in his long legs was unmistakable. This moment had to end; she wanted it to last forever. Longing stirred, strangely welcome. "I did not see you clearly."

He looked at her for a long moment as if waiting for her to say more, to offer further explanation. She thought, *I shall tell him everything, everything about Thomas.* But her lips would not part, the words clogged somewhere in her throat. Sebastian despised her; how could she leave her soul naked to his scorn?

"I see," he said, and released her. When he stepped away, it was like being thrust out of a warm, well-lit room into the dark, cold night. She clasped her hands at her waist. Worse, it was like stepping into the night because she feared what would befall her in the room. If she had not lied, he would still hold her. What a fool she was.

"I misspoke when I told you I despise you," he said, folding his arms across his chest.

She looked away. "Why should you not despise me, Sebastian? I did not lie to you when I said I despise myself." If she could not tell him about Thomas, she could confess this much.

Silence answered her. She looked up to find Sebastian staring down at her through narrowed eyes. She waited for him to speak or to look away. He did neither, watching her as if trying to value what he saw.

Goaded by his silence and the pressure of his stare, she cried, "Do you not believe me?"

He looked at her for a moment longer and shook his head. "No. I believe you. But I do not know why."

"How should I not scorn myself?" she cried. "I have done things that shame me."

"You said yourself you have done penance for your sins," he said irritably, unfolding his arms and planting fists on hips. He was tall and strong, his shoulders broad against the sunny summer sky.

Longing stirred again, making her aware of her body, her skin suddenly alive to the brush of sleeves and skirts, the constraint of her pair-of-bodies, the breeze lifting the lappets of her hood to tickle the back of her neck. And her distress, the moil of emotion churning in her heart, only heightened her awareness, made its tooth sharper. If he had not held her, would she feel this now? It did not matter.

"I am still ashamed," she said. The more shamed now because she had not let George Conyers handle and caress and kiss her out of desire for him. No, wearying of Thomas's accusations of infidelity, she had finally given in to the impulse to be as black as her husband painted her, to taste the pleasure of sin since she got no pleasure from goodness. In the end, she had not found pleasure anywhere.

"I cannot help you," Sebastian said.

"I do not ask it of you."

"My lady Manners!" An usher trotted along the path toward her, a square of white in his hand. Joining them, he bowed and offered her the square. "This arrived for you."

Beatrice took it and turned it over, revealing the crest pressed into the wax sealing it closed. The Manners arms. The last time she had seen the ring that made this mark, it had been on Thomas's hand. She shivered. Oh, for the day when she would be shut of the whole house of Manners.

"What is it?" Sebastian asked.

"A letter from my stepson by the look of it," she said, and broke the seal.

Unlike her sister, she did not read easily, so it took her a few minutes to understand what the letter said. Even after reading it a second time, she could not believe the contents. The strutting lickspittle thought to deny her right to her own things. Anger, banked but not dead, flared up. Surely he would not dare.

She held the letter out to Sebastian. "Please, if you will, read this and tell me what it says." Her voice was milder than she had thought it would be. So all the hard lessons Thomas had taught her were not lost; she could sound placid as a milch cow while resentment and annoyance curdled beneath her breastbone.

He took the letter and quickly scanned it. "It says the jewels you demand belong to the Manners family. You have no valid claim on them."

I will flay him for this.

She took a deep, calming breath. "That is what I feared it said."

I will crush his bones to powder.

She was a mere woman, unable to harm anyone, schooled to meekness and submission, but at the moment, as fury swelled her heart, she thought she might have the strength to tear a man in two.

"What jewels does he mean?"

"Baubles my lord gave me. Nothing from the Manners hoard. He was very clear when he gave them to me that they were mine."

Some of her anger must have revealed itself, for Sebastian stepped back, spreading his hands in a placating gesture. It stung.

"Do they matter so much? Do you value gauds so highly?"

No, she wanted to say. *I hate every stone, every ounce of gold. But I wept whole oceans and endured more than I dreamed I ever should for them. I deserve to keep what is mine.*

"I will not allow a puffed-up popinjay, a preening bladder stuffed with bombast, to steal what is mine. I will not stand idly by while a thief who dares to sign himself my loving son robs me." She clamped her mouth shut, afraid of what her flash of anger would provoke in Sebastian, yet unable to regret a single spoken word. *Let him beat me, I do not care.*

"Do you think I shall give you nothing?" he said, frowning. "Do you think me so poor?"

I think you will not give me anything because I am the last woman you would choose. Summoning the skill to smother her temper, a skill honed before Thomas's greater provocation, she took a deep breath, ribs straining against the confines of her pair-of-bodies, and let it out silently. Sebastian must never know how she had to gather her patience, just as Thomas had never known.

"My lord, this is a relic of my past. I did not mean to disturb you with it."

He scowled at her. "Do not turn a soft face to me, Beatrice. Do you think I cannot buy you gauds to make up for the ones you lose?"

Thomas had said and done far crueler things, yet he had never made her as angry as she was now. "Do you wish me to speak plainly?"

He folded his arms across his chest again and she thought of a fortress drawing up its bridge, lowering the portcullis, defending itself. "I do."

She folded her hands at her waist and straightened her back. If he struck her, he would not knock her down. "I have no doubt you have wealth enough and more to replace the poor things I claim. But all your wealth will not undo theft."

"Is it disdain for theft that makes you so wroth?" he asked. "Or is it greed?"

She spread her hands, holding them with their backs uppermost so he could see that the only ring she wore was her wedding band. "Are these the hands of a greedy woman?'' She pressed her hands to her bare neck. ''Are there chains about my neck set with pearls and rubies? Is this the guise of greed? Is my hood bedecked? Oh, yes, I am a greedy woman. Do you not fear for your strongboxes when I come into your home?''

''Your tone ill becomes an obedient wife.''

''You are right, Sebastian. But you have not yet claimed me.''

He stepped closer, so close he leaned right over her as if to overawe her. If that was indeed his intent, it nearly succeeded. Something—stubborn pride, a determination not to cower again—kept her spine straight and her head lifted. She met his eyes, refusing meekness while inside something quivered as if in fear. But it did not feel like fear.

''Shall I claim you?'' he asked. ''Will that still your tongue?''.

''You bade me speak plainly. If you do not desire plain speech, do not give me leave to speak it.''

''Shall I claim you, Beatrice? Answer me truly.''

The fountain of courage and pert words inside her ran dry. She stared up into his eyes, dark between his glinting golden lashes, exhilarated and terrified. But not terrified of him. Terrified of something she saw burning in the depths of his eyes. *Yes,* she thought. *No…I do not know.*

''You promised to claim me at Michaelmas. Is that not soon enough?'' Her voice, low and with a rough whisper in its depths, did not sound like her own, nor did it seem to come from her throat. She sounded as if she spoke from the depths of her flesh.

Sebastian licked his lips. ''No,'' he whispered, ''it is not.'' He swallowed and stepped back, his mouth drawn in a tight, thin line. "Do not start this with me, Beatrice. You will not make a fool of me." He stepped back again. "I must go. I do not think I shall see you again before you return to Wednesfield. Ask your father for the terms of your dowry if you wish to know them."

"Where do you go?" she asked. It was a question she should not have asked—it was not her place—yet she could not let him go yet.

He frowned. "Do you dare question me?"

If I say yes, he will be very angry and rightfully so. If I say no, I will lie. She stared at him. *That was a fool's question, my dread lord.*

When she did not answer, he sighed, the frown fading, his tension dissipating. He looked as weary as she felt, yet in his eyes, she saw the same sparkle she felt to the ends of her fingers and toes. *How is this? How shall I feel this now, with him? And how long shall he feel it, too?*

"You are addled and now I am addled, too," he said, and for the first time in years there was nothing but rueful amusement in the tone he used with her. "I go to visit my uncle Isham in Kent. I will not be able to go there and come back in time to join you on the journey home."

Without his anger and scorn to anchor her, she was adrift. How could she answer him when she no longer knew how he would respond? "God be with you, my lord."

His gaze traveled over her face and down her body, as tangible as if it had been his hand. Her mouth went dry.

"Until we meet again, my lady."

Chapter Seven

When Sebastian, accompanied by servants and guards, rode out of the lane leading to his uncle Henry Isham's house outside Canterbury three days later, he found the family gathered before the great door, prepared for his coming by the man he had sent ahead. Gilded by the late-afternoon sun, Henry stood at the top of the shallow steps before the door. His son Kit stood beside him, his daughter Anne behind them. Henry's expression was neither welcoming nor forbidding, a mask designed to reveal as little as possible.

Sebastian halted his horse before the steps. He swung down from the saddle and, pulling his gloves off, climbed the steps to the waiting Ishams. Kit bowed, Anne curtsied, but Henry stood straight as a poplar, his brilliant blue eyes warm despite their wariness. He spread his arms; Sebastian moved into his hard grip.

"Why are you here?" Henry asked, softly enough not to be overheard.

"You will know soon enough," Sebastian replied, and stepped back to be welcomed by his cousins.

"That is a fine doublet for riding," Kit said, his gray eyes shining. "Do you wish to awe us, Cousin?"

"Sebastian was at Court," Anne said. "All his things must be very fine."

Henry said, "Anne, hush."

Anne ducked her head before lifting it to stare at Sebastian. Kit stared, too, the two pairs of eyes fixed on him with ravenous interest. What did they want him to say? *Yes, they are fine. Very fine indeed. And far too expensive for my purse, but I was at Court and had no choice.*

He made himself smile once more. "What, Cousin, would you have me arrive shabby as a beggar?"

"Let us not stand about chattering like magpies," Henry said. "Go within. My men will tend to your horses and my steward to your men."

With Henry leading the way and his children trailing Sebastian, they went to the parlor above the hall, a snug room that faced west and was filled, at this hour, with golden light. Henry insisted that Sebastian sit in his great chair, an honor that seemed faintly edged with mockery. Though Henry respected the difference between his rank and Sebastian's, he was not over-awed by it and the honor he paid Sebastian as a no-bleman was leavened by the knowledge that Sebastian needed his counsel.

When they were settled, he asked, "So, Nephew, what news?"

"I am betrothed to the Earl of Wednesfield's elder daughter, Lady Manners."

Anne gasped and clasped her hands. Kit sat back, mouth slightly agape.

"Does she not have a husband? From Norfolk?" Henry asked, brows drawn together.

Sebastian shook his head. "No. She is widowed."

"When was this? I had dealings with her husband nigh unto Midsummer's Day."

"A fortnight ago."

Henry's frown deepened. "She changes her estate quickly."

Sebastian narrowed his eyes. Was this one of Henry's subtle criticisms or was it no more than it seemed? "What do you mean by that, Uncle?"

Surprise sparked in Henry's eyes as if he had not expected that Sebastian would need to ask. "No more than I said. This is speedy work."

"Only a fool lets a good match slip through his fingers," Sebastian replied, discreet before his wide-eyed cousins. "I had it in mind to marry and had begun to look about me for a wife. I can imagine no better family to ally myself with than Wednesfield's."

"He is short on kinsmen."

"Then he will be all the more glad of me. Although, through Beatrice's mother, there is a connection to the Nevilles."

"Who are not the family they used to be." Henry sighed and gripped his knees. "I am not sure you could not do better."

The memory of Beatrice outfacing him in the Coleville House garden rose in his mind's eye. With her face flushed and her eyes bright, she had looked like a woman consumed with desire. And though he had known her heat was anger, his body had responded as if she radiated passion. Since then, whatever his mind and heart said, his body had insisted marrying her was far from disastrous.

"It cannot matter, Uncle. I have signed the contract."

"Did not Lady Wednesfield's grandsire marry a Benbury daughter?"

"Lady Wednesfield's grandsire's grandsire. Lady Manners and I are not within the forbidden degree of consanguinity." He and Beatrice had known that since childhood. Their common ancestors were further back than four generations, so far back they were nearly lost to memory.

"Humph." Henry shifted his weight and rearranged the folds of his long gown. "I expect you did not ask your mother about this."

"No, Uncle, I did not." He considered adding that his mother lived too far away to consult, but discarded the idea. Henry knew where his mother was as well as he did.

"When do you marry?"

"Michaelmas," Sebastian said.

"So long?" Anne asked wistfully.

"She is newly widowed," Henry said. "Do not interrupt your betters, girl."

Uncomfortable silence followed Henry's untoward sharpness. To ease it, Sebastian said, "You must be at the wedding as my guests."

Henry nodded. "You will need witnesses of your own."

"I should wish for your attendance in any case," Sebastian added. He looked at Henry. "And it please you, Uncle, I should like to speak to you of business when you have the time."

If his uncle was surprised, he hid it, merely nodding as if he had expected the request. As perhaps he had— very little escaped him.

"Why not now? Come with me to my counting room."

The counting room was a tiny chamber behind the hall, so full of tables piled high with ledgers that there was barely room to move. After lighting a few tallow candles, Henry dropped onto a stool set before the largest table and motioned with his hand for Sebastian to sit on the stool in the corner. Sebastian pulled the stool forward until it was within five feet of Henry's and sat, facing his uncle.

Henry waited without speaking. His patience reminded Sebastian of the earl and all the earl's tricks. How not? Between them, Wednesfield and Isham had raised him to honorable manhood. It was fitting that they should be alike.

"You will call me fool, Uncle, when I am done with my tale."

"Perhaps. What have you done that I should name you so?"

"There is more to my betrothal than the wish to capture a rich prize."

"Your mother wrote me that you intended to pursue the younger Wednesfield daughter. Is the elder so much richer?"

Sebastian sighed, unwilling for just a moment to speak his sorry tale. Let him put off for a minute or two his uncle's inevitable displeasure and censure. "No, but it does not matter. I pledged myself to Lady Manners five years ago."

All the expression left his uncle's face, the warmth gone from his eyes. The silence in the room was as heavy as lead.

After a long moment his uncle asked, "Was the pledge binding?"

"Binding enough."

Henry's eyes narrowed. "Then it was not unbreakable. Can you still get out of it?"

"I do not wish to."

Henry stared at him, his eyes hard and probing. "You cannot befool me. You do not desire this betrothal."

"No, I do not. If I had not made a binding promise, I would not be here now. But I did make a binding vow and I will not be forsworn."

Henry's gaze wandered away from Sebastian's face, traveling around the room as if he might find wisdom in his stacked ledgers, in the dusty corners of the floor. His gaze returned to Sebastian. "Why does this betrothal not please you?"

Sebastian rubbed his palms on his thighs. "I do not trust her."

Henry waited, patient as time.

"She dishonored her marriage vows."

"How did she betray her vows? Was she disobedient? Or did she—"

The truth lodged in his throat as if he betrayed her by speaking it. "She took a lover."

Henry's brows rose in surprise. "Are you sure?"

"I discovered them in such a way that I could not be mistaken." Conyers's arm around her waist, his hand on her breast... Sebastian shoved the memory aside with the ease of long practice.

"I must confess I do not understand your determination to marry this woman." Henry's eyes were shrewd and worried, his mouth tight. "If she has so little sense of honor, surely you cannot continue with this."

"I am married to her." Sebastian sighed, groping for the words that would explain his reluctance to repudiate Beatrice, his desire to preserve what honor he had. "I cannot change that by lying."

"You are a fool."

"I know, but I am not a dishonorable one."

"What value is honor if it costs you a son of your loins? Do you want another man's get to inherit Benbury? Put her aside," Henry said sharply.

"I cannot," Sebastian said. "Believe me when I tell you if I could, I would. However, I will not lie and I cannot get out of this marriage else. As you love me, accept that Beatrice Manners is my wife."

Henry sighed, a heavy gust of exasperation. "Very well. I will do as you ask because I love you and because I will not deprive myself of the pleasure of saying I told you so later. In the meantime, how do you intend to keep her from straying?"

"I have not thought so far ahead," Sebastian said.

Henry snorted. "If I had a farthing for every time you did not think ahead, I should be rich as Croesus. This is the true reason you are here, is it not? You wish for me to think for you."

"I do wish for your counsel and I will endure your calumnies to get it."

A smile flickered, quick as lightning, over Henry's face before he answered. "The answer is simple enough. You must bind her to you with love."

"What?"

"Woo her to love, win her heart. Look you to your aunt. When she wed your uncle, she was as willful a girl as I have ever seen. Edward won her heart and through her heart her willing obedience."

"A wife owes her husband obedience."

"And a dog owes his master obedience, but without proper training will not offer it. You can beat submission into a wife, as you can a dog, but when you have done, you are left with a dog or a wife who cringes and whines when you come near. No, as you train your dogs with sweet words and rewards, well mixed with chastisement, so must you train your wife. Woo her. Blind her to the blandishments of other men.''

''I do not wish to love her,'' Sebastian said stiffly.

''Pish-tush! I am not talking of you. I am talking of a woman, who is weaker and more easily tempted than a man. Fix her eyes and heart on you, and you need not worry her flesh will stray.''

''You make it sound simple, Uncle, but I doubt me it is as easy as that.''

''How not? You are well made, clever, smooth-spoken. Surely you have won women to your bed— the only difference here is that this one you will not turn off when you tire of her.''

Somehow it did not seem the same, seducing Beatrice as he had once seduced light-minded, light-skirted Court ladies. Court ladies felt no more love than Court gentlemen; it had always been a game of lust and boredom. Whatever her sins, Beatrice was not a Court doxy.

''Women are fickle, Uncle. I may win her love and it may last through the winter, but what of spring?''

''By then she will be heavy with your son and no man will desire her. If no man hunts, shall the hart fall?''

''There is one difficulty that you cannot overcome. I despise the lady.'' Despised her, desired her, could not stop thinking of her. It all churned in his mind, dangerous and alluring.

''I'll wager that is not all,'' his uncle said gently.

''What of it? I cannot play this game.''

"Is it a game? Or do you reform an errant woman and make of her a good wife?"

"I do not think she can be a good wife."

His uncle shook his head. "I long ago gave up the hope that women would behave as I expected, Sebastian. They will always surprise you. Lady Manners might make an excellent wife." He hesitated, glanced at Sebastian as if gauging his trustworthiness, and added, "I dealt with Lord Manners for many years. He was no steadier than a weathercock, turning to follow the prevailing wind, and had an excess of choler. A man like that might drive a beautiful, high-spirited wife to another man's arms, if that other man spoke to her sweetly enough."

"You excuse her."

"No, I do not. I simply offer understanding. I have found that understanding why another man behaves as he does aids me in my business. As for Lady Manners, if I had my way, you would be free of your entanglement with her. Since you will not choose that path, I must help you make the most of the path you have chosen."

"You need not."

"We are kin. What you do must concern me." Henry paused. "There is another matter which you must consider. Earlier I spoke of another man's child inheriting Benbury. I am more concerned that none will. Lady Manners was four years wed with no sign of quickening once. You may have taken a wife of barren stock. If so, naught will come of this marriage."

"She is not barren. Old bulls do not get calves, even on fertile cows. She will bear a child."

"You cannot know that."

Sebastian sighed. "I know. But I can pray."

"Lie with her."

"What?"

"Lie with her before you are wed. If she does not get with child, repudiate her."

"I cannot do that!"

"Does not Benbury come before your qualms? Do you want everything your forebears built to revert to the Crown because you could not stomach bedding a woman you claim as your wife?"

"I can stomach bedding her." He could more than stomach it; the thought made his flesh stir. The stirring discomposed him, suggesting that he might be led where Beatrice willed by the tether of his lust. "What I cannot do is cast her aside."

"You must be ruthless to protect what is yours."

"But not dishonorable."

"I do not urge you to dishonor, only to consider what you owe your estate."

His service to Benbury had earned Henry the right to speak of its future. If it had not been for him, Benbury would have sunk beneath the weight of debt Sebastian's father had accrued. Patiently, steadily, Henry had taught him how to manage his income so that it might cover his expenses as well as mitigate the burdens he had inherited. If Sebastian threw away his patrimony, he also threw away Henry's unremitting and selfless work.

What a damnable coil this was, a tangle he could not smooth. Whatever he did, whatever action he took, he would betray someone. To whom did he owe loyalty? His uncle? Himself? Benbury?

"I make you no promises, but I will not forget Benbury."

"I can ask no more," his uncle said.

"There is one other matter I wish your help with," Sebastian said.

"What is it?"

"The late Lord Manners gave gauds to his wife, Lady Manners. Her stepson refuses to return them to her."

"You wish me to get them for you."

"You could persuade the sky to give up the sun," Sebastian said.

His uncle snorted. "I have no use for flattery."

Sebastian grinned.

His uncle sighed. "Very well, I will handle this for you." He rose. "Come, let us return to the family. In the morning, you will write to your mother of this betrothal and I will send the letter to her."

As they left the counting room, it occurred to Sebastian that if he wooed Beatrice he ran the risk of being caught once more in the web of her beauty. She still moved him, as much as he wished she did not. Unless he kept very much on his guard, he ran the risk of being trapped in love, rather than trapping Beatrice.

He would have to be very careful.

Chapter Eight

Beatrice knotted her thread and cut it. The last of her father's shirts was mended and for now, she had nothing to do. In the fortnight since she and her family had returned to Wednesfield Castle, she had kept busy, helping her mother and her mother's women as they worked. Looking up, she saw a patch of blue sky, a smudge of white cloud, through the high, small window of the old solar. If she sat here with idle hands, she would begin to think of things she did not want to consider.

She was not Ceci, who could read as fluently as she spoke or sing for the other women in the solar. She lowered her gaze to her mother, sitting across the room where the light was brightest while she examined Wednesfield's accounts. "Madam, have I your leave to go?"

Her mother looked up, a question in her eyes. Whatever she saw in Beatrice's face must have satisfied her, for she nodded. "Nan, attend Lady Manners."

"Yes, my lady." Nan was one of the newer maids at Wednesfield, a short girl, plump as a partridge, whose round face always looked as if it would smile at the least provocation. Beatrice liked her best of all the women attending her mother because of her cheeriness.

Half an hour later she and Nan, wearing wide-brimmed straw hats against the sun, stepped out of the house. Beatrice turned her face up to the sky and closed her eyes. Taking a deep breath, she waited, as she had waited since arriving at the castle, to feel the return of the peace she had known in childhood. It had not yet returned, it did not return now.

She opened her eyes and looked through the great gate in the curtain wall to the green world sleeping in sunshine beyond the confines of the castle. Her mother, and no doubt Nan waiting patiently a pace behind her, expected her to go to Wednesfield's garden, planted against the walls of the house itself. She ought to go; the garden had been one of her refuges growing up.

Another more valued one had been a little place along the banks of the placid river Wednesford where a bend in the bank allowed the river to form a small pool. Sebastian, her brothers Jasper and John, and some of her father's pages had swum there in the summers. She and Ceci would sit under the willows on the bank to watch the boys swim and wrestle and torment one another like puppies bred with fish.

Most other days she would choose the order and fertility of the garden, but today she wanted the pool. She wanted to hear the soft burble of the water as it eased past the bank, the sigh of the wind as it lifted and stirred the willow leaves. There, with the smell of water in her nose and the brush of the breeze against her skin, she might find the peace she sought.

But she could not go alone. She glanced back at

Nan. "Follow me," she said, and began walking toward the gate.

She waited for Nan to protest—any of the other maids would have, with good reason—but Nan held her tongue, even when Beatrice left the lane and began walking across the fields.

Arriving at the place under the trees, she saw that it had hardly changed. One willow had lost a branch and the stones pushing through the turf were mossier than she remembered. But the river still murmured quietly, and sun and shadow still flickered on the turf amid the tree roots as the wind stirred the leaves and branches overhead. She put out a hand and touched the nearest trunk, the bark cool and rough under her palm. Trees lining the far bank glittered as the same wind tossed their leaves.

She glanced back at Nan. The girl stood with her hands at her sides, waiting without impatience as her eyes moved from tree to turf to river and back.

"Come. Sit and talk with me," Beatrice said. She settled herself where she knew the roots and trunk cupped a comfortable seat facing the river. Nan sat opposite her on the turf, her skirts spread on the ground around her.

Beatrice took off her hat and leaned her head against the tree, watching lozenges of sunlight pass over Nan sitting in the pool of her skirts. Sheep grazed the hillside across the river, fat as clouds as they drifted across the green turf. A breeze rippled across the pool beyond Nan and fanned Beatrice's face, sweet with the perfume of grass and river.

Every prickling fear, every edge of doubt, regret and recrimination, every ache of sorrow faded, then disappeared, leaving silence and cool calm. Peace. Elusive, longed for, found.

They sat in silence for uncounted time. Little by little, Beatrice's regrets crept back, but now they were not as difficult to endure. Peace had come once; surely it would come again.

A moment later two men on horseback crested the hill on the other side of the river. Beatrice sat straighter, alert and wary. While Wednesfield land was in a general way safe and no one should harm her so close to the castle, she could not be sure of her security. She narrowed her eyes and tried to see if she knew either man.

Sebastian.

She knew it was he even before she recognized the way he sat astride his mount, the particular line of his shoulders and the lift of his head. Her heart began to pound, her legs and arms tightening as she resisted the desire to leap to her feet and run away.

"That is Lord Benbury," Nan said.

Beatrice glanced at her. "Do you know him?"

"No, but I know his man, Ned Makepeace. His father did business with mine, long ago."

Sebastian and his servant rode forward until they were at the shore of the pool, Sebastian's horse with its forefeet in the water. Sebastian was dressed very plainly, in doublet, bases and hose that had seen much wear. His knee-high boots, however, were new and well cared for, the fine leather glossy in the sunlight.

"Greetings, Lady Manners."

His voice washed over her, waking the memory of how he had felt pressed against her as he caught her in her near swoon. The desire to feel him again traveled in a warm wave from breasts to belly.

"My lord." She could think of nothing else to say.

"Wait for me. I will cross downstream and be with you in a trice."

More than ever, she wanted to run—but not from fear. The shaking inside her was never fear. No, it was excitement almost too great to contain. What did it mean that the sight of him should stir her so? She pushed the question aside.

Within minutes he rode toward her along the river's edge on this side, Ned trailing behind. She rose to her feet, waiting for him to ride to her side where he could overawe her with his height astride.

But he did not ride all the way. When he was perhaps fifteen feet away, he halted and dismounted. For a long moment he looked at her without speaking. His gaze was thoughtful, with nothing of his former scorn and anger in it. Where had they gone? She offered look for look, half thinking that to release him from her stare would be to free him to return to his contempt of her.

"Ned. Water the horses."

"Aye, my lord." Ned swung out of the saddle and came forward to take the reins from Sebastian.

Had Sebastian decided he did not want Ned to witness one of their brangles? Perhaps not, but *she* did not want Nan to see how poorly she and Sebastian fared together. "Go with him, Nan. It would not do for him to be found, a stranger on Wednesfield land, with no Wednesfield people by."

"Aye, my lady."

Ned led the horses forward, passing Sebastian and Beatrice to bring them upstream. Nan joined him as he went by. Neither Beatrice nor Sebastian spoke until they were out of earshot.

"I did not expect to find you here," Sebastian said.

"I did not expect to be here," Beatrice replied. Alone with him, she felt his nearness too clearly and eased away from him until she felt the tree at her back. Sebastian followed, standing so close her skirt brushed the toe of his boot.

She ransacked her mind for something to say, afraid of what might come of silence between them. "Did you find your kinsmen well?"

"Well enough." He paused, looking at her. "I asked them to attend the wedding."

She nodded. "How many shall there be?"

"A dozen, no more." He looked away, freeing her from his gaze. In a careful voice, as if he warned her, he said, "They are merchants."

"Yet gently born, Sebastian," she said. "I still remember that much."

One corner of his mouth curled up in a rueful smile as he turned back to her. "I had forgotten how much you know of me." There was warmth, true warmth, in his eyes as he looked at her. How could this be? What had he seen or done in the past fortnight to so change his opinion of her?

"Yes, I do know of you. And you know of me." She shook her head. "But, if you will give me leave to say so, I do not think we *truly* know one another."

His smile disappeared. "What do you mean?"

She sighed, groping for words. "Four years have passed since we could speak kindly to one another, Sebastian. I think we have both changed and are no longer the boy and girl who promised to marry one another."

A short laugh jerked out of him. "For a certainty." He sobered. "If we are strangers to one another, why may we not find amity? I do not wish to live at odds with you, Beatrice.''

''Nor I with you,'' she replied.

''I knew you did not when you asked my pardon in London.''

Her cheeks burned at the memory, and at the memory of his refusal to give her the pardon she had asked for.

''I spoke in haste then,'' he said. ''I cannot trust you blindly, but I do not suspect you of dishonor.''

It was no more than she had a right to expect, but it still stung. She wanted to say, *You can trust me. You can trust me because I have learned in a hard school the costs of deceit and dishonor.* Looking up into his face and seeing the steadiness of his gaze, she knew he had offered all he had to give. She must be content with it.

''Very well.''

He smiled at her, the smile like a hand reaching out to her. ''Then it is settled. We shall fight no more.''

She wanted to believe him, but could not. How could they leave behind so many years of dissension so simply? ''If you so desire.''

Silence fell between them, heavy and still. Sun, filtering through tree limbs and leaves, fell in spangles across his face, catching in the clear blue depths of his eyes, passing over the contours of his wide, firm mouth. His smile evaporated as he stared into her eyes. Her heart turned over beneath her breastbone.

''I do so desire.'' The world faded as it had in the garden in London, lost in a mist while his gaze moved over her face as if he had never seen her before. ''How fair you are.'' He reached out and ran his finger along the curve of her cheek. His fingertip was hot and a little rough.

Under its caress, her skin prickled and her mouth went dry. He was so close she could feel the heat of his body even through all the layers of their clothing, warm and radiant as sunlight. She waited for him to look away and resume his distance from her, the beating of her heart trembling in every inch of her body. His bright eyes were dark as a night sky, the planes of his face tight. With a jolt of fear and excitement, she recognized the look as desire.

"Let me kiss you, Beatrice."

His low voice hummed under her skin. She nodded, unable to speak even to save her soul, and lifted her face for him. He lowered his head and kissed her, his mouth just brushing hers, his mint-sweet breath warm against her cheek. When she did not pull away, he set his mouth on hers as he might set a seal, but he touched her nowhere else. The caress of his lips, hot and gentle at once, was all that held her. If she wished, she could break free of him simply by turning her head.

But she did not want to break free. She sighed, her lips parting, opening to his kiss. His breath caught and then his tongue lightly traced the inside of her lips before slipping deeper within. The shock snapped through her, even to her fingertips, and set the world beneath her feet to spinning. Dizzy, she reached up to clutch his shoulders lest she fall. He was broad and strong under her palms, bones and sinews sturdy even through the padding of his doublet.

Sweet saints, desire. She had forgotten how it felt. The last time she had felt anything near to this had been in Sebastian's arms, so long ago it might as well have been a hundred years.

Underneath the scents of leather and wool, horse and man, she smelled something else. Something that seemed the essence of Sebastian and went curling into the depths of her belly. She leaned toward him, hungry to be closer.

As though her touch had been enough to release him from restraint, he shifted and pressed against her from breast to hip, his mouth moving over hers, his tongue caressing hers. If she had been kissed before, if she had thought she had found pleasure in kisses before, she had never known anything like this.

Hot, red darkness blinded her. Heat soaked her body as Sebastian's arms went around her, crushing her against his strong length. *Yes. Oh, Sebastian, yes.* This was what she wanted, the touch of his mouth harder, demanding more, his hands on her waist, pulling her closer. So close, she shook with the force of his heartbeat. Her arms moved along his shoulders, her fingers diving into the soft, wavy hair at the nape of his neck, and her back arching because no matter how tightly he held her, it was not tight enough.

His hand came up to cup her jaw and the side of her face, his thumb moving in a languorous caress along her cheek. He kissed the corners of her mouth and then the edge of her jaw, the touch of his mouth featherlight yet striking her through to her bones, her flesh struck by lightning.

"Beatrice, sweet Beatrice."

She pressed her forehead against his neck, gasping for breath, her knees useless. If he let her go she would fall. "Sebastian."

He bent his head and kissed her shoulder, his mouth

hot on her skin, while his hand trailed a path from her throat to her shoulders and then came to rest on her breast. She quivered all over, heat licking her from head to toe.

"Ah-hh. Sebastian." She wanted more, her appetite growing, gnawing her, but her thoughts stirred sluggishly and she could not think what shape "more" would take.

"Sweetheart. Oh, yes, so sweet." He pressed his cheek against hers, his fingers caressing the side of her breast through her bodice, pleasure burning under his fingertips. Her gasp sounded like a sob. Sebastian replied with a shuddering breath. "You are sweeter than honey." He kissed her eyes, her nose, and then her mouth, parting her lips once more with the urgency of his kisses.

The heat and pleasure she found in his embrace was greater than anything she had ever known. He spoke truly: it was sweeter than honey. It also threatened to overwhelm her. She broke the kiss, reached up and covered his mouth with her fingertips. His mouth and tongue moved over them; she felt their touch in the depths of her belly and tears sprang to her eyes.

Oh, sweetness, such sweetness. Sebastian half lifted her; she could feel every inch of his length as if it were her own body, and he was still too far away. *This is why priests warn us against sin. Because it is so sweet, such temptation.* She could drown here, now, in the demands of her appetite. *I never knew. I never knew how sweet the sin of lust could be...*

Sin.

She stilled, the word reverberating in her mind.

This is sin.

Her blindness lifted, the red darkness cooling. In her

mind's eye she had a picture of herself, her clothing rumpled by the caress of a man's hands, her mouth made red and swollen by a man's kisses.

I am guilty of the sin of lust.

In a moment he could have his hand in her bodice and she would allow it; the moment after that he could have her on the ground with her skirt pushed up around her waist and she would welcome it.

As if she had been flung into the river, cold reason and colder anger doused the heat of her desire. She wrenched herself out of his arms, shaking in the backwash of hunger for him and disgust at herself, panting raggedly.

How quickly and easily she had slid along the old path, and with a man who had reason to doubt her honor. All he had needed to do was come upon her and ask to kiss her and she had been in his arms, allowing him to kiss and caress her with more ardor than was seemly. Worse, she wanted nothing more than to step back into his arms and let him continue, to follow the path of her desire to see where it led. To see what else he knew to raise such delight in her.

"Beatrice…" His voice was hoarse and the hand he stretched out to her shook. "Sweetheart."

"No!" Backing away from him, she pressed her hand to her lips. "No. I will not behave so."

He moved toward her. "You are my wife. You know that. There is no sin in this."

She shook her head. "I will not be tupped in a meadow like a goose girl." Heat and longing rolled over her. Witling that she was, in this moment she wanted him enough to lie with him anywhere he asked. Speaking as much to herself as to him, she whispered, "Even if I am your wife, I will not."

"Bea, please." Sebastian stepped closer, his hand within inches of her.

She looked up into his face. His eyes were still dark, his face still taut. His lips looked swollen; she wanted their touch on her mouth, her throat, her breasts. Wanted it with an edge that cut.

She stumbled on her skirt. If she stayed here a moment longer, she would take the hand he held out, take everything the look in his eyes offered. Lifting up her skirts as she had not done since childhood, she turned and ran home to Wednesfield.

Chapter Nine

Sebastian leaned against the tree trunk, his face pressed into the crook of his elbow, his body taut as a bowstring with the pull of unfulfilled desire. He had known he wanted Beatrice, but he had not thought that the touch of her lips on his would scatter his plans, his very thoughts to the four winds. Kissing her, he had only been aware of the taste of her mouth, the softness of her body pressed against his, and the growing weight of his arousal. Years ago, kissing her had been pleasant enough, but nothing like the wild delight that had filled him today.

"Fool, fool, fool," he muttered. He ached for her, burned for her; desire consumed him. He had dreaded this, knowing how she could bewitch him with a look or a touch. And yet, he could not wish he had not kissed her. If the fierceness of his desire surprised him, at least no harm had come of it and he had learned enough to be more wary.

He pushed away from the tree. The earl had sent for him; he did not have the time to stand out here like a greenling pining for his ladylove. He had to find Ned and resume his journey to Wednesfield. He walked away from the tree and onto the faint trail of bruised grass left by his horses along the riverbank. As he left the pool behind, the burble of the river as it flowed over the rocks in its bed grew louder, gentle music in his ears. Beneath it, he thought he heard the lilt and sparkle of a woman's laughter.

He drew close enough to see Ned and Nan through the screen of boughs, their heads close together until Nan threw hers back and laughed. From the sound of it, hers was the laughter he had heard before. She slid away from Ned and, as Sebastian pushed through the last of the leaves barring his way, she cast a saucy glance over her shoulder. Ned stepped closer to her. The air between them hummed with dalliance and Sebastian did not know whether to be amused or annoyed.

"If you are done, girl, your mistress has returned to the castle," he said. He spoke more harshly than he intended, but so be it. The girl was a fool to remain out here alone, prey for any clever-tongued caitiff who came along.

Glancing warily at Sebastian, she murmured something to Ned. With a quick curtsy in Sebastian's direction, she hurried past him down the path. Ned, meanwhile, wound the reins in his hand through his fingers, refusing to look at Sebastian.

"And if you are done, perhaps we might finish our journey to Wednesfield."

Ned flicked a glance at him, assessing how angry he was. Sighing, he led Sebastian's gelding forward. Sebastian swung into the saddle and nudged the horse forward, leaving the path to get out of the trees. The jingle of tack and the thump of hooves told him Ned followed close behind.

He made for the road to Wednesfield; finding it, he urged his gelding into a fast walk. The road wound along the low hillocks, too narrow for a quicker pace. Cutting across the earl's fields was shorter—long ago, that had been the only way he had ever arrived at Wednesfield—but he was no longer that kind of visitor, a neighbor crossing onto friendly land making a visit. Now he was something else altogether.

The household at Wednesfield was well run, so that when he rode in through the great gate in the old curtain wall, one boy ran to the main house while another hurried to rouse the grooms. The earl's steward had come into the yard to lead him within before he even dismounted. With Ned at his heels, Sebastian followed the steward to the earl's chamber above the hall.

The earl sat by the room's only window, his elbow on his chair arm and his chin on his fist, listening to a man with a harp sing in a thin and reedy voice. His eyes were half closed, his thoughts apparently far from here. The steward, a step ahead of Sebastian, coughed quietly.

The earl looked up. Seeing Sebastian, he made a quick gesture with his fingers. The harper stopped singing, laying his hands across his harp strings. "You may go," the earl said to the harper. "Come in, Sebastian. Join me."

Sebastian dismissed Ned and accepted the earl's invitation. Behind him, the door closed softly.

The earl rose and came forward to embrace him. "I am told you came with only one attendant. Surely that was not needful." He moved to a table with ewer and cups in readiness. Taking his cue, Sebastian followed to serve him and poured two cups of ale.

"I do not take your summons lightly, my lord. Besides, my men are needed at Benbury, preparing the house for its new mistress.''

"Sit. Let us talk." The earl indicated the countess's chair, set near his own. To Sebastian's knowledge, she was the only one to use the chair. In bidding him to use it, the earl paid Sebastian no small honor.

And then it struck him soundly, like a blow. In six weeks he would be married to the earl's daughter Beatrice, finally connected to the earl by ties stronger than friendship. He sat. In all his resentment, in all his thought of what his honor cost him, he had lost sight of what he gained by marrying Beatrice.

"I did not expect you to return from your errand so quickly," the earl said. "I trust all is well with your family."

"It is, my lord." Sebastian sipped his ale. "While I was there, I asked them to be my guests at the wedding, an it please you."

"How should it not? What man goes to London and does not learn the name of Henry Isham? He may be a merchant, but he is a prince among them."

"You are too good, my lord."

"Sebastian, soon you will be my son by marriage. My sons do not say 'my lord' to me when we are closeted like this. Call me sir."

"Very well, sir."

The earl grinned. "Very well indeed." He drained his cup and set it at his elbow. "Lady Wednesfield has gone over Herron's books to be sure naught is amiss. She tells me all is as it should be, but no doubt you will wish to examine them yourself."

If a woman had examined them, he most assuredly would. "I did not know you allowed Lady Wednesfield to see your books."

"Allow?" The earl snorted. "I would make such a muddle as would not be righted in a month of Sundays."

"Surely you must have a man who does your book-keeping," Sebastian said.

"I do, but Lady Wednesfield checks his work. She has a finer head for numbers than any man I have ever known. I should be a fool not to make use of that." He folded his hands, hooking one thumb on the gold chain crossing his chest. "Beatrice has the same skill. It is not for me to meddle or pry into your affairs, but if you will take the advice of a man who was old before you were born, you will let her watch your books for you. She will be able to account for every farthing spent anywhere on your land."

Give her that kind of power? He would woo her into love as his uncle had counseled—but he would not trust her with anything of value.

"No doubt you wish to know why I sent for you," the earl said.

"I am grateful for your advice, but I did not think you would send for me to offer it." Sebastian took another sip of his ale, determined that for once, he would outwait the earl.

The earl smiled as if he saw Sebastian's move and approved it. "It is nothing ill. I wish to ask you to remain as my guest here until you marry Beatrice. I had thought we might ride to Herron together so you may look it over before taking it."

"You are kind to think of it, sir," Sebastian said.

"I may take it as read then," the earl said.

"You may, sir."

"Then you may go and enjoy the freedom of my house and lands."

"And Herron? When shall we travel to it?"

The earl unclasped his hands, putting one up to ward off discussion. "We will talk of that later, tomorrow perhaps. We will not need to leave for at least a week." The earl smiled at him. "Go, find my daughter and greet her. I am certain she will be glad of the sight of you."

Sebastian doubted it, but that was nothing to say to her father. He rose, bowed, and left the room.

He did not see Beatrice again until dinner. By the time he had washed off the dirt of the road and changed into his household finery, it had grown too late to go in search of her. Knowing the earl preferred to dine with his family in the new way, Sebastian, with Ned once more at his heels, went to the solar.

Pausing in the doorway and scanning the room, he found Beatrice standing near her mother's chair. Dressed in black velvet slashed to show the stark white linen of her undergown, her black gabled hood edged with pearls, gold and jet, she looked a far different woman than the plainly clothed one he had kissed by the river. One not so easily approached, for one thing; a sadder, more vulnerable one, for another. But was her vulnerability a lie, the faint air of sorrow clinging to her no more than a reflection of her black clothing? As well as being sad, the mourning seemed faintly reproachful, as if she wore it to register her disapproval of their marriage. Or perhaps she wore it to warn him away, to let him know she would not be cozened by kisses.

It is too late for that, my lady.

He made his bows to the earl and countess, but before he could join Beatrice, the servants came in and laid the cloths on the table. Sebastian watched Beatrice from across the room. Looking at her, no one could ever guess how she had kissed him that afternoon, how sweet and willing she had been in his arms. Part of it was her lowered eyelids and the sober line of her mouth. The rest was that accursed clothing, armoring her, making her a pale creature of the shadows, half alive.

No more black for you. I shall persuade you to colors. And we shall see what happens then.

Once the table was laid, the family took their places, he and Beatrice seated side by side. She greeted him without looking at him, but in the stark frame of her neckline, her breasts rose and fell quickly. She was not as unmoved by his closeness as her apparent calm implied. Through the courses of the meal, he spoke to her and to her brother's wife on his other side, keeping up a flow of easy talk and making sure to offer Beatrice the finest portions. The gesture made color flow into her face; the blush encouraged him.

John and his wife excused themselves as soon as the covers had been drawn and the fruit, cheese and sweetmeats laid out. Now he could give Beatrice his whole attention and begin his campaign to get her out of her weeds.

He leaned close to her. "Why do you still wear black?" His mouth was mere inches from her cheek, its rose-petal smoothness tempting his fingers, resting on the linen tablecloth, to touch her once more. They tingled with the effort not to reach up and caress her.

"To the world, to all in it, I am a widow," she murmured. "I shall leave off my black the day I marry you."

Against the darkness of her gown, her skin had the

same luster as the pearls on her hood, the tops of her breasts surging round and full above the square neck of her bodice with every breath she took. He wanted to lift those breasts in his hands, he wanted to bury his mouth in the shadow between them.

He looked away, his body tightening in response to his wayward thoughts. Thinking of her in such a fashion had no part in his plan. He would not be led by lust. When he had command of himself and his unruly flesh once more, he turned back to her. "Clothe yourself in blue, if you wish to please me."

She slid a glance at him through the veil of her lashes. "Why will it please you if I wear blue?"

"Blue for your fine eyes."

"You flatter me," she said.

He thought of denying it and then discarded the thought. "Is it flattery to tell you the truth?" he asked. "You have always been fairest in blue."

"You also—you ought to wear nothing else," she said, looking up at him. Her eyes were doubtful and wary, as if she sought to know true reasons he spoke so.

"I shall wear whatever pleases you. Name the color."

She allowed a faint smile to curve her lips, a smile she had no doubt learned at Court. He had a whole host of like expressions, masks made to deceive. "I leave you to choose your own colors. I shall be best pleased by that."

He laid his hand over hers on the table, trapping it. "Choose a color for me, and promise me you will wear blue."

Her hand moved under his, trying to get free. "This is unseemly."

"How so?" he asked. "We are betrothed."

"I know, but…"

"I am come as a suitor to win your favors, Beatrice. Will you not grant me this single boon?" He had not intended the pleading note in his voice, but her hand stilled and her eyes searched his face. Looking for the truth? Or mere reassurance? He could offer her one but not the other.

"Why? Why do you do this, Sebastian?" Her voice was very low; he had to lean forward to hear her.

Perhaps he could offer her some truth, after all. "Because it is not enough to me to live without quarreling. I want there to be harmony between us."

Color tinged her cheeks and she bit her lip. The memory of her mouth on his was so vivid that he had to swallow the heat that rose from his depths. Looking from her mouth to her eyes, he saw them darken.

"Why did you kiss me?" she whispered.

"Because you are fair, Beatrice."

The roses in her cheeks darkened. "Do not say so." Under his, he could feel her hand tremble.

"You are fair, and it was no more than a kiss," he murmured to reassure her.

"It was far more than a kiss," she replied.

Far more than a kiss, indeed. He wanted to kiss her so badly he ached with it, only it was not just her mouth he wanted to kiss. He wanted to kiss her breasts, her belly, her throat, her fingers, her toes, every pearly, rosy inch of her.

Where had this incontinent desire come from? Surely not from something so simple as a kiss…

But the kiss had not been simple. It had lit him on fire, the kind of fire not even the most practiced caresses had ever fed, so that now he burned for her as much as he distrusted and doubted her. Given the chance, he would go to her bed without a backward glance, a moment's regret. He had to have her, and he could not wait until Michaelmas.

And he would have her, as soon as he could persuade her to yield to him. He glanced at her, comely and a little sad in her widow's black beside him. Her body promised riches, her passion this afternoon promised delight.

Lie with her.

His uncle's voice spoke in his mind, insidious and tempting. He would make no plan to seduce Beatrice into anything but loving him; he could not in honor do anything else. Yet if wooing her to love also wooed her into his bed, he would not repine.

Chapter Ten

Beatrice sat up in her bed and, sighing, rubbed her tired, itching eyes. She had barely slept all night, her thoughts turning like a mill wheel as she tried to understand what Sebastian was about, if indeed he was about anything.

For five long years they had been at odds, each slashing the other with taunts and gibes whenever they met for more than a moment or two. As soon as she had been promised to Thomas Manners, Sebastian had changed, acting as if she had betrayed him when in truth he had betrayed her in failing to claim her. He should have said, "You are mine," if he had felt so, instead of standing silent and staring when she told him another man desired her.

She drew up her knees and rested her chin on them, gazing at the faint light marking the gap between the bedcurtains at the foot of the bed. True, she had not said, "Am I yours or no? Do you wish to claim me? Or am I free to accept this man's attentions?" Yet should he have needed prompting? There was no way to know the answer without asking him, and she did not have enough courage to do that. Sometimes she wondered, on nights when sleep would not come, how different her life might have been if she had asked instead of keeping silence.

Now, after her foolish attempt to put things right between them, he returned from visiting his uncle with a heart that seemed changed. But was it changed? Had he truly decided to accept her apology? He behaved as if he did, but something within her doubted him. Why was that so? Why could she not believe the evidence of her eyes?

He wants something.

Those years she had spent among the foxes at Court had taught her about deceit and its many faces. Something indefinable in Sebastian's manner made her think of every courtier who had smiled at her and spoken sweet words to her while attempting her undoing. The recognition made her heart ache. She had always believed Sebastian was different than other men, even when he had been so angry with her.

You were wrong about Thomas. Can you be sure about anything?

There was the rub. It had been a witling's mistake to marry Thomas believing his appetite for her was so great that she could easily cozen him. If she could be so wrong about Thomas, how could she be certain of anything ever again?

You are certain this marriage will be as disastrous as your other one.

Other *marriage?* Disgusted memory crawled over her skin.

Her time with Thomas had not been a true marriage, and all she had endured had been for nothing. She had suffered his slaps, pinches and incontinent rages, obeyed his command that she give up the stitchery and gardening she loved, borne his persistent, futile attempts to bed her and accepted his insistence that if she was a good wife to him his desire would rise for her.

He had smelled of death; death had been in his cold fingers as he'd caressed her, in the bones that had thrust through his thinning flesh, in his failure to plant life in her aching, child-hungry womb.

Thank God she need never again lie still while he touched her, parted her legs and lay atop her, breathing the scent of cloves and decay into her mouth as he tried and failed yet again to consummate their marriage. She shivered.

At least she would not suffer the same with Sebastian. Heat swirled from her throat to her breast and belly. When he had kissed her by the river, the fervor of his mouth had spoken unmistakably of his appetite for her.

A hand slid between the bedcurtains and drew them open, revealing Nan. Beatrice had been so far lost in her thoughts she had not heard her maid rise and dress.

"It is dawn, my lady," Nan said, pushing the curtains fully open. Beyond her, the rim of the sky showed pale through the windows, the heights still dim with night. After the darkness of the curtained bed, the shadowed room seemed bright. "What shall you wear today?"

"The black brocade skirt and bodice, the black brocade sleeves," Beatrice replied as she swung her legs over the side of the bed. The question was the same every morning. Why should her answer have changed? "The black hood, the jet necklaces. Dress me in black, Nan, I am but a crow."

"What of your white sleeves, my lady? Shall you

not wear those instead, and white underskirt to go with them? Surely you must leave off some black, with you so soon to wed.''

Beatrice shook her head. ''I shall wear black until I marry.''

Nan nodded, her merry face puckered with trouble. Beatrice sighed, feeling the pull of Nan's regret and her own disgust of her weeds. Why did she persist? She did not mourn Thomas in the least and, betrothed already, no one could fault her for leaving off her sad colors. And she was sick of black.

''Nan, wait,'' she said. ''Dress me in blue.''

Nan's face lit as if Beatrice's change of heart was a gift to her. While Nan combed out her hair and put it up, and laced her into her clothes, she bit her tongue against the desire to cry, *No, take this off, dress me in mourning.* By dressing in blue when Sebastian had said it would please him, she gave him leave to continue his new pursuit of her, a pursuit that might lead her to his bed long before they married.

Yesterday he had reminded her that if they lay together, it was no sin because they had married one another. Fear had made her flee him, fear of her desire, fear of what he would later say to her if she let him seduce her. In his behavior after finding her with George, he had shown himself willing to believe ill of her without concern for the truth. Yet she had not been able to cast his words out of her mind. ''You are my wife. You know that. There is no sin.'' They had kept her appetite for him from dulling, so that when he had leaned toward her and spoken to her last night, it had taken all her will to listen to him through the dry-mouthed ache that burned through her.

How could she desire him so after just one kiss?

And how could she contain her hunger until they married?

You need not. He is your husband and there is no sin.

Nor, as a widow, was she expected to prove her maidenhood. There would be no display of sheets this time as there had been the first, when Thomas had cut his own foot to hide his shame. She could lie with Sebastian anytime during these weeks in safety.

Safety from what? Safety from death? Thomas would have killed her if she had ever lain with anyone while he lived, but lying with Sebastian was different. Safety from shame? As Sebastian had said, lying with him was no sin. Safety from recrimination?

Ah, recrimination. There was no safety from that, nor from regret. She could not be sure Sebastian would remember in the years to come that he had claimed there was no wrong in lying together. How could she be sure that she would not rue yielding to him, if indeed she yielded?

Can I trust him?

She was afraid of how he might hurt her, if she yielded too much of her heart and soul to him. Yet she wanted him, her body cried out for him. Could she yield one and not the other? Could she lie with him and keep herself heart-whole and safe? The only way to know was to take the risk and lie with him.

"What jewelry, my lady?" Nan asked, breaking into her thoughts.

She opened her mouth to tell Nan to find the pearl carcanet her parents had given her when she married Thomas. The memory of Sebastian's gaze passing across her skin when she offered him her bare throat, breast and arms as proof of her poverty checked her.

"None," she said. Would he understand why she wore no jewelry? Did she? It did not matter; she could not put on any of her gauds.

When she was dressed, she went to the chapel and prayed; she had missed Mass. Her soul eased, she went to her mother's solar. At the door she hesitated, the enormity of her decision to put off widow's black clear as it had not been in the safety of her chamber. What if her mother disapproved? However much the countess had disliked Thomas, she could well expect Beatrice to give her late husband's memory its due.

I have given him his due and more. The defiance of the thought collapsed; woe betide the child who failed to meet the Countess of Wednesfield's exacting standards. Beatrice swallowed to loosen the tightness in her throat and nodded to Nan to open the door.

The room that had been humming with soft talk fell silent. Sitting in her chair of estate, her mother looked up from her stitchery. Her brows lifted in surprise as she noted the blue brocade. Beatrice straightened her spine, torn between the wish that she had remained in black and the first stirrings of rebellion.

And then it did not matter. Her mother's surprise melted into a smile, the expression as welcoming as an outstretched hand. Beatrice's tight wariness eased. Since their return to Wednesfield, her mother had been kinder, revealing the softness beneath her prickly exterior like a hedgehog who no longer rolled into a ball of spines.

"Come, child, sit with me."

Beatrice went to sit on the stool beside her mother's great chair. As she settled herself, her mother held out her needle case. "Take a needle and help me with this altar cloth. It is for the abbey church and I can trust no one else to aid me. None of the maids sews as finely as you.''

Beatrice took the needle case, chose a needle and threaded it. Lifting one end of the cloth, she found the place to begin and started stitching, the old pleasure in creating beauty stealing over her. How much of her childhood had been spent in this room, needle in one hand, cloth in another, while she stitched and dreamed?

Her skill with needles had seemed small when compared to Ceci's scholarship, even after her father had asked her to stitch a missal cover as a gift for the queen. Any woman could sew a fine seam, make pictures with needles and silk; how many could read French and Latin as well as English? As for the beauty that had drawn so much praise, it had been a gift; even when her vanity had been greatest, she had known that she was not as good as her face proclaimed her to be. She had not been made beautiful because she was good.

''My eyes are not what they used to be,'' her mother said with an impatient sigh. ''You will have to set these stitches.'' She handed her end of the cloth to Beatrice, where the vine was delicate, its leaves tiny. Beatrice exchanged needles and brought the cloth close so she might see it more clearly.

''I shall miss you when you are gone,'' her mother said softly.

''Because I can sew finely.''

''No, child. I will miss your company.''

Beatrice lowered her stitching and looked into her mother's face. It had softened, her eyes shining as if she fought tears.

"I will not be so far away. Benbury is only three miles from here."

"I know. But it is sweet to sit with you."

It had always been sweet to sit in the solar, making beauty out of thread and cloth. She had dreamed of Sebastian over shirts for her father and brothers. What had she dreamed? Perfect love, perfect harmony, endless days of sunshine filled with Sebastian's smiles and the feeling that he would lay the world at her feet if he could.

Beatrice paused, her needle halfway through a stitch. She had taken him for granted, taken his love as a given, due homage to her beauty. Of course he had loved her. Who had not? Her mouth twisted as she pulled the needle through the cloth and set the next stitch. No one had loved her the way she had thought. No one could. Her vanity had made her foolish.

Well, Thomas had cured her of that. Her beauty had mattered only in that it made men envy him; she had been a bauble, a pretty toy, less than that when he had been frustrated. He had forbidden her to sew, claiming it would ruin her eyes, reddening and swelling them; she had come to believe that he denied her because it gave him pleasure to do so.

It was a sin to thank God for a man's death. If it had not been, she would have given thanks every day. Was it a sin to be glad she was free? Please God it was not; she did not know how to confess it, nor knew what penance might be asked for it.

She and her mother had sewn in easy silence for a good hour when a boy slipped into the room and bowed to the countess. "My lady, Lord Benbury asks if his betrothed wife, Lady Manners, might join him below in the hall."

Beatrice raised her head. Sebastian, asking for her? Why? What did he want? *To woo you,* a voice murmured as if from her bones. Her stomach rolled over.

The countess looked at Beatrice. "That is for Lady Manners to decide."

Go, she thought. Stay. If she was wise she would remain where she was... But Sebastian had never openly asked for her company before.

"If you have no need of me, madam, I should like to join him."

"I have no need of you greater than your lord's, child. Go."

Beatrice pushed her needle through the cloth as if she would only be gone a moment. "I shall return anon."

Mischief and mockery shone in her mother's eyes, as if she knew how unlikely it was that Beatrice would return anytime soon. "Go."

Her heart beating in her throat, Beatrice left the solar and descended the stairs, emerging behind the dais into the jewel-bright brilliance of the hall. Morning sunlight streamed through the stained-glass windows along one wall, scattering topaz, ruby and sapphire on the flagstones and rushes underfoot. Sebastian stood amid the glory, golden hair glinting, lozenges of color splashed against the blue of his short gown and doublet. When he saw Beatrice, he grinned.

"How now, my lady," he said, coming forward to meet her. He took her hand and raised it to his mouth, pressing a warm kiss on its back. His thumb brushed over her knuckles. "What, still no jewels?"

She listened for mockery, but heard none. His blue gaze was innocent, as if he had never accused her of greed, and warm, as if he had never scorned her. She decided to answer the question as if he had asked it sincerely.

"Until my stepson returns what is mine, I shall wear none," she said.

"Then it is as well that my uncle pursues this for both of us."

She swallowed and looked more deeply into his eyes, seeking the truth and finding only the clear warmth that she did not wholly trust. Was it a lie? Or had he truly changed toward her? She would never discover whether or not she was right in her wariness if she did not risk a little.

"I will be glad of any aid."

"It is my pleasure." He turned her hand over and lifted her palm to his mouth, his breath hot against her skin. "Now that is settled, let us walk in your mother's garden."

"Why?" The question came out before she could stop it.

He smiled at her. "Because it will be pleasant to do so."

"Your will is mine."

He placed the hand he still held on his forearm and led her toward the pantry arches and the door that led to the gardens behind the house. As they passed into the sunlight of the garden, he turned, facing her. His smile was as sunny as the August morning, his eyes bluer than the summer sky above them. No matter how hard she looked, she could see no lie in him; his pleasure seemed genuine. She wanted very much to believe it was.

"I meant it when I said I wished there to be harmony between us."

"I wish it, also."

''Good.'' He led her onto the path.

Contained within the castle, the garden at Wednesfield was larger and older than the garden at the house outside London. Golden walls, not the turbid Thames, bound it, their stone holding and reflecting the sun's warmth so that this garden bloomed as the other could not. Wandering the knotted paths, Beatrice smelled green growth, the clean, complex scents of the herbs in their beds released by the heat confined within the walls. She would miss this place, these green beds. She did not know in what state the garden at Benbury had been left after Sebastian's mother remarried, except that it could not match this verdant world.

''Can you make my gardens as wealthy as these?'' Sebastian said, leaning close.

Her thoughts spun into meaninglessness. Was it his nearness or was it the way he seemed to have read her mind that made her head swim? She neither knew nor cared; she was growing to crave the way his breath, soft and warm, felt on her skin. ''No, but I can make them richer than they are,'' she murmured, ''if that is what you desire.''

''It is.'' He slowed. ''Did you make Manners's gardens richer?''

''No,'' she said carefully, holding herself still to lessen the pain. ''My lord said it was not meet for me to worry over herbs when he had gardeners to do so.''

He turned to face her, gold-tipped lashes shadowing his eyes. ''Did it mean so much to you?'' he asked, his tone a curious mix of gentleness and skepticism.

What to say that answered both? No soft answer that she could devise—only the truth would suffice. ''Yes, it did. There is little enough I know how to do. To be forbidden to do those few things...''

"I will not forbid you to tend my gardens. You have my word on it."

"Thank you," she said. "I do not know how to repay you."

"Smile for me. That is payment enough."

Because she could not resist him when he was kind to her, her mouth lifted and with it, her heart. In answer, Sebastian's mouth curved, one corner rising higher than the other in the tilted grin that had led her into mischief all those years ago.

"Is it so hard to smile?" he whispered.

Her heart jumped, as if it had missed a beat. "No."

"Be happy, Bea."

"Yes."

She saw the kiss in his eyes before he bent his head and pressed his mouth to hers. His touch was gentle, with none of yesterday's demand, yet heat still enveloped her, the earth still swung beneath her feet. He lifted his head, looked at her and bent to press a kiss to her brow. The tenderness of it caught in her throat.

"I want you to be happy."

A strange note in his voice made her pull back and look up into his face. Something flickered in his expression that she would have named guilt in anyone else, but not in Sebastian. He had no reason for guilt. Even his condemnation of her, which seemed to have burned away like morning mist, had been warranted. How could it be wrong to call her a whore when she had behaved like one?

"If you are kind to me, I shall be, Sebastian," she said.

He brushed the backs of his fingers along her cheek. "Then you shall be the happiest woman alive."

Blindly, unable to stop herself, she leaned into his

hand as it caressed her. He turned it and cupped her cheek. Gently, so gently that the slightest hesitation on her part would break her free, he drew her close again, tilting her head up. She followed his lead, drifting toward him as if his touch had somehow dissolved her doubts and worries. But for all the gentleness of his approach, when he kissed her, heat flared, blinding and red. As soon as his mouth brushed hers, her lips parted, welcoming him. His free arm encircled her waist, pulling her hard against him.

The fire that had burned her yesterday afternoon by the river roared back to life as if it had only been banked, not quenched. She gripped his arms, the weight of his strength under her palms. If George had made her feel such burning sweetness, would she have been able to keep him from her bed? No, never; she could not have resisted the temptation to sup more of this delight. Sebastian nipped her lower lip, the scrape of his teeth setting her mind awhirl, spinning with pleasure. Somewhere, in the drowning depths, a small voice whispered, *How shall I resist him?* and then it was gone, swept away in a flood of desire. He shifted, or she did, so they pressed more tightly, bodies fitting neatly together, as if made for it. *We are married. There is no sin.*

As if he heard her thought, Sebastian lifted his head, pressing kisses, gentle as rain, on her sensitive mouth. "You are sweeter than I dreamed, Bea," he said, "but this is not the place for such things." He nodded at Wednesfield's windows, bright as eyes.

She pulled herself free of his hold and backed up two steps, putting distance between them. To keep him away? Or to keep herself from reaching for him? She did not know who she feared would be tempted.

"I beg your pardon."

"No, Bea," he said, bridging the distance between them in a single step. "The fault is mine."

All her fearful wariness leaped up. "Can you mean that?" she asked, and heard her own plea for reassurance. She longed to believe he did mean the words he spoke, that he claimed the censure their behavior warranted.

"Yes," he said. "I can. I do."

She waited for something within to tell her if he lied, listening for the little voice that had aided her toward the end of her marriage to Thomas. The voice had warned her when his fury was brewing, warned her when to tread softly and when to clothe herself in the remnants of her pride. But now it was silent, leaving her to gauge the sincerity in Sebastian's bright, deep blue eyes as best she might.

I want to believe you, but I am afraid, sore afraid, of being mistaken in you. Prove yourself to me, Sebastian, please.

She could say nothing; she must hold her doubts close, as if they were gold and she a miser. If she did not trust him easily, how could he trust her? That was the niggling heart of her worry. She did not know what had prompted his change of face; until she did, she could not believe that the change in his behavior truly betokened a change in his heart.

He took her hand and drew it through the crook of his elbow. "Let us walk. I will not kiss you again."

Together they resumed moving along the paths, but now the silence between them was charged, as if lightning might strike at any moment. She could not think of anything but the tension in Sebastian's arm under

her fingers, the way his legs brushed her skirts, the
heat of his body so close to hers.

"What will you need to make the garden at Benbury
as fine as this?" he asked suddenly, as if their prox-
imity troubled him, as well.

She took a deep breath and let it go on a sigh, trying
to clear her head. "I shall need time, more than anything else. This is not made in a year or even two."

"You will have the time. We will not be at Court."

Thank God. To know she was free of the wolves
and the foxes, the staring eyes and the bitter, malicious
tongues... "I am glad."

"Do you not care for Court?" he asked, sudden
tension in his voice.

"Court was my undoing," she said. "How should
I wish to return?"

The path crunched beneath their feet. As her relief
subsided, she considered Sebastian. Why did he turn
his back on Court? As far as she knew, he had been
well thought of, rising higher and higher in royal favor,
his feet firmly on the path to preferment.

"I have no desire to return, either," he said suddenly, as if he had heard her unspoken question. It was
the second time he had replied to an unsaid remark.
She shivered. "Are you cold?"

"No," she answered softly. "I am well."

"You must tell me if you grow chilled."

"I shall." They walked a little farther. "Why do
you not desire to return? Surely you did well there."

"It costs too much and returns too little," he said.

She thought of her own sorry career. "So it does."

"Then we are agreed," he said, putting his free
hand over hers and pressing it. "A quiet life for us."

"Yes," she said.

They walked in silence for some while longer, Sebastian apparently at his ease. Beatrice could not relax, a skeptical voice in the depths of her mind murmuring questions she would not ask. *Why are you so kind to me now when you were so scornful a fortnight ago? What do you want of me that you cannot command?* And underneath the voice there was the memory of fear, as if Sebastian was like Thomas, playing a game to shame her.

Sebastian would not be so unkind, the voice of her heart said, but would her heart not speak what it wanted to believe? She did not know, she could not tell. She had thought she could see, but had found she was blind; she dared not trust her judgment when it had betrayed her so badly in the past.

"What ails you, Beatrice?" Sebastian asked, his voice quiet.

"Naught ails me," she said. Even if he had wanted to hear them, she could not speak of her doubts.

"You walk as if you might cringe at any moment. Do you fear me?"

"No." It was not a lie. Above all else, she feared her own foolishness.

He halted. "Then what do you fear? For you do fear something. I can see it in your face."

Could he? If he could read her now, why had he not been able to read her in the past? He had been wrong in so many ways about her—how could he be right now? Perhaps it was a shot aimed in darkness, in the hopes it might strike true. If so, he had been lucky in it.

"Beatrice."

"I cannot tell you."

"Cannot? Or will not?"

"We have spoken of this before," she said, lifting her eyes to his, expecting anger.

She found calm and patience. "I know. But this time I will not upbraid you. Can you not tell me?"

She shook her head. "I do not have the words." The words she did have must not be spoken.

"If you fear me, it is without cause. I shall not harm you."

There is harm and harm, she thought, remembering the cut of scorn and cold words, the red battery of fists. She remembered Ceci's certainty that Sebastian's kindness toward his animals, the way he did not beat either his horses or his dogs, meant he would show equal gentleness toward his wife.

"I fear grief and disillusionment," she said quietly.

"You can trust me," he said as quietly.

"I cannot."

She caught her breath. The words had slipped out, eased into breath by his gentleness. She waited for his offended anger, for the kindliness and calm to vanish. How not, when she had said he was not worthy of her faith.

"Then I must win your trust," he said, and lifted her hand to his mouth.

"How can I trust you when you leave London so angry you cannot look at me and then return to me as if we never quarreled? I cannot help thinking of those men at Court who prey on unwary maids, all smiles and sweet words to cover deceit and knavery beneath. When they have gained what they sought, there is no longer any kindness or flattery, only japes and mockery." She stopped, breathless and tense, waiting again for the storm to break over her head.

He did not release her hand, holding it loosely in a

clasp that was strangely comforting. "I am sick of fighting with you, Beatrice, that is all. If we are to spend the rest of our lives together, I wish for there to be pleasantness between us, not anger and bitterness. Is that so hard to believe? And if I wish to smooth the way with a little flattery, a smile or two, how does that harm either of us?"

"It frightens me," she said simply. Pain rose in her chest and her eyes filled with tears. "I can believe your anger. I cannot believe your kindness."

"Give me time to prove I mean you no ill."

She blinked her tears away. "Oh, Sebastian, I am yours to command. You do not have to win me. I will always do as you bid."

Something shivered across his face, gone before she could read it. He sighed. "We will come to no agreement today. I do not want to speak and then watch you weigh what I say for truth and falsehood. I want you to believe what I say because it is the truth. *That* you cannot give me out of obedience, however perfect."

There was no answer to that. If he did not want her obedience and obedience was all she had to give, where did that leave them? Yet she had to say something. She could not leave his last statement hanging between them.

"I pray you, give me time."

He touched her face, light as swansdown. "You shall have it."

Chapter Eleven

Sebastian leaned against the wall near the dais and watched a laughing and graceful Beatrice dance with John. In the past week he had wooed her, speaking soft flattery, seducing her with gentle touches and, when he could claim them, gentler kisses, trying to gain her trust. Every night he left the hall or the solar certain he had breached her defenses and had only to exploit his advantage to win her. Every morning he found she had repaired the walls she held against him, so that he had all his work to do again.

He shifted his weight, his gaze following them as she and her brother moved in the dance's intricate figures. How could the kisses that made his head spin and his flesh burn fail to move her? How could he come so close to winning her and yet still fail? Was she wary of him because of her previous mistakes? He saw in his mind's eye Beatrice in Conyers's arms, clinging to him, kissing him. Anger stirred in his depths, anger that would wreck his efforts to win her if he did not master it.

Swearing under his breath, he closed his mind's eye to his memories and pushed away from the wall to find another resting place, watching Beatrice as he went.

The beat of the music gathered speed. With John as her shadow, Beatrice turned with the rest of the dancers, her eyes shining as she leapt and spun. The light from the candles and torches licked over her skin, glinted on her teeth and gleamed on her lips. Desire bit him, hard. Even if he could not persuade her to love him, his gnawing appetite demanded that he bed her. He could never contain himself until Michaelmas.

When she is your wife, you will be able to take her as you list.

But she was his wife now, or nearly enough that it made no difference. Despite her watchfulness, she responded to his caresses with a heat that fired his own. Though she tamped her response down as quickly as it flared up, she must surely yield soon…

John said something that made her glance flick to Sebastian and away. Why did she fight the desire he knew she felt? Did the past have so great a hold on her? Whatever images came to torment him, the past was done. He was not Conyers and she was not Thomas Manners's wife. If he could see it, why could she not?

With patience he could wear down her resistance, but he feared he did not have it in him to be patient. He looked at Beatrice, laughing with her brother as they whirled by. By'r Lady, he did not know if he had the patience to wait out the night, never mind wait out her fears.

The dance ended. Sebastian straightened, ready to follow Beatrice wherever she went. If he could not kiss her nor caress her, he might still hold her hand, speak to her, turn and move with her in the public intimacy of a dance. She put her hand on John's arm; John turned toward Sebastian. Beatrice looked at him and, despite the distance, he could see doubt and something else cloud her eyes. John turned, said something, then he and Beatrice crossed the hall to Sebastian.

"I bring you a fair lady," John said.

"Fair indeed," Sebastian said, looking at Beatrice.

She tilted her head in acknowledgment of the flattery while the musicians began a slow pavanne.

"And now, having done my duty by both of you, let me find my wife," John said, and left them.

"Will you dance with me?" Sebastian asked.

Her eyes met his. "Gladly."

He led her to join the other handful of dancers, her fingers curled around his. For a minute or two they simply danced, no words spoken.

"You looked as if you enjoyed dancing with John," he said at last.

She smiled. "I did. I should have lost my place if he had not aided me."

"This is very different."

"But pleasant, too."

"Yes."

They moved forward, back and forward again.

"I like dancing at home better than I did dancing at Court," she said suddenly, and it was a measure of his success in wearing her down that she had begun to offer information rather than waiting to be asked for it.

Still, the remark surprised him. She had spent her time at Court surrounded by admirers. If he had thought them unworthy of her, she had still seemed to enjoy their attentions. "Why is that?"

She sighed, her brow faintly creased. "Because I

need not be so on my guard at home. When the men at Court flatter a woman, half the time it is in aid of a plot to do her an ill turn.'' She glanced at him sidelong. ''You may flatter me, Sebastian, and I may wonder why, but I do not think you are trying to harm me.''

''Do you not? I see you doubt me.''

She laughed but the sound was as skeptical as it was amused. ''I still wonder at your kindness to me. I wonder when it will end and I wonder what it is in aid of.''

''Have I been so unkind?''

''Yes.''

He stumbled a little, surprised by her forthrightness.

''You asked, Sebastian. I would not have said so otherwise.''

''I have not been unkind since I came to Wednesfield.'' It was all he could say.

''No, no, you have not.''

He let the dance move them through the hall without answering, trying to absorb what she had said. In any other woman, he would interpret frankness as a weakening of defenses, the first intimation that her walls were coming down. With Beatrice he could not be so sure.

If you will give me leave to say so, I do not think we truly know one another.

He heard her voice again, speaking soberly, almost sadly. He had agreed with her that day under the tree because it had suited him to do so, not because he had put any thought into what she said. Yet every day he spent with her only underlined the truth she had spoken. She was a mystery to him, unknown despite the years they had been acquainted. Would he ever know her? He could not be sure of anything she might do and if the uncertainty made him angry, it also made her alluring.

The dance ended, the music silenced. He kissed her mouth lightly, then lifted her hand, palm up, to be kissed, as well. Under the chatter of the other dancers, he heard her gasp as clearly as if the room had been silent. He looked up in time to see heat flare in her eyes. Encouraged by it, he lifted her other hand and pressed his mouth first to the center of her palm and then to the inside of her wrist.

"Do not," she whispered, but she left her hand in his.

"Why not?" he whispered in reply.

"I…" She swallowed. "I should prefer it if you did not."

"Do you dislike it?"

Her eyes met his, full of entreaty. "No. I—I like it too well."

"You said you do not believe I will do you harm."

"I said I do not believe you try to do me harm. There is a difference."

"Words," he said. Was it words that came between them? Was that the source of his difficulty? If he ceased using words, set them aside in favor of action, would he breach her defenses? Would she yield to him?

"Words that speak the truth," she said.

"Words conceal, as well."

"Yes," she said. "I only dare judge by actions and even then I cannot be certain."

"Then let my actions speak for me." What else could he say? The music began again, a livelier tune. "Dance with me."

She turned her hand in his, her acquiescence answer enough.

Later that night Beatrice turned over onto her side in her wide, empty bed and stared into the darkness. Just under her skin, tension thrummed, keeping her awake. How could she sleep when she could not relax into the deep comfort of her bed? When she kept feeling Sebastian's touch, his hands and his mouth on her? When she kept seeing his eyes, dark blue and intent, stare into hers? Desire drove away sleep, gnawing, maddening desire such as she had never known. Whatever she had felt for George Conyers, it had been no more than a trickle to this flood.

She turned again, the ropes underneath the mattresses creaking faintly, and sighed. If it were only her own desire to fight, she would vanquish it. If it were only Sebastian's, she would resist it until he gave up his siege. But to successfully combat her desire and his? She did not know if she had the strength. With her appetite working from within and his from without, how long until her defenses were breached, her walls undermined and collapsing? Even now she could feel herself weakening, hear the little voice in her depths whispering softly that it would be better to yield and have done. She was his wife, was she not? Or at least so nearly that it made no difference…

Give me strength. Give me wisdom.

She did not know what to do, caught in a fever of lust and longing. She ached for Sebastian, the tooth of her desire sharpening day by day. Would she yield in the end simply because she could not endure the pain of denial any longer? Please God let it not be so. Sebastian would never understand how he had driven her to it, nor believe that he alone could have brought her to such a pass. She feared that if she yielded to him, all his new kindness would disappear, replaced by anger and contempt. She feared he tested her without knowing that he had power over her that no other man in the world had. He was the one man she feared she could not resist.

Beatrice sighed and turned once more, rolling onto her back. She folded her hands over her stomach, staring into the blackness above. Let sleep come, let her have surcease from the endless mutter and complaint of her fears and doubts. She closed her eyes and sank into darkness…

A minute or an hour later awareness returned. Had she slept? And if she had slept, for how long? The longing in her depths had not abated, its edge still sharp. What would it be like to turn to find her husband with her? What would it be like to turn to him and welcome his touch?

Do not think of that, do not. She would make herself mad if she did not learn to master her wayward thoughts. If she was going to keep from thinking of Sebastian, she would have to think of something else, anything. Plan the garden at Benbury, she thought. That is something. She turned onto her side, letting her eyes close. Rosemary, rue, lavender and sweet marjoram….

Adrift in the bed, she opened her eyes. Her garden… No, she had not been thinking of the gardens. She had been thinking of something else, something that unsettled her. What?

Hands. She had been dreaming of hands, only these had not been Thomas's hands, they had been Sebastian's, and everywhere they touched, she burned, so hotly that even now, remembering the dream, desire drowned her in long, red waves.

She pushed her face into her pillow, trying to blot out the memory. When it would not be driven away, she sat up, drew up her knees and pressed her forehead against them. Her hunger for Sebastian robbed her of sleep, of sense, of certainty. Knowing the high price of having him only made her want him more.

What is to become of me?

His hands, his mouth, hot and sweet as they brought her delight... Beatrice moved to sit on the edge of the bed as if the dream lingered in the place where she had lain. Through the gap in the curtain, she could hear Nan's faint, steady breathing. She slid her hand into the gap, parted the curtain and eased her feet onto the floor. The night candle guttered in its dish, casting flickering light across the walls. In the windows, the sky was a deep gray rimmed with red. How much sleep had she had? Her eyes were gritty as if she had not slept at all.

Nor would she sleep now. She could not remain in her bed, tormented by memory and longing. Moving quietly, she went to the press and pulled out her plainest clothes, a bodice and skirt she could get herself into without Nan's aid. She dressed quickly and tucked her plait into a simple coif. If she went to the garden to see what she might like to plant at Benbury, she would still have time to return to her room and dress properly before the sun was well up.

Outside, the air was chill enough to bite, raising gooseflesh on her arms when she stepped through the door. After the fever of the night, the cold was welcome. She took a deep breath and lifted her head to look at the lightening sky.

The stars had faded and the gray and scarlet she had seen from her window had become sapphire-blue faintly tinted, over the top of the wall, with rose and peach. The garden was full of shadows, the corners of the walls blurring into darkness. As she stared, one of the shadows moved. Her heart jumped, slamming against her ribs. The shadow moved closer. She stood still, poised to flee, yet not truly frightened. No one could enter Wednesfield in the middle of the night, nor would any within its walls harm her. A bird called indistinctly, like the voice of a man half awake, and was answered by another call, as drowsy as the first.

The shadow became Sebastian and if one tension relaxed, another tightened. Why was he here? Had he, too, spent a sleepless night, wrestling with a hunger that would not abate? He drew closer, so close she could see the blue shadows under his eyes.

"Good morrow, Beatrice. What do you here?"

"Good morrow," she said, and took a deep breath, trying to calm the riot under her breastbone. "I could sleep no more, and… And I thought I might find ideas for the garden at Benbury here. What of you?"

"I do not know why I am here, except I could not sleep, either." He smiled and stretched out his hand. "Since you are here, will you walk with me?"

How could she resist that smile, crooked and full of sweetness? She slid her hand into his, his palm hot against hers in the cool morning air.

He drew her with him as he retraced his steps into the depths of the garden. For a while they walked in silence broken by the crunch of their feet on the path and the songs and calls of the birds, growing in volume as the day brightened. When they reached the bottom of the garden, where the deepest shadows lingered, Sebastian halted. As if this was what she had agreed to by joining him, he lifted the hand he held to his mouth, turning it to press one kiss into the center of her palm, another on the inside of her wrist, the same caress as the night before. Once again, pleasure cascaded through her; once again, she gasped. His mouth drifted from the point where her heart beat against her skin, nibbling the skin of her forearm. She shivered as slow waves of delight traveled from hand to breast.

Sebastian pushed her loose sleeve up and kissed the bend of her elbow. A wave of heat crashed in her lower belly as if he had put his wandering mouth there. Her face burning, she put her free hand between Sebastian's mouth and her skin, the only denial she could bring herself to make. He seized her hand and pulled it away, pulling her into his arms in the same movement. She looked up into his eyes, unreadable in the half light, and at his mouth, at the curves of his upper lip and the corners that always seemed ready to smile.

Please, she thought. The heat of his body, long and strong against hers, pushed through her bodice and shift to caress her skin. Without the armor of her pair-of-bodies and her petticoats, there was almost nothing between them.

No. Break free of him. That was wisdom, drowning. *Sebastian, please.*

As if he heard her thought, his eyes narrowed. She saw the kiss in them before he lowered his head, his mouth open and hot on hers. She wrapped her arm around his neck so she would not fall when her knees gave way, and parted her lips for him. Heat surged through her, blurring thoughts, wishes and good intentions into a red, dark haze. The world narrowed to Sebastian's arms across her back, Sebastian's mouth devouring her, Sebastian's body pressing against hers, so close nothing could come between them, and yet too far away.

He lifted his head and kissed her eyes before resting his chin on her head. "Beatrice," he said softly. She clung to him, amazed by the speed and heat of the fever he raised. "We cannot stay here, sweeting, where anyone may come upon us."

Come upon us and see what they ought not. Come upon them as Sebastian had once come upon her and George. Beatrice pulled away to stare at him, uncertain of his intent and afraid of her own.

He cupped her face in his hands. "I cannot stop touching you." He kissed her gently, but underneath the gentleness, he burned. "Please, Bea, come away with me to a place where we will not be disturbed."

His mouth was on the corner of her lips, the corner of her eyes while his fingers brushed her throat, her ears. Her desire leaped to meet his, burning, burning. The walls she had built against him collapsed and with them went her ability to resist him. She nodded, afraid and exhilarated, lust itching beneath her skin with such ferocity that if she did not soon scratch, she would run mad. When Sebastian pulled her toward the old tower, his hand tight on hers, she followed despite a voice in her head crying, *This is madness. Say him nay.* It was wisdom, but she could not heed it. She wanted to be strong, but was weak; she wanted to be honorable and chaste, but was wanton. She ought to care, but did not.

Sebastian could do with her whatever he wished.

Chapter Twelve

Desire burned through Sebastian. Where could they go where no one would see them? If they remained in the open, they would surely be interrupted by the gardeners and, as surely, Beatrice would flee him. He had to touch her, kiss her; he had not spent a sleepless night in a fever of lust to be denied now. Somehow she had failed to rebuild her walls; he must take advantage of her weakened defenses before she had a chance to strengthen them.

He glanced at the house with its irregular roofline, the old tower bulky and graceless beside the soaring roof of the hall, and his mouth quirked. So few people ever entered the tower that when John had stolen the mead on Twelfth Night, he and Sebastian and Beatrice had known there was only one safe place to drink it. How fitting would it be to go there now and woo Beatrice into yielding to him? Wordlessly, Sebastian walked to the old tower, pulling Beatrice in his wake.

The door opened on half-lit gloom and the unexpected smell of newly sawn wood. Sebastian pulled Beatrice inside the tower and shut the door. Early sunlight drifted through windows that were hardly more than slits in the thick walls, providing just enough light to see the stairs that led to the floor above.

He drew Beatrice close, pressing her against him with her hand, still clasped in his, against the small of her back. With his free hand, he caught her neck, drawing her mouth near enough to kiss.

She yielded as soon as his mouth touched hers, her lips opening hot and sweet underneath his. Red shimmered beneath his eyelids, burning through his bones and sinews and dropping heavy and powerful into his loins. His arms tightened, drawing her still closer as if he might absorb her. He wanted to throw her down, feed and douse this fire in the curves of her body. He wrenched his mouth away and rested his forehead against hers, dragging air into his body as if he could not get enough.

He held himself still; if he moved, he feared he could not contain this lust, excessive, outsize and inexplicable. How could it have grown to such monstrous proportions in so short a time, fed only by a few kisses? He was no green boy, he was not controlled by his appetites.

With an effort of will, he put aside the thought of breasts and thighs and the pleasure he would find in them, at least until he could think clearly, and then he considered Beatrice. He did not want to overmaster her into compliance.

He took a deep breath and tried to think of something unpleasant, something that would distract him and cool his fever. *London*. Stinking streets, stinking river, noise and dirt…

Loathing rose up in him, enough to calm him. He drew her deeper into the room, looking for blankets, straw, anything that would soften the floor. There was nothing, the flagstones swept clean as they had not been in his memory. Perhaps on the next floor…

"Come," he said, and led her to the stairs, hoping that the light would enable them to see the worn and damaged places in the rise.

But the stairs had been repaired, broken treads fixed, holes filled. The smell of newly sawn wood grew stronger as they ascended, sweet and dry in his nose as they emerged through the opening in the floor. It was not as dim up here as it was below, the light sufficient to see details, such as they were.

The floor had been mended, the new wood bright against the old. There were no furnishings, not even the broken and worm-eaten benches that they had used in the past. The room was empty but for a stack of lumber against the far wall and stones for repairing the stairs piled beside it.

It is enough, his body said, lunging against restraint like a dog maddened by the scent of a hart. If they had been lovers of long standing, it would have been enough, the chance to snatch private pleasure outweighing the rude accommodation. But they had never lain together and whatever her past, he did not want to treat Beatrice like a common doxy.

Yet he could not stop touching her. As if she heard his thought, Beatrice turned to him, a question in her eyes. He caught her free hand and pulled her against him. She came willingly, slipping her hands free of his and placing them on his chest.

"We are private now," she murmured.

He looked down at her. Did she seduce him? His kisses had swollen and reddened her mouth, and her breasts, soft and white against the darkness of her gown, rose with the force of her breath. Yet she did not eye him with a wanton's boldness and her fingertips plucked at the facing of his doublet as if she were nervous.

Almost without his volition, his hand lifted and his fingers came to rest against her exposed skin. It was soft, softer than anything he had ever felt, smooth under his palm. As he touched her, her eyes half closed and her lips parted, the look invitation. He bent his head and kissed the cleft between her breasts. Her breath caught, her sigh skimming across his hair like a caress. His other hand lifted and cupped her breast, full and round without the restraint of her pair-of-bodies. In answer, her hands clutched his doublet, her eyes half closed. His mouth went dry, his thoughts blurring.

He kissed the tops of her breasts, her skin silky and cool against his tongue. His mouth wandered to her throat and her head fell back, giving him easier access. She was sweet in his arms, all that he had dreamed she would be. His hands wandered, as well, spanning her waist, brushing her breasts, before lifting to remove the coif concealing her hair. He combed his fingers through her plaits, loosening their weave. Catching fistfuls of soft hair, he drew her mouth to his and kissed her, breaking open her mouth. *Burn for me.*

She released his doublet, insinuating her arms around his neck and arching against him. He lifted his head to glance at her and to gauge her response. Her eyes were heavy-lidded, veiled by her long, straight lashes. She licked her lips and his groin tightened painfully, the red weight of it heavier. He released her hair and dropped his hands to her hips, half lifting her to where his need raged.

It was not enough; he did not have the strength to

both hold her and press her close, not with this fire burning his flesh. The lumber would have to do; there was nothing else. Touching her, caressing her, kissing whatever inch of sweet flesh came under his mouth, he half carried her to the stack of lumber and lifted her atop it so that she sat hip-high. He put his hands on her knees and parted them. Running his hands along the outsides of her thighs to her hips, he stepped between her legs and fit himself to her, groin to groin. She sighed and pressed her face into his shoulder, acquiescing. His fingers fumbled at the knot in her bodice lacing, suddenly too thick to do the work. Break the laces, he thought, struggling. The knot gave and the front of the bodice parted, exposing white skin to fingers, lips and eyes.

Heat and hunger washed through him, dissolving the remnants of thought, leaving only the sharp, greedy awareness that to find surcease in her heat all he need do was push up her skirt and free himself from the confines of his codpiece. Doing it would take no more time than it took to draw two breaths. Her breath coming in gasps and sighs and the way she moved under his hands encouraged him. He bent and grasped her hem, straightening to kiss her protests away before they formed. His palm skimmed over her knee to the warm skin of her thigh. Her skirt bunched over his arm, rustling like the wind in leaves; moist heat spilling from the apex of her thighs flowed over his thumb. His mouth went dry and his groin tightened unbearably. He closed his eyes.

Go! his flesh cried.

Pleasure Beatrice, another voice said, and his thumb moved, following the heat to its source, to the place where experience had taught him touch led to joy.

Through her skirt, Beatrice's hand clamped on his wrist. "No," she whispered.

Do not deny me. His arousal, in the stiffened confines of his codpiece, was so intense it hurt. He pushed against her hand, reaching for her.

Her grip tightened on his wrist, insisting. "No."

He looked down at her. Tears rimmed her lower lids, gleaming in the half light.

"Why?" he asked harshly. He did not know if he asked why she denied him or why she wept. The tears made him ache; the ache was not desire.

"I cannot do this," she said. "I cannot let you use me so."

He brushed his thumb over the skin of her thigh. She swallowed and closed her eyes, as if sensation drove out sight. When she opened her eyes, there was shame and a spark of something else in their depths.

"You have reason enough to doubt me as it is. I will not give you more."

"Do you think I will doubt you if we lie together now?" he asked. Desire was a lead weight in his belly, drawing him down; he was within inches of ease, if only he could persuade her to yield.

She searched his eyes, looking for something. When she shoved at his wrist, trying to move his hand from her thigh, he knew she had found it.

"Do you think I have not learned a man will say anything to get a woman into his bed?"

"You are my wife. There is no sin."

"When you have had your fill of me, will you remember that I yielded to my husband, or will you not think that if I yielded to you easily, I will yield to others easily?"

"I would not think that."

Her eyes narrowed. "Do not lie to me." She pushed against his wrist with both hands.

He put his free hand over both of hers to still her. "I want you and you want me. I am willing to risk anything to have you. Will you not do the same?"

Her anger dissolved, washed away by bleakness. "No, I will not," she said. "The worst thing I have ever suffered is your contempt. There is nothing I would do to risk that. I cannot."

He pulled his hand from underneath her skirt and seized her hand. He pressed it against his codpiece, letting her feel by his hardness the force of his desire.

"I *want* you," he said through clenched teeth, desire and pity and frustration fusing together, forged into anger. "Does that mean nothing to you?"

She stared into his eyes, her lips parted, until the bleakness in her gaze dried to desolation. Her lids dropped and she turned her head away, her hair shielding her face like a golden veil. "If your desire so overmasters you, take me and have done," she whispered.

His hand tightened on hers, and he pulsed in response. A treacherous voice whispered, *Take her. She is yours.* He wanted her so much he hurt with it; there was nothing to stop him from possessing her here and now. As his wife, she could not refuse him. If he pushed up her skirts now and pushed into her, she would not fight him, lying obediently beneath him while he found relief.

And when he was done, would he not have destroyed all hope of binding her heart to his, and all for a tumble he had not fully enjoyed?

After a long moment, while he fought his hunger for release, he lifted her hand from him and kissed it, holding it against his mouth. "Forgive me," he said, his voice rough. "I have been unkind."

She turned to look at him, her face wet. Desire howled in his belly, straining against the leash of his will, but he would not yield to its demand when the cost was so high. Drawing her skirt down, he stepped from between her legs and closed her thighs. He took her hands and held them loosely; if she wished, she could pull them free. She let them rest where they were. He looked down at them, small and white between his own, veins tracing pale blue beneath the skin of her wrists.

"You are angry with me," she said.

He rubbed his thumbs across the veins. "No." What he felt was not anger. "I should not have pressed you."

"I tempted—"

"I am not a puling boy to be led by my codpiece." He looked up, meeting her doubtful, tear-drowned eyes, and cursed himself for frightening her. "I want you, you know how much, but the first time I lie with you, it should not be atop a stack of lumber. You were right to say me nay."

She eased one hand free of his grip and wiped her wet eyes with her fingers. He had a sudden, vivid memory of her doing the same at fourteen, when her brother John teased her about her vanity. That day she had seemed curiously untouched, despite the tears and rage blotching her face, as if nothing could pierce the armor of her pleasure in herself and her prettiness. He was surprised to recognize that her sleek self-satisfaction was gone. How long ago had it faded? A year? Two? Or had it begun to erode the day she married Manners?

"I am yours to do with you as you please," she said, her voice flat, as if she had learned the words by rote.

"It does not please me to touch you when it gives you no pleasure."

She lowered her head, shielding herself from his gaze. "But it does give me pleasure." She looked at him, the wariness in her eyes at odds with the trustful way her hand rested in his. "That surely makes me the wanton you have said I am."

"If you are wanton, what am I?" he asked. "I would not have said no to you, yet you denied me for your honor's sake."

"You said you despised me."

"I was a fool and liar when I said it."

She swallowed. "Do not lie to me now, Sebastian."

Here was a lesson if he had the wit to learn it: she was not as easily cozened as he might wish. The only thing that would do now was a piece of the truth.

"You were right when you said that I have wondered if you would yield to another man as easily as you yield to me."

"Though I have not yielded to you," she said quietly, braced as if for a blow.

A blow he must deliver. To ease it, he spoke as gently as he could. "No. But you did yield to Conyers."

"So I must surely be lewd and unchaste all the days of my life." She tried to pull her hand out of his.

He would not let it go. "Will you be?"

"No!" she cried, jerking her hand free. She clambered down from the lumber, shoving him out of the way. "I had little enough joy from Sir George. Why should I risk my name and destroy what remains of my honor for any man? Even you, Sebastian. What do you offer that makes it worth the price?''

No joy of Conyers? If she had had no joy, why had she lain with him? He knew what Conyers had felt—how not? Standing before him with her hair tumbled like a river of gold around her naked shoulders, her eyes blue as flame with anger as she refused him for honor's sake, she was so fair that desire knotted hard in his belly, harder still in the midst of his chest. If she had been any other woman but Conyers's leman, he would have admired her for the courage with which she disdained his effort at seduction. As it was, she was worth any price it might cost to have her, body and heart.

''I promise you pleasure. You will have joy of me, I swear it.'' *And if I give you something he did not, so much the better.*

''I have heard that before and it was worth less than the breath that spoke it.'' She pulled the laces of her bodice tight and knotted them.

''You were nigh to swooning not so long ago and you said I pleased you. Did you lie?''

''No. I will not lie to you. There was pleasure.'' Her voice broke. ''But after pleasure, what then? Pain and scorn and contempt. Can you promise me, on your honor and your immortal soul, that you will not despise me after giving me this pleasure? I care nothing for pleasure. All I desire is to be free of pain.''

''Do you think I will hurt you?''

''You have!'' she cried, and burst into tears. She turned away and stumbled to the other side of the room, colliding with the curving wall. Like a sapling caught in a summer storm, she shook under the force of her weeping, her sobs echoing in the hollow space.

Sebastian crossed the room to her and laid his hands on her heaving shoulders. She jerked her shoulders free and moved away from him, sliding along the wall, her distress hardly checked by her transit. The harsh sound of her weeping made his throat ache and he wondered if he should stay or go, if he did more harm than good to his cause by remaining. The question was bootless; he could not leave her like this. Slowly, warily, he rested his hands on her shoulders once again. Minutes passed, her grief in full flood, until at last her sobs began to slow, interrupted by hiccuping sighs. He might not have been there for all the heed she seemed to pay.

"What did I do to hurt you, Bea?" he asked. "Tell me."

She shook her head. "I cannot," she said, her voice muffled.

"Cannot or will not?" he asked quietly. Anger drove her into silence and oblique answers. Perhaps mildness would coax her into speaking the truth.

She turned. The tears had swollen her eyelids, rimming them in pink; her nose was red and shining. "Does it matter?" she said. "Whatever my reason, you do not like my silence."

"No, I do not. Can you not trust me? Must we continue to play these games of doubt and suspicion?"

"But I am not the only one who plays, Sebastian. Do you not doubt and suspect me?"

How could he not have some doubt, when she had betrayed him, betrayed Manners?

"You cannot answer me, can you?" she said. "You cannot deny it, either. What is to become of us, always staring at each other out of the corners of our eyes?"

What indeed? Somehow they must find their way out of this. "Did we not agree we want peace?"

"We did."

"Can you not trust me enough for it?"

"You are not the only one I distrust."

He frowned, unsure of her meaning. "I do not understand."

"I do not trust myself," she said. "How should I when I let George Conyers handle me like a woman from the stews because my pride was hurt? I am a fool, Sebastian—I have no more wit than a hen. I thought I need not follow the rules of conduct my mother laid down as befitting her daughters. I knew I was beautiful—how could I not?—and for that, I thought no harm could come to me. But I was wrong, wrong." She caught her breath, curling hair floating about her pale face in a cloud of gold. "I was wrong about everything. How can there be peace between us when I am afraid you will hurt me?"

He could not follow the erratic leaps of her mind, but this last he could answer. "I would never strike you unless you needed lessoning," he said.

"I know that. But, Sebastian, do you not know that fists are not the only things that hurt?"

"Have I ever hurt you?"

"Yes!"

"How? When?"

"You broke my heart."

"And you broke mine. What of it?"

She stared at him. "When? When did I break your heart?"

"When you broke your word to me and married Manners." He took a deep breath to calm his anger, surging as fiercely as if the old hurt were new made. "Did you ever intend to keep your promise to me?"

"I?" she cried, tears and sadness burned away, her voice low and furious. "What of you? If you had honored your promise and claimed me, I would not have married Thomas. But you did not claim me. You let me go without so much as a farewell. Do not blame me if that broke your heart."

"Was it for me to cry you nay when you told me you were going to marry him?"

"I told you he had asked, not that I would marry him. I had returned no answer to him when I spoke to you. If you had betrayed by so much as a breath that you honored our promise, I would have refused him."

"You should have refused him as soon as he asked!"

"And waited another year or five or ten for you to speak to your father? Is that what you think I ought to have done?"

"Why would you not wait for me?" he cried, the question echoing in the round room.

"You did not ask me to," she said.

He could not have; pride would have stopped up his mouth before he had the chance. Yet... "If I had asked it of you, would you have waited?"

She took a quick breath, ready to launch a furious assent, and then the expression in her eyes changed, as if she had caught a glimpse of something unexpected. Her eyes widened and then she sighed. "No," she said sadly. "No, I would not have. I told you I was a fool."

What had he expected? That she would have waited? Yet he was disappointed, old hurt mingling with old anger, both of them bootless. The past was done. "You cannot undo your mistakes."

She flushed and lowered her eyes.

"No," she said, her voice choked, "we can neither of us undo what has been done. Can you not accept that I know what a fool I have been? I do not think you know how much I want to live in peace with you."

"I do not doubt you," he said.

"When I was with Lord Manners—" she began.

"Bea—" *It will avail us nothing to do this.*

"Hear me out, Sebastian." She folded and unfolded her hands as if taking a fresh grip on her courage. The fear in her gesture silenced him. "When I was with Lord Manners, there was neither peace nor kindness between us. I do not think I could endure to live like that again. I will do anything you ask, try to be anything you wish, if it means we will have peace at Benbury."

If you make me listen to part, you must tell me all. He would not be satisfied with less than everything. Ignorance only made a fool of a man.

"Is that why you lay with Conyers, because Lord Manners was less than kind to you?"

Her hands tightened, the knuckles white. "No."

Everything, Bea.

"Why did you lie with Conyers?"

She raised her eyes and for a moment she looked like her fierce, fearless mother. "Do you truly wish to know?"

No, I do not. He had started this for pride, continued it for hurt pride, when he did not want to know what she had done with Conyers, or why she had done it. Anything she told him could only fuel the images he had never been able to cast out of his mind, of Beatrice shivering with delight in another man's arms. Anger in a dark wave flooded him once more. He still wanted to kill Conyers for taking what was his.

She belongs to me.

He went still.

It should have been me.

The truth broke over him like sunlight.

He was not, had never been, angry with Beatrice for betraying Lord Manners. He was angry because she had betrayed *him.*

"No," he said. "I want to know why you did not lie with me."

Chapter Thirteen

Beatrice stared at Sebastian, her heart thumping in the base of her throat and striking with such force that her whole body shook.

"He pursued me," she said, forcing the words past her heart. "You did not."

That was only part of the truth, sauce on the meat of it. She had chosen to allow Conyers to touch and kiss her because he had plainly desired her and she had needed to be desired. Had Sebastian wanted her, as well? If he had, he had not shown it.

"It should have been me, Bea," Sebastian said, a note in his voice that was both hard and soft. The sound of pain; she had made it often enough that she could not mistake it. *Oh, Sebastian.*

"Was I to chase you and offer myself to you?" she asked. "Whatever you may think, I am not a doxy."

"You offered yourself to Conyers. If you had to offer yourself to someone, why could you not choose me?"

"I did not offer myself to Conyers. He came to me."

"That does not answer my question, Bea. Why *him?*"

"Because he desired me." How shameful it sounded, spoken aloud. If Sebastian believed anew that she was light-minded and lewd after hearing it, she could not blame him.

"I do not believe you."

"Whether you believe me or not, I have told you the truth. Sir George was the only man I knew who wished to lie with me."

"Aside from Lord Manners."

"No." Her throat closed; she fought it open. "Lord Manners found me—" She could not say it. Clenching her fists to drive her nails into her palms, she took yet another breath. "He did not desire me."

Sebastian stared at her and shook his head. "He was an old man. If his flesh would not rise to the battle, it could not have been for lack of desire. You have mistaken the case."

Mistaken the case? She could not have mistaken Thomas's meaning at all. Impatience with Sebastian's persistent disbelief freed her tongue. "He told me I sickened him."

And with that, something inside her gave way and she was flooded with pain and shame, spilling through her on a tide of memory. She turned, walked to the other side of the room and pressed her forehead to the cool, rough stone of the wall. Thomas had been sick the first time he had tried to lie with her. He had put his cold hand on her breast and then had rushed to the pot in the corner of the chamber where he had vomited. After he was done retching, he had commanded her to cover herself. Shocked and bewildered, she had hesitated—and had been slapped for it.

She squeezed her eyes more tightly shut as if doing so would close out her memories, and wondered if there would ever be an end to them.

"What did you do?" Sebastian asked, his voice rough.

"You were at the wedding. Surely you saw me bedded." What had she done to so disgust Thomas? She still did not know; nothing George Conyers had been able to say or do had erased the fear that she would repel him, too.

"No," Sebastian said. "When he said you sickened him—what did you do?"

Do? After that blow, she had dared nothing, attempted nothing, too shocked to do anything but nurse her cheek and stare at the aging stranger she had married.

"What could I do? He was my husband. I had no redress."

"Did you not try to please him?"

"He was my husband, my master. How should I not try to please him? And yet I failed. I failed, Sebastian." And the one thing she had been sure of, her beauty, her ability to waken a man's desire, had been shown for a sham. If she was not beautiful, what was she?

Footsteps crossed the room toward her and then fingers parted her hair, trailing along the back of her neck.

"Do not weep, Bea."

"I am not weeping."

His fingers caressed her neck and shoulder, gliding across her skin, gentle and soothing, offering more comfort than an embrace could have. Standing between her and the room, the stairs and the world beyond, Sebastian protected her, shielding her from her own memories, while his fingers massaged the tension from her neck and shoulders. As she relaxed, her body's response to his touch changed, heat blooming under her skin, desire stirring. God help her that even half distraught, she could not resist him.

"Manners was a fool. How could he not desire you?" His hands still moved over her skin. She wanted to lean closer, she wanted to pull away. She had no will, could make no choice but to stand still under his touch. Her eyes drifted closed as he caressed her. "Bea," he murmured, and then his mouth was warm on her shoulder. She sighed and his mouth was on her throat. "Bea, please. I want you so much I ache with it. Lie with me."

"You will scorn me," she whispered, her voice and her will weak.

"I will not, I swear it." His lips brushed her ear and she closed her eyes, undone. "Do not deny me."

"Michaelmas…" Something about Michaelmas…

"I cannot wait." His arms encircled her, pulling her against him and cradling her close. "Do not torment me."

"Sebastian…" Her will was crumbling, her barriers falling. She wanted him so much that tears leaked from her eyes, slow as honey.

"Say yes, Bea, I pray you. We are all but married. There is no sin."

"I do not…"

"Please." His whisper was harsh in her ear, the note of pain sounding again.

Desire surrounded her, filled her, more hunger and longing than she could withstand. She nodded.

His arms tightened. "I will come to you tonight."

"Wait…"

He turned her, cupped her face and kissed her as if he drank deeply. "I cannot, Bea. Do not ask it of me."

"Promise me." She was drowning, drowning in him.

"Anything."

"Promise me you will not abuse me for it later."

"I promise you I will not. There is no sin."

"Then come."

"Sweeting," he said roughly, and pulled her into his arms.

His mouth was hotter and hungrier than before; she responded like dry tinder devoured by flame, consumed in an instant. His arms were hard around her ribs, his thighs hard against her thighs. Released from restraint, her desire for him burned down to her bones, and she knew why she had chosen George Conyers over him. No matter the risk, she would never have been able to say no to Sebastian; she would have lain with him without a thought for the danger. She pushed her fingers into his hair, its heavy waves silky against her palms. He broke the kiss, his breath ragged in her ear.

"Sebastian," she whispered, her mouth against his throat, his pulse beating against her lips, swift and hard. Or was it her own? "Oh, Sebastian."

"If we do not stop now, I will not be able to stop later," he said. "I must go. I cannot stop touching you if you are near." There was a shaken note in his voice, as if somehow this kiss had destroyed his composure in a way the others could not.

"Then go," she said softly. Stay, she thought, do not leave me. But he must, she knew that. She watched him leave until he could not be seen below the floor.

A moment after he disappeared the door creaked open and banged shut, and she was alone, bereft, afraid and exhilarated.

The memory of Sebastian's mouth, ardent and demanding, on her own, sent a wave of heat cascading over her skin, scalding and sweet at once. A voice inside her cried, *This is madness!* It was madness, but she could not abjure it. Something within compelled her into Sebastian's arms, made it impossible for her to say him nay. Perhaps it was the work of the devil, but would the devil bid her lie with her husband?

She was a fool, but there was no helping it. Desire for Sebastian, the knowledge that they were married, both conspired to weaken her, undermine her defenses, allow her lesser nature command her. If she had any strength, she would deny Sebastian.

She had none.

Sebastian crept through the sleeping castle toward Beatrice's chamber, his candle barely able to penetrate the darkness. His heart pounded with excitement, desire and trepidation, yet he went on, moving through the night. He had gone too far to back out now.

When he came upon Beatrice's door he opened it without hesitation and slipped within. A candle burned on a table by the windows, casting vast dancing shadows across the curtains shrouding the bed in the center of the room. Despite the candle, the complete silence in the chamber made him wonder if he was all alone. Had Beatrice fled this meeting? He stepped further into the chamber. A floorboard squeaked underfoot.

The curtains drew back from the corner of the bed and Beatrice's head poked out. "Who goes—Sebastian...?"

"Yes, Sebastian." He blew out his candle and crossed the room to set it on the table, deferring the moment he joined her.

She had disappeared when he turned back to the bed. His heart's pounding redoubled, he began to undress, unlacing and stripping off his doublet, untying and dropping his bases, kicking his shoes off his feet. He pulled his shirt free of his trunk hose and grasped its hem to pull it over his head before pausing thoughtfully. The first time he and Beatrice made love was going to be awkward enough without thrusting himself on her naked at the outset. Let him woo and seduce her first. He had promised her pleasure, not discomfort.

And all the while, a little voice in the back of his head cried jubilation that this moment had come at long last.

He parted the curtains at the foot of the bed. Another candle stood on a little shelf above the bed and cast yellow light over Beatrice, her hair spilling loose and bright over the mounded pillows. Shadows gathered in the folds of her night rail, concealing the curves of her body, one shadow jumping in the hollow of her neck, steady as a heartbeat.

Across the distance separating them, their eyes met. She said, "I am afraid."

"So am I."

Her eyes widened. "You are? Why?"

"I promised you I could give you pleasure and now I fear I shall fail. What do you fear?"

Her gaze lost its doubt and became thoughtful, reminding him of the garden in London when she had weighed him and found him wanting. He held his breath.

"I fear pain. I fear I shall disappoint you."

"You cannot disappoint me," he said, and climbed onto the mattresses. The ropes underneath creaked under his weight and the bed shook as he crawled to its head, approaching her. She waited, biting her lip, her eyes growing wider the closer he came. He reached her and sat beside her on the mattress, his weight trapping her under the coverlet. This close, the linen of her night rail was thin, thin enough that he could glimpse the shadow of her breasts. He swallowed.

"Do you wish me to lie down?" she whispered, her hands knotted together in her lap.

He put his hand over that knot and brushed his thumb across the back of one hand. "We have time, Bea. We have all night."

He waited, thumb rubbing the back of her hand until her clasp loosened, her fingers parting company. He laced his fingers with hers, willing to sit quietly with her until she grew used to his presence and relaxed. As much as he wanted her, he could wait.

With her hand in his, he felt it when she eased. He waited a moment longer, then lifted her hand to look at it. "Such pretty hands," he murmured, and lifted the hand he held to his mouth, sliding his fingers free so he might kiss her pink palm and then nibble the length of her fingers one by one. He watched her to gauge her reaction.

She sighed beside him, her lids lowering to veil her eyes. From her hand he moved to her wrist, resting his lips against her pulse point long enough to feel her blood beating against her skin. He pushed her sleeve up and followed it to her elbow. He licked the inside and scraped it with his teeth, and heard her gasp. His groin tightened.

All night, all night, we have all night. But he wanted

her now, he wanted her to lie down, lift her night rail and let him ease himself. He had waited too long for this—years of desire pressed against him, clamoring for release.

Wool, he thought. Think about wool. How great will this year's yield be and how much gold will it fetch?

The hard edge of his lust dulled, though its weight still pressed him. This last, short wait while he readied her was almost too much to bear. But he would bear it because without it, she would have no joy of this night. And that he would not accept.

From her arm he moved to her neck, placing one small kiss on the tender spot under her ear. He turned her face to his with a gentle hand so he might kiss her, kiss her sweet, hot mouth until the blood roared in his ears and he could think of nothing but the burn of his lust and the hungry discomfort of his arousal. He reached for her breast and a groan shook him when the weight of it filled his hand, her nipple hard against his palm. He caressed her, his hand lifting her, and she tore her mouth from his, her breath harsh and fast in the enclosure of the bed.

Forgetting all his resolve he pulled her into his arms, across his lap, shoving the coverlet aside when it threatened to keep her from him. Her hair spilled silk across his hands as she pressed her forehead against his neck, allowing him to explore the warm, soft contours he had only guessed at before.

He could not stop touching her, caressing her. His free hand wandered to the hem of her night rail and slipped underneath, sliding up her shins to her knees and beyond to her hot, silky thighs. In the back of his mind he waited for her hands to reach down and stop him as they had before when he had touched her so.

Instead they clutched his shoulders, gripped his hair. She trembled in his arms, her breath coming in little sobbing gasps that made his desire pulse hard in his flesh.

Wool. Wool. Think of…

Her hip was round and satin-soft under his hand, sloping inward to her waist. He spread his hand across her belly, across the cradle of her hips, dizzy with hunger.

"I cannot wait anymore," he muttered. "I need you."

She turned his head and kissed him, her mouth hot and wanton on his, the kiss demanding and ardent. Was she ready? She kissed him as if she was, but he wanted to be sure. He let his hand drift downward, to touch her to be certain. His finger slid between her thighs, to slick heat. She tightened her thighs, stiffening in his arms.

"Sebastian…" she whispered. Her voice sounded shocked.

"Has no one ever…"

"No."

"Relax. Let me please you."

London. Think of London, the stink and the noise and the expense. He remembered everything he hated about the city, about Court, concentrating on his distaste and scorn. The fire in his blood subsided, enough that he could touch Beatrice without being overwhelmed by the desire to throw her down and have her, to end the endless waiting.

She relaxed, letting him touch her and stroke her. He kissed her mouth and her eyes and her face, swallowing her moans and gasps. She frowned, biting her lip, moving under his hand in short, jerky bursts.

"Oh. Sebastian, Sebastian…" She put her hand over his. "Please. I cannot bear it. Come to me."

London burned away, consumed to ashes in an instant. He lifted her away, stretching her out over the mattress, and stood to strip away his hose, points ripping in his haste. He tore his shirt off and, naked, crawled back onto the bed. He pushed her night rail up, exposing her white flesh, her round breasts, her tight rosy nipples. His mouth went dry. If he had thought her beautiful clothed, it was nothing to her magnificence now.

"Take it off," he said, his dry throat hoarse.

She knew what he meant without further explanation, pulling her night rail off and flinging it aside. Her glance dropped to his hips and she swallowed, blushing so intensely that it was visible in the candlelight, the color spilling to the tops of her round breasts. He leaned over and licked the edge of the color, then settled over her. She parted her legs for him, releasing heat that bathed him and beckoned to him. It took every bit of restraint he possessed not to thrust into her immediately, to hold himself back long enough to kiss and touch and stroke her until she bucked underneath him.

Now, he thought and eased into her.

He encountered resistance. Beatrice stiffened, gasping as if in pain. He pushed harder and she clutched his forearms, her fingernails digging into his skin.

"What…?" And then he knew. As unbelievable as it was, Beatrice was a virgin. He would be the first, after all.

"Do not stop," she whispered. "Please."

Her plea, the drive of his body toward release—both overwhelmed him, impossible to resist. He could not stop; his hips moved. The barrier gave and he was enclosed by her, tight and hot. He shuddered, the pleasure of her clasp intense. It blotted out thought as desire possessed him and carried him under its red flood, driving him into her, bearing him furiously toward climax.

He exploded, his release a fierce convulsion. He burned down to the marrow of his bones, leaving nothing but ash. When he came back to himself he was shaking, hollowed out. It had been a long time since he had lain with a woman, a lifetime since he had begun desiring Beatrice.

And what of her? How had she fared? He lifted his head and looked down into her face. Her eyes were closed, wet lashes shining, silvery tracks trailing from the corners of her eyes into her hair. Remorse stung him and he withdrew as gently as he could. He had not meant to hurt her.

"Oh, Bea. Why did you not tell me you were a virgin?" he whispered.

"I thought you knew. When you wondered if I had ever…"

What had he asked her that could have led them both so far astray? He thought hard of what had gone before. His hand had reached up to the juncture of her thighs, those thighs had tightened…

"I was asking if you'd ever been touched," he said.

"Oh." She wriggled beneath him and winced. "You crush me."

He rolled off her. "I did not want to hurt you." If he had known, he would have been more gentle. "But you should have told me." One man's wife, another man's mistress, and still a virgin—if he had not felt the evidence himself, he would have thought it impossible. But, inconceivable or no, it was true, and something deep within him exulted. He had been the first, the only man, to know her with such intimacy.

She sat up, reached for her night rail and pulled it on. "I thought I had." The nightgown enveloped her in thin folds, concealing her.

As if it had a will of its own, his hand reached out to her, fingertips grazing her hip under the soft linen. "If I had known, I could have lessened the hurt."

She glanced over her shoulder at him, her eyes unreadable. "It does not matter."

Though he had possessed her, she still had the capacity to lift her guard against him. He sat up, pulling the coverlet over his hips, clothing himself because she was clothed, however inadequately. "How can you say it does not matter? You let me believe you had lain with Conyers. You lied to me."

"You never asked me what I was about. You should have known better but you condemned me without a hearing," she said, gathering her hair into her hand.

"You should have told me the truth," he said.

"Would you have listened to me if I had tried? Or would you have accused me of lying to you?"

Unexpectedly, she had struck home with her question. He had done everything in his power to avoid her after discovering her with Conyers. By doing so, he had made it impossible for the truth to be aired. Instead of knowledge, he had had to make do with unreliable anger and imagination.

"If you will tell me now, I will listen."

She turned to face him and for a moment, as she had in the tower, she looked like her proud, fierce mother. "Are you certain you wish to hear this?"

He did not want to hear her out, he wanted to pretend she had never lived as Manners's wife, never dallied with Conyers. But the things she had not told him kept ambushing him, the surprises unpleasant even when they overset his unkind assumptions about her and her behavior these past few years. She had kept her mysteries long enough. Let there finally be plain speaking between them.

"I am certain. Tell me."

"Very well." She sighed and tilted her head back, her eyes closed. "I told you I disgusted Thomas. What I did not tell you was that when he attempted to lie with me, I so sickened him that he vomited." Her voice was flat and hard, as if she dared not allow expression in her voice. Had she also closed her eyes so she might not see how he heard her? Curiously he wanted to comfort her, yet he feared that if he touched her, she would fall silent and no amount of cozening or commanding would compel her to speak of this again. Or least not until the next time she sprang one of her traps. "He tried to lie with me almost the whole of our life together. When he failed, it angered him. He beat me for it."

She fell silent. She had flinched in the garden in London, throwing her hand up as if to protect her face from a blow. How many times had Manners struck her that she reacted without thinking? He did not want to know. Let him hear what he needed to hear and no more.

As gently as he could he asked, "And Conyers?"

She did not open her eyes. "I wanted to know I did not sicken every man I met. Sir George desired me greatly. It addled me so much that I gave him everything he asked, save my maidenhead." She opened her eyes and looked at Sebastian, her gaze unflinching, as if she challenged him. "I would not risk getting with child."

"Why risk anything at all?"

She shook her head. "I do not know, except that after being told day after day that I was so foul no man should ever want me and seeing how I sickened Thomas, I lost my wits when I roused someone else to real desire." Her mouth tightened and she looked down. "I was a fool and I am sorry for it."

What could he say in answer to that? Unable to think of a single thing that was neither cruel nor dishonest, he reached out and took her hand, lacing her fingers with his. They sat in strangely companionable silence for a long, peaceful moment, their only point of contact their joined hands.

"Do you hate me?" she asked, not looking at him.

Did he? Had he ever? He did not know what made his heart ache, but it was not hate.

"No."

She lifted her head and looked directly into his eyes. "I will never do anything that foolish again. I have learned the cost of that kind of folly and it is too high. You may not believe me, but I do not lie."

He thought of every witless thing he had done in the last five years, everything he had learned by painful experience not to do. If he confessed them all to Beatrice and swore never to do any of them again, would she believe him? Or would she believe that if he had made a mistake once, he must by his very nature make the same mistake over and over again?

"I wish that you had not married Lord Manners, and I wish even more than you had not held yourself so cheaply before Conyers," he said slowly. "I cannot forget either one. But I do not doubt you regret both and I think that will deter you should any man tempt you."

"How should I desire a man enough to dishonor myself? I— Forgive me, Sebastian, but I found no pleasure in you." Color, vivid enough to be seen in the uncertain light, filled her cheeks. "I liked your touch well enough before…I knew it should hurt, but not how much."

He sighed, exasperated with both of them. If only he had known… "Will you not let me try again? I swear there can be pleasure. I have brought—" He bit the words off before he spoke them.

"Other women to pleasure?" Beatrice asked. "I pray you, do not tell me of these other women, however much you pleased them."

"Do you now understand why it angers me to hear of Lord Manners and Sir George?" he demanded.

"You ask about them, so I must answer. I have not asked about the women you have lain with."

"Because you did not find me with any of them." He knew his annoyance was unwarranted, that he snapped at her because he was ashamed of himself for bringing his sins into this bed when he did not want hers there. *Fool, fool, thrice-damned fool.*

"I have not asked because I do not wish know," Beatrice said, frowning. "You ask when you do not want the answer, you berate me when I keep silence and berate me again when I answer. I do not know what you want of me, Sebastian. I have not known for years. I have begun to wonder if the reason I do not know is that you do not know, either."

"I wanted a wife I might trust."

"You have one, if you will but see it. Would it be better to marry a maid as heedless as I was, who trusts her virtue cannot be assailed for no better reason than it has yet to be tested? Or is it not better to marry a woman who knows how quickly danger may come upon the unwary and who guards herself, her honor and her soul accordingly? I am no longer so proud I think I cannot be led astray. I guard myself well.''

She shifted on the bed so that she was half turned away and gathered up her hair. White fingers flashing in the candlelight, she separated her hair into three sections and began to braid it. ''You ought to go,'' she said without looking at him. ''It will not do for you to be found here.''

She was right, but he did not move. As quickly as it had flared up, his irritation had died down. This room, this bed, seemed as if they held all the warmth and sweetness in the world, while all without was cold and dark. He did not want to go.

Her hair almost bound in a neat plait, Beatrice glanced over her shoulder at him, eyebrows lifted. ''Do you not go?''

''No, I do not. Let me stay awhile longer.''

Her eyes widened, her cool, stern expression giving way to uncertainty. ''It is not safe,'' she said, a faint breathlessness undermining the confidence of her words.

He leaned forward and, cupping the back of her head to hold her still, he kissed her, the kiss deepening as her lips parted under his. She twisted toward him, putting her hands on his shoulders, clutching him as if for balance. Her plait loosened, the waves of her hair clinging to him. Desire kindled, leaping from spark to flame in a heartbeat. He pulled her against him, to feel her soft curving body yield to his. She leaned into him, hands clenching and relaxing on his shoulders as if she did not know what to do with them.

He lay back, drawing her with him. The awkwardness of the movement broke the kiss. Beatrice lifted her head to look at him, gaze moving across his face.

"Sebastian...?"

"I will go before it is light. We have a few hours. Do not make me go."

Doubt and longing, pushing her close, pulling her away, fought in her eyes. He reached up and brushed her cheek with the backs of his fingers.

"Please."

She lowered her eyelids, long lashes shadowing her eyes. "You have only to command me, Sebastian. I am your wife and must be obedient to your will."

"Not for obedience," he said softly, running the pad of his thumb over her soft, swollen mouth. "Only because you wish it."

Chapter Fourteen

Beatrice closed her eyes, still dizzied by the kisses, by Sebastian's soft touch and softer pleas. How could she say him nay, when the ache of desire was greater than the ache of his too-rough lovemaking? She could not even remain angry with him.

"I do wish it," she said, opening her eyes and lowering her head to kiss him.

His arms tightened around her and he kissed her as if he might consume her whole. Against her belly she could feel him hardening, telling her that the kisses and touches affected him as they did her. Half drowning in the ardor of his kiss and the rising flood of heat it generated, she waited for him to grasp her and roll so that she lay beneath him once more. As much as she dreaded the renewal of pain, as much as she knew it was too soon to accept him again, she would still yield to him, partly because she owed him obedience and partly because the pleasure he had found in her body had soothed a good portion of the hurt Thomas had done. Despite all Thomas's claims to the contrary, she *was* desirable.

But Sebastian did not roll. He reached beneath her

night rail to stroke the backs of her thighs, her buttocks, her hips, his hands moving restlessly as if he could not touch her enough. His mouth traveled, trailing kisses, to her throat. As if it bathed her, she could feel his hunger for her; the flood of his desire broke through the gates of her own. She shuddered and gasped, unable to breathe, sinking beneath the surging heat he roused and drowning in it.

Now he turned, rolling her onto her back, but he did not cover her. He lay beside her, half raised on one elbow, and his eyes glittered in the candlelight as he reached out and brushed the tips of her breasts with his palms. Lightning forked into the depths of her belly and she gasped in surprised pleasure, a great wave of dizzy delight swamping her. She had never felt like this, never. With Thomas there had been disgust and fear of the cruelty his failures engendered; with George there had been fear of discovery and consciousness of sin.

Sebastian leaned over her and put his mouth where his palm had been, caressing her through the linen of her night rail. She arched toward him, struck again and again by lightning.

"I promised you pleasure, Bea. I will not hurt you again," Sebastian murmured, his voice soft as a caress.

"If you... You will hurt me if...if we..."

"I know. So we will not do that. Let me touch you, let me find what pleases you. I promise I will not hurt you."

No man had ever said he wished to find what pleased her. George had been certain he knew what gave her delight and though he had been wrong, she had not dared tell him. Thomas had not cared in the least what she felt.

She opened her eyes and looked at him. "Do as you will."

He took her hand and, watching her with eyes alight with heat, he traced the crease across her palm with the tip of his tongue. She shivered.

"No. I shall do as pleases my lady." He bent to her.

With his hands and his mouth, with delight and fierce concentration, he set about discovering the touches and caresses that gave her pleasure, that made her gasp and writhe and speak his name like a plea. She tried to be still and silent, but again and again she lost command of herself, crying out, arching into his touch, into the pleasure he gave her.

She was sensitive in places she had never imagined. His fingertips brushing the swell of her breast along her ribs made her gasp; his mouth behind her knees made her head swim. She was limp with delight and tense with it; her flesh felt like a bowstring slowly growing more taut. Heat and drugging pleasure bereft her of her wits; the whole world had become Sebastian's hands, mouth, the blue flame of his eyes burning into hers as the bowstring pulled tighter, tighter.

The tension made her sob, "Please, please," but she did not know what she asked for. Drawing her close, Sebastian touched her, stroked her in the most intimate of places, his mouth on her neck, his arm supporting her. He touched her again, a sliding caress, and the bowstring snapped and she snapped with it, shattering into white-hot fragments. She hung suspended in delight for an endless moment before sinking, bright as a falling star, into Sebastian's arms. His mouth on her hair, he held her trembling body close, trembling himself.

"Oh, Sebastian," she murmured. Where she had

been tense, she was now heavy with relaxation, her body at peace. *So that is what release is.* It was an apt name; she understood as never before why men worked so hard to get women into their beds. She, too, might say anything, do anything to find this overwhelming pleasure. "I did not know."

"I cannot believe you have not known pleasure," he said gently.

In her lethargy, she spoke the truth. "I have known pleasure. *That* was…"

"That was what?" he asked.

"I do not have words."

His arms tightened. Lying so close to him, she could not mistake that he had not been satisfied; he was hard against her hip. She turned her head to look at him. "What of you?" she whispered. Should she touch him, caress him as he had her? She did not think she could give him such pleasure, but she might yet ease him.

"I am well enough."

"You are—"

He put his finger over her lips, silencing her. "I stayed longer than I intended and I must go soon. All I want is to hold you."

She nestled closer, puzzled by his abstinence but willing to believe that he did as he pleased. Surely he must know he could do with her as he chose. And it was sweet to lie in his arms, his skin soft under hers, his heart thumping steadily under her ear. Slowly, imperceptibly, like the tide moving in, she grew drowsy, lulled by the warmth of his body and the profound relaxation of hers. She was almost asleep when Sebastian shifted, easing her onto the mattress without him. It awakened her.

"Where…?"

"It is nearly light. I must go." He bent down and kissed her, a kiss he could not seem to end. Her body responded, heat glimmering in her depths, as if knowing the delight that was possible made her easier to arouse. "Will you let me come again tonight?"

"Tonight?" she asked, puzzled. Was it not night now?

He smiled, the old, alluring, crooked grin. The heat in her depths expanded, washing over her. She wanted him so much that it took all her strength not to pull him to her.

"It is morning, sweeting. We have burned through the night."

Only the remnants of pride kept her from pleading with him to remain. "I will be waiting for you."

His eyes darkened. "I will be hard-pressed to wait until then. If you do not see much of me today, that is why."

"That will be as well for me," she said. "Go, before I beg you to stay."

His breath caught, his nostrils flaring. He bent and kissed her hard, bruising her mouth. "Do not tempt me."

"Go," she said, "and do not tempt me."

A hand shook her, jostling her. "My lady, arise."

Beatrice buried her head more deeply into her pillows, groaning. She ached all over, but there was pleasure in the ache; she wanted to stay in this bed where she had known such happiness and sleep until Sebastian came to her again.

"My lady, it is well past dawn. You must arise." Nan's voice was sharp.

Beatrice rolled over, flinging her arms wide across

the mattress. Her hair was in a tangle all around her, her night rail bunched up at the top of her thighs. No doubt she looked as wanton as she felt but for the first time in years she did not care.

"My lady, your courses," Nan said.

At that Beatrice opened her eyes. Nan was staring at the bedsheet near her hip. Following her gaze, Beatrice found a reddish-brown stain half the size of her palm beside her on the linen. She gaped at it. Where had that come from?

Sebastian, groaning as he found his release. Burning pain overwhelming the first kindling of her desire. The stain was the remnant of her maidenhead, the proof that she had lain with Sebastian last night. Why had she not thought of this? *Fool!*

"It is not my courses," she said, and wished she had held her tongue. If it was not her courses, what could she tell Nan it was?

"Then what has befallen you?"

"I am well, Nan. Nothing has befallen me."

"But, my lady—"

She sat up so that she looked down on her maid instead of up at her. "Do you dispute with me?"

Nan's eyes lowered. "No, my lady."

"You must not speak of this, Nan. I am unharmed, I promise you."

Nan looked up, her eyes shrewd. "You are my lady, I shall not betray you. And if you are well, it is my joy. Shall I have the linens changed? You will not like to sleep in them."

"That would please me." She swung her legs to the side of the bed. "Dress me in blue again, Nan." *Dress me in the colors Sebastian prefers.*

"Aye, my lady."

She drifted into a haze of memory as Nan dressed her, recollecting Sebastian's touches and whispers, the things they had said and done in the night. Her heart wanted to lift, rising on a tide of excitement, and yet doubt kept it moored as if ready for grief. She sighed. When the trees began to leaf out in spring, did she not take joy in their new greenness, forgetting by choice the cold gray days that April also bred? Why should she not do the same with the green newness of her heart while it lasted? It would end soon enough, destroyed by disillusionment or Sebastian's weariness of her, or something else she could not yet imagine. Happiness did not last any more than spring did. Why not take pleasure in it while she could?

And what else could she do, when the desire to be with him drew her toward him as if they were bound by an invisible rope. Descending from her chamber to the hall, she wrestled with herself, her sense of duty pitted against the pull of that rope. If she were a good, dutiful daughter, she would return to the solar and the altar cloth her mother wished to finish. Yet when she stepped into the hall and found color from the windows splashed across the flagstones as it had spilled over Sebastian a fortnight ago, she knew with abrupt certainty that she could not immure herself in the solar. She turned on her heel and began her search for Sebastian.

He was not in the chapel, nor was he in the garden or the old tower. Outside the tower door, enveloped in a cloud of fragrance from the herb beds, she paused. Was she a fool to pursue him? She looked up at the castle, at the solar windows high above the garden. If she had a particle of sense she would go up there right now and cease this folly.

She resumed her search.

She found him with her brother John in the dusty yard near the stable, both men dressed in no more than shirt and hose as they faced each other over crossed swords. For a moment, no longer than a heartbeat, she thought they dueled in earnest, but the mocking twist to Sebastian's mouth and the gleaming pleasure in John's eyes reassured her. This was a game, no more, the kind of game they had played as boys. She crept to the edge of the crowd of grooms and ushers that had gathered on the edges of the yard and watched.

Sweat dampened Sebastian's shirt. It clung, nearly transparent, to his broad shoulders and strong back. The sight made Beatrice's nerves hum. She wanted to grip those shoulders and to stroke that back, letting her fingertips follow the line of every muscle that bunched and lengthened under the veil of his shirt. She had thought she had felt desire before, but it had not been like this. Nothing in her life had been like this.

Sebastian was no true match for her brother—even with her small knowledge of swordsmanship, she could tell that. Again and again, John stopped the bout to show Sebastian a shrewder stroke, a stouter defense, a piece of clever footwork, resuming the duel when Sebastian had learned what he had to teach.

"Halt!" John cried suddenly. He grinned and nodded toward Beatrice. "Your bride awaits yonder."

Sebastian turned. He did not smile at her, but the heat in his eyes dried her mouth.

"Good morrow," he said softly.

"Good morrow," she replied, and wondered how she could speak.

The grooms and ushers nearest her drew back, staring. Sebastian handed his sword to John and crossed the yard to her side.

"I thought we agreed we should stay away from one another," he said in a low voice, pitched for her ears alone.

Her face burned. He was displeased. Oh, why had she come? "I—I could not stay away."

His gaze dropped to her mouth. "You madden me," he said, his voice rough and something tense in the center of her back relaxed.

"Shall I leave?"

Do not make me go, I pray you.

"No, stay and watch. Walk with me afterward." He looked away, glancing around the yard. "There. Go sit on the mounting block. I want to finish this."

Obediently she crossed the yard to the heavy stone block nearest the stables. The grooms and ushers eased away from her as if afraid to touch her, some of the very young men in their midst staring at her pop-eyed. Surely they had seen her before? Perhaps not so closely, but did it make a difference? It had been a long time since anyone stared.

She settled herself on the block and arranged her skirts so they gathered the least amount of dust and grime on the hems. Sebastian reclaimed his sword and he and John began to work anew, blades clanging as they met. John was holding back, containing himself and his skill. It showed in the opportunities he did not take, the openings he ignored; it was plainly visible in his checked jabs, feints and swings.

If Sebastian noticed it, as well, she could not tell. His concentration was complete, so narrowed on John and their swordplay that she might well have been in the solar with her mother. Each time John broke their play to show him yet another attack or defense, he listened and watched intently, aping John as if his life depended on it. As perhaps someday it might. She shivered and crossed herself against the unchancy thought.

As she crossed herself, they resumed once more. The strain of fighting, of attacking and defending was beginning to wear on Sebastian. His shirt was soaked, his face dripping sweat. Even John's hair had grown damp enough to wave. How much longer could they go on? When did they reach the point where no good could come of more?

As if he had heard her thought, John flung off his restraints and began to attack Sebastian with skill and daring. Beatrice, even in her ignorance, could tell that John's work was far beyond Sebastian's capabilities, far beyond those of anyone she knew. Sebastian knew it, too; even as he tried in vain to defend himself against clever strokes, delivered with lightning speed, his eyes widened in admiration. Backing away from John, he flung up his sword in a gesture of surrender. John ceased his attack and put up his own sword, grinning devilishly.

"Where did you learn to do that?" Sebastian cried.

Since the match was clearly finished, Beatrice rose and moved toward them.

"In Paris and in Rome," John replied. He crossed to the scabbards leaning against the wall and sheathed his sword. "It fed me."

"You offered your sword for hire?" Sebastian said. His tone was odd, as if he was torn between admiration and displeasure.

"I did not care to starve," John said, and handed Sebastian the other scabbard.

Sebastian shook his head. "How could you leave Wednesfield?"

"At the time, it was easy enough to do." John wiped his forehead with his sleeve. "And that is all I will say." He turned to smile at Beatrice. "Let us go into the garden, where the smells are sweeter."

Beatrice glanced at Sebastian. He stared at her as if he could see through all her garments to her naked skin, his face tight. Desire crashed over her, the strongest wave she had felt this morning. How was she going to survive until they married if this is how she felt after one night of love play? And if she gave herself up to him now, would he not tire of her all the sooner? He had said he wanted harmony and she had claimed the same, but now she feared she would want more.

"Or perhaps you would rather walk in the garden with only Sebastian for company," John said softly. "I can as easily find my wife and see how she fares."

Sebastian looked at John. "I am sure she would be glad of your company."

I am not, hung in the air, unspoken.

John grinned as if Sebastian amused him. "Let me take your sword within. Shall we meet again in the morning?"

"I should like that," Sebastian replied. He handed his sword to John, picked up his doublet from the ground and turned to Beatrice. "Come."

They did not touch as they walked toward the garden, yet it felt as if he caressed her, held her; the distance between them crackled with awareness. She absorbed the smell of his clean sweat and the other indefinable scent that was his alone. It had filled her nostrils last night when he touched her; catching it now reminded her with aching vividness of all they had done together. The fine linen of his shirt still clung to his skin, no concealment for the strong muscles of his arms and back. He moved gracefully, sinews and muscles well-knit and balanced, his walk as pleasing as a dance.

The garden was empty when they entered it. Beatrice did not know whether to be pleased or dismayed. The emptiness tempted her to do things she ought to leave until nightfall.

"You wore blue again," Sebastian said, and took her hand.

His skin was a little rough, brushing against hers. "I wished to please you."

"You do."

At that she turned to look up at him. His mouth was tight as if he fought pain. "Sebastian," she whispered, offering comfort, responding to the desire in his eyes, speaking blindly in lieu of a touch. She did not know which she did.

"Bea, this is madness."

"I know." She ought to apologize for her disobedience but she could not find the words, not when he looked at her that way.

He tugged on her hand and drew her closer. Her heart cried, *Danger!* and her flesh cried, *Yes!* Encouraged by his eyes and the way he pulled her nearer, she reached up, thrust her hand into the damp hair at the nape of his neck and pulled his head down to kiss him with all the hunger she felt. He responded instantly, mouth opening to hers, arms crushing her close against the strong, lovely length of him.

Her mouth bruised, her heart hammered, hot tension built in the depths of her belly. He was hard against her, his arms were hard around her, she wanted to crawl under his skin and never come up to the light of day.

He put her away from him, his mouth leaving her bereft.

"No, Bea, no more."

Shame cascaded through her. She had been wrong, she had misunderstood him.

As if he could hear her thought, Sebastian shook his head. "Do not look like that." He laughed uncertainly. "It is not your fault. It is mine." Color seeped into his face. "I cannot contain myself."

"We said we would not meet until tonight," she whispered. "And we were wise. But I could not stay away."

He brushed the back of his knuckles against her cheek, the caress she was coming to love. "If you had not come to me, I would have come to you."

Only by force of her will did she keep herself from yearning into him. Taking a deep breath, she stepped away from him, out of the worst of the peril. She could not make herself leave him altogether.

"Then if we are to be together, we must be careful," she said. "I do not want to shame myself."

"Nor I," he said, sighing. "Very well. I will keep an arm's length away."

She walked a few steps away from him along the nearest path, listening for his footsteps behind her. When the sound did not come, she turned. He was where she had left him, frowning at the garden.

"What is it?" she asked.

He shook his head. "I do not wish to walk here." He looked at her, the frown clearing. "Come with me to the pool."

She looked at him doubtfully, aware that far from

spying eyes they were more likely to behave as they ought not. Her skin prickled with heat on that thought and a little demon whispered, *Is that not the very reason to go?*

"Yes," she said.

Together they left the castle, passing under the arch of the gatehouse into the wide world. Though the pool had been their favored meeting place when they were younger, she had never gone there in Sebastian's company. The constraints of her girlhood rose up, whispering that it was unseemly for her to leave the castle without escort. She silenced the voice with the reminder that she was no longer an unmarried maid who must be strictly careful of her honor. In the world's eyes, she was a widow, a woman with a certain amount of freedom. More to the point, she walked in the company of a man who was for all intents and purposes her husband.

At the pool he spread his doublet on the ground for her to sit on. When she was settled, he stretched out on the turf beside her, head pillowed on his hands, long legs crossed at the ankle. She was surprised that he did not touch her and her surprise told her that she had imagined, in some hidden place in her heart, that he would seduce her as soon as they arrived. She had not expected that he would take her remark about needing to be careful so much to heart that he obeyed its dictum here, where no one could see what they did.

Still, despite the uneasy hunger of her flesh, she was glad he had not tried to lie with her here. She had warned him that she would not be tupped in a meadow like a goose girl and she had meant it. Perhaps the vow also stayed Sebastian. Whatever the source of his restraint she could not fight it, not when it gave her the safety she had asked for. Let her enjoy this peaceful time with him as best she could.

She moved closer to the tree until her back pressed against the trunk, wriggling until she found a comfortable seat amid the roots. Sebastian, his eyes closed and his chest rising and falling in slow, deep breaths, did not stir beside her. She leaned her head back and closed her eyes.

With sight closed off, her other senses came alive. Below her, the river whispered against the shore, the sound cool and silky. Above, birds sang and shouted, a riot of noise against the barely audible rustle of leaves. The breeze brushed against her face, sweet with the green smell of the river. Her breathing slowed and her heart calmed; she remembered the peace she had found a fortnight ago. It was back, grown a hundredfold, not least because of the man drowsing beside her.

How could this be? Did she dream? Or had the long painful years with Thomas been the dream? It did not matter. If she dreamed she did not wish to awaken.

"Bea."

Sebastian's voice was pitched low; if she had been sleeping it would not have roused her.

"Yes?"

"Is there anything else you have not told me?"

She opened her eyes and looked down at him. His eyes were still closed, his body still relaxed as if her answer could not matter to him.

"I do not know what you mean."

"You did not tell me you were a virgin. Is there anything else you have not told me?"

She cast her mind over all the secrets she had kept—Thomas's heavy hand, her virginity, her reasons for lying with George—and all the things that had shamed her. Sebastian knew them all. There was relief in that—there was nothing left for him to discover, nothing that might turn him away from her. His kindness in the past fortnight even gave her some hope that he might turn toward her.

"No, there is nothing else. You know the worst of me."

He opened his eyes. "And the best of you, too."

She remembered his rough voice demanding that she strip away her night rail and blushed. He grinned and levered himself up on one elbow.

"Have I ever told you how beautiful you are?" he asked.

"Yes," she whispered, abashed by the look in his eyes, a mixture of laughter, desire and something else, something that made her breathless.

"Did I ever tell you that when you blush you look sweet enough to eat?"

Her face burned. "No."

"Kiss me, Bea."

If she kissed him that would lead them into danger, the danger they had agreed they must avoid.

"I dare not."

"One little kiss. It can do no harm and I will stop there."

One corner of his mouth was higher than the other in the smile she could not resist. She bent and pressed her mouth to his. His hand cupped her cheek, thumb gently stroking her cheekbone and the corner of her eye. His mouth was soft, gentle on hers, its touch building warmth, not heat. No kiss she had ever received had been so sweet. Slowly, reluctantly, she lifted her head, looking down into his eyes. The mischief and desire had fled, leaving only warmth. Holding her gaze with his, he groped for her hand and pressed a kiss in the center of her palm, then laid her hand on his chest. Under her palm, where the kiss still tingled, his heart beat, steady and strong. Her own heart skipped, made foolish by the look in his eyes.

"Did I not say I would do you no harm?"

"Yes," she said distractedly.

He frowned. "What is it?"

"T-the kiss. It addled my wits."

His uneven grin widened his mouth. "Would you care for another?"

"Oh, yes," she said, and bent forward again.

This kiss was as sweet and warm as the one that had preceded it, Sebastian's mouth and hands as gentle. He stroked her cheek, her neck; his touch made her shiver. She sank deeper into the kiss, drowning in its sweetness until breath left her. Putting her hands on his face, she lifted her head.

"That has not cleared my head," she said.

His eyes glinted. "I did not promise it would. I only asked you if you wished for another. Give me a third, dearling."

"No," she whispered.

"Sweetheart," he said in a pleading tone.

"No," she said again, attempting sternness and finding laughter instead. Her heart felt as if it had been fashioned of swansdown, floating lightly within her breast. Exhilaration sang in her veins, source of the laughter that bubbled up within her. Her joy frightened her but she could not quell it.

"I shall die without it."

"I think not." By dint of will, she glowered at him.

"You are cruel, fair lady."

"The better to win your love."

"You have it," he said, grinning at her.

"I beg leave to doubt it."

"Kiss me and know my heart is true."

"And aid you in achieving your end? I am no fool."

"Bea, please."

Quickly she leaned down and kissed him, a bare touch of her mouth to his.

"There." She gathered herself and began to rise. "You have had your kiss. I must go."

As quickly as she stood, he shot to a sitting position and seized her around the hips. Tripping on her hem, she staggered and began to fall. Sebastian caught her and eased her onto his lap, his arms tight around her.

"Now, sweetheart, you are my prisoner. You must buy your freedom with kisses."

She glanced at him through her lashes, the flirtatious look she had not practiced in years. Where once she had used it in calculation, now she used it in play. "And if I do not desire my freedom?"

His arms tightened, his eyes glinting hot blue. "Then I may kiss you to my heart's content."

Despite knowing how unwise it was, she leaned closer to him, tilting her face up to his. His eyes darkened and she waited, her stomach quivering with excitement and longing, for his mouth to swoop down on hers. It had been a hundred years since she had played like this and her happiness was shot through with sorrow for the wasted time.

"My lord!" The voice came from near the lane.

Sebastian stiffened, his face darkening. "If he does not have good cause for seeking me…"

"Let me up, Sebastian," Beatrice murmured, her happy mood crashing down as she had known it must.

It had been too short a time... "Do not let him see me so."

"Wait." He grabbed the back of her neck and kissed her, his mouth hot and hard. "We will finish this when I send him on his way."

With that he lifted her to her feet and stood. His man strode across the field toward them, his cap off. He reached them and bowed, his gaze fixed on Sebastian as if she were not present.

"A man at the gate said you might be here, my lord. His Grace the Earl wishes to see you as soon as I may find you."

"Do you know why?"

"I am not in His Grace's confidence, my lord."

"Do not be a fool if you can help it. You are cleverer than that."

The man sighed. "Aye, my lord. A rider came in earlier with letters for the earl. I expect he wishes to speak to you about one of them. He did bid me hurry, so you might attend him all the sooner." Go *now*, his stare said.

Sebastian sighed. "Very well. I shall return to the castle. Go, tell the earl you have found me and I follow."

"Do you not wish me to wait for you, my lord?"

"Ned, if I wished you to wait, I should say so. Go, do as I have bidden you."

"Aye, my lord." He bowed again and trotted the way he had come.

Sebastian turned back to her, his mouth twisted in a rueful smile. "I'll warrant your father is good enough cause."

She stepped into arms that seemed to open for her, resting her hands against his broad chest and finding more shelter than she had expected. "So he is. It is probably as well. I dare not think where paying my forfeit might have led."

He kissed her forehead. "I have not released you from payment. I have only deferred it. I will claim it in your bed tonight."

"As you will it," she murmured.

He grinned, mischief and laughter returning to his eyes.

"Remember that."

Chapter Fifteen

Sebastian walked Beatrice back to the castle, unwilling to leave her by the pool without even a maid to attend her. She had smiled at him when he said so, her whole face lighting as if she were a candle. The sight made his heart squeeze, a painful clench beneath his breastbone he rubbed to ease. How long had it been since he had seen her smile like that? Years, no doubt—certainly not since her marriage to that caitiff, Manners.

The ache sharpened. She had been ill used by the men in her life, himself among them. He had failed to claim her, her father had failed to protect her from Manners, Manners had failed to treat her with courtesy and gentleness, and Conyers had failed to honor her. How could she smile now, as if the sun had come out after days of rain, as if her heart's desire had been granted her?

He took her hand and tucked it into the crook of his elbow, covering her fingertips with his hand. Incontinent desire was one of the hungers driving his need to touch her, but it was not the only one. Touching her satisfied another hunger, one he could not so easily

name, one he would not examine closely enough
to name.

In the hall, they parted, Beatrice to go to her
mother's solar, he to join the earl in his closet. At the
foot of the stairs, Beatrice turned as if to catch a last
glimpse of him. Seeing him watching her go, she
smiled as if he gave her a great gift. His heart clenched
again. It took all his strength of will not to join her.
Still smiling, she turned away and disappeared up the
stairs. Freed by her absence, Sebastian went to wait on
her father.

In his closet, the earl sat alone, his pen squeaking
on the paper as he wrote. Sebastian entered the room
and closed the door.

"Sir, I have come as you bade."

The earl glanced at him, nodded and continued writing, scowling at the page, his mouth a thin line. After
two more lines, he flung down the pen and shook sand
over his handiwork. He scanned the letter, tossed it
aside and looked up, his frown easing into a look of
welcome.

"Come, sit down, lad."

When Sebastian had settled in the chair he had taken
on his arrival a fortnight ago, the earl spoke.

"I have received a letter from my steward, shortly
to be your steward, at Herron. It seems that some kind
of quarrel has arisen between two tenant families and
it has grown past the poor fool's ability to resolve. A
month ago I should have ridden to Herron myself to
knock sense into a few thick heads, but Herron will be
yours soon. I think it wise that you accompany me and
have a say in how this is resolved. You will have to
live with the decision, not I."

"I should be glad to join you, sir. When do we leave?"

"As soon as it is light tomorrow."

So quickly? How could he leave Beatrice? "That seems very soon."

"I do not wish to let this boil fester longer than it must. The sooner we leave, the sooner there will be peace on your land."

The earl was right, wise in his decision-making. Sebastian had known that for a long time, but he did not want to be wise, not when wisdom meant leaving Wednesfield. Beatrice would be here, more than reason enough to stay.

But it was not reason enough to turn his back on the earl's shrewd counsel.

"That is true, sir. I will be ready."

"Good." The earl sat back in his chair. "I have heard you and John indulged in swordplay this morning."

"As the cat and mouse play, sir. I am no match for him."

"No doubt he will be able to teach you a trick or two."

"I hope so, sir."

"It's a wise man who learns from anyone with something to teach and a proud man who thinks first of his teacher's station and second of his teacher's wit."

"Yes, sir," Sebastian said, puzzled.

"I am saying you are wise to learn from John despite disapproving of the way he acquired his skill."

Ah. Surely this was John's doing; he had always preferred being frank, whatever the cost, to dissembling. Well, let Sebastian be equally frank. "It is not seemly for an earl's son to hire his sword out as if he were a common man.''

"No.'' The earl sighed. "It is not. However, unseemly or no, he has an uncommon skill. And he has come home to England to live as a good Englishman. I will not repine over what may not be amended. Nor should you.''

"I do not, sir. I am glad he is home.''

The earl looked away, his eyes bright. "Not as glad as I, lad, not as glad as I.''

Silence, easy and peaceful, fell between them. As she did whenever he had a moment's ease, memories of Beatrice filled him. Crying out as she reached joy. Confessing that she had never known the kind of pleasure he had given her. Nestling in his arms, sweet and warm. Dressing in blue again as if his pleasure counted with her. Her skin had glowed pearl-pale against the dark blue of her gown; seeing it, he had remembered its softness against his own and it had been all he could do not to carry her away right then. Somehow he had thought he would desire her less once he had lain with her. He had been wrong. He had not known what sweetness she had to offer before; now he craved it as a drunkard craves wine.

Old feelings stirred, longings he had thought dead and gone. He wanted to lay the world at her feet, to offer her silks and brocades, jewels and gold, beautiful things to adorn her beauty. He could afford to do none of it. If his finances were in a better state than they had been when he had inherited his estate, they were still not rich enough to do all he imagined. And even if he were rich enough, would he do it?

"I could wish John had not married a foreign

woman,'' the earl said suddenly. ''I fear me that Jasper's heir will be his brother's half-Italian get.''

''Is there no sign Jasper's wife has quickened?''

''No, no sign, and I do not look for one.'' The earl sighed. ''Enough of that.''

''John's son shall be raised an Englishman,'' Sebastian offered. The earl had never spoken so frankly to him, nor had he ever revealed his concerns. What could he do in response but offer what comfort he might? ''Surely that will be enough.''

The earl shot a hard stare at him, the stare proof that Sebastian had startled him. Abruptly the earl grinned. ''There are some that say I am a Welshman, born at Pembroke as I was,'' he said as if it were a matter for pride. ''If I am English enough for this title, my grandson shall be, too, whatever his mother is. I thank you.''

''It was my pleasure, sir, though I do not know what I did.''

''You reminded me of what counts in managing this estate. You waste your cleverness here. If you will take my advice, you will think again about returning to Court where that kind of wit has uses.''

''It is costly, sir, and I gain less than I spend.''

''You will be my son-in-law. That alone will make a difference. I am serious in this, Sebastian. You could be of service to me.''

On those terms, how could he refuse? It would mean long partings from Beatrice, for how could he trust her in the morass of Court? *When I have tired of her, I will go,* he thought.

''I will consider it, sir.''

''Do not forget Beatrice. She was well beloved of the queen when she was in the queen's household and if she returned with you, she could be of great assistance to you. Do you but say the word and I will obtain posts for you both.''

He could not refuse the earl outright, but he would not put Beatrice's fragile honor at risk. ''I pray you, let me marry Beatrice before I make any decisions.''

''Very well,'' the earl said agreeably. He sat forward and picked up his pen. ''I have much to do. You have my leave to go.''

Sebastian rose. ''Yes, sir. How long shall I plan on being away?''

''A fortnight, perhaps longer. While we are there, I thought you might wish to inspect the property and refresh your acquaintance with your past tenants. There is no need to hurry any of that.''

Everything he said was ripe with good sense, yet Sebastian's heart sank. As much as he had once wanted to see Herron again, he did not want to leave Beatrice for so long a period of time. A child wishes things might be different, he thought. A man bows to necessity.

That evening, Sebastian told Beatrice of the plan to go to Herron as they danced a pavanne, stately and slow, in the hall after supper. ''We leave at dawn.''

''Tomorrow?'' Beatrice whispered. A frown shivered across her face, breaking her composure for an instant. ''Why so soon?''

''The sooner we go, the sooner the quarrel at Herron will be amended. So your father said. I think he has the right of it, Bea.''

''Will you come tonight?''

''Nothing could keep me away.''

She glanced at him as the dance moved them

through the hall. "I did not think I should ever act this way," she said, her voice barely above a whisper.

"How?"

"Welcoming you to my bed in secret."

Welcoming a man to her bed in secret had been the sin he had condemned her for. Her words ought to wake that old anger but did not; despite her past mistakes, she was not wanton, not light-minded. She lay with him now because she believed, as he did, that they were married before God.

Abruptly he realized that they *were* married, whatever the truth of that confused promise made so long ago. The vows they had exchanged at Coleville House, solemnizing their public betrothal, and their lovemaking last night had married them as finally as if they had spoken vows before a priest. Something in his chest shifted and settled as if the world, that had been narrowly off balance, had righted itself. Unwilling to consider the implications of the sensation, he let the dance carry them away.

When Sebastian slipped into Beatrice's room, the bedcurtains had not been drawn, revealing Beatrice, gold and white, against the pillows. As he had the night before, he blew out his candle and set it on the table in the corner. He unlaced his doublet, aware of the tension under his skin. If he had been visiting her chamber openly as her husband, he would be clad in his nightshirt under his robe. If he were here simply to lie with her, he would remove everything. But he was not here in either guise, for either reason. He wanted the pleasure of seducing Beatrice though he was certain, given her willingness to meet him, that she would not refuse him. He glanced over his shoul-

der at her; she watched him, her expression impossible
to read at this distance, in this light.

He pulled his doublet off, crossed the room to the
bedside and leaned forward to kiss her. At the touch
of his mouth, her lips parted and the kiss deepened.
As if freed by that small touch, lust roared through
him, obliterating everything else. He hauled Beatrice
into his arms, crushing her close, one hand in her hair,
the other pressing her hips to his.

In response, she arched against him, arms around
his neck, her mouth hot, her kiss maddening. He
pushed, she pulled and they fell together onto the mattress. His thigh thrust between hers; her legs wrapped
around his waist. She moved against him and sank
biting kisses into his throat, her breath harsh and quick
in his ear, her wantonness overwhelming him. If he
did not have her now, it would kill him; his hunger
was too vast to be contained a moment longer. He
lifted himself to fumble free of his clothing and sank
into her.

The shock of pleasure was as stunning and abrupt
as a plunge into cold water; he groaned, driven nigh
to delirium.

Beneath him, Beatrice murmured, "Oh." Then
louder, "Oh!"

She tightened around him, eyes closed, mouth
twisted in a grimace. Then, in a rippling cascade that
sent hot shivers to the base of his spine, the spasms of
her release clenched him, grasping him in waves. He
burst in one great pulse, the pleasure of it shaking him
to the core. More pulses. More pleasure. He heard himself groaning through a roaring torrent of sensation, as
if a flood swept through him and into her.

When he came back to himself, his arms and legs

shaking and weak, it was all he could do to lift himself onto his elbows to keep from crushing her. He looked down at her. Her eyes were still closed, a small smile playing with her lips. Her skin gleamed, glowing like a pearl under a sheen of moisture. He threaded his fingers into her hair and lowered his head to kiss the corner of her smile, the rounded point of her chin, the velvety hollow of her shoulder.

"Forgive me that I did not wait," he murmured. He thought he had satisfied her, but if he had not…

She half opened her eyes, her look seduction. "I could not have endured to wait."

He kissed her mouth, losing himself in the sweetness of it. "Do I crush you?" he asked when he could speak.

"No. Do not go," she answered, and pulled his head down for another kiss, intoxicating as mead.

The kiss lingered, spinning out endlessly like a dream, like the moment between waking and sleeping when the day was new and anything was possible. Beatrice was round and soft beneath him, warm around him; he could stay here forever, entangled with her, kissing her. He shifted his weight onto one elbow and with his free hand cupped her lush, heavy breast for the simple pleasure of it. She gasped into his mouth and stroked the length of his back to slide under his shirt and stroke upward on his naked skin.

He felt himself begin to harden again in response. Beatrice must have felt it, too; she moaned softly, her hand clutching his shoulder. His legs still trembled with weariness; he did not have the strength for this. Beatrice quivered and he responded, his body reacting as if he had not been wrung dry a scant fifteen minutes before.

"Sebastian," she whispered, and licked his neck, scraping it with her teeth.

He groaned. "Do you trust me?"

If the question surprised her she gave no sign. "Yes."

"Good. Do not fight me."

Gathering the dregs of his strength, he clamped his arm around her waist and rolled with her, coming to rest when his back was against the mattress, Beatrice above him straddling his waist, their bodies still joined. Her eyes were wide with shock, her mouth wide in a delighted grin.

"Sebastian!" she cried, and giggled.

The sound of her laughter went through him like a blade; how long had it been since he had heard it? He pushed the thought away before it could make him weep. "Use me as you will. I do not have the strength for anything else."

Her eyelids lowered in a look of mingled calculation and allure. "Then I control our play."

"You do."

"Oh, Sebastian," she murmured. "I think I shall like this very much."

She leaned forward and kissed him, a long, lingering kiss. Through her night rail and his shirt, the hard tips of her breasts pressed into him; where shirt and gown had rucked up, the silky skin of her lower belly slid against him. Her hair fell around them in a curtain of gold, soft as feathers against his neck. He was submerged in sensation, soft as her hair, her flesh, all of it pressing down into his groin. Beatrice straightened and stripped off her night rail, revealing herself to him. Color tinged her cheeks and she eyed him with a mixture of trepidation and triumph.

He let his gaze travel the length of her body. Candlelight burnished her firm white flesh with gold, shadowing her round breasts and rounded belly, the long curves of her thighs gripping his waist. Her beauty took his breath away. He lifted a hand to cup one of her breasts because he could not stop himself; her eyes closed and she licked her lips. He caressed the curve underneath the side that met her ribs, the rosy point. Slowly, Beatrice began to rock her hips, moving against him. He slid his free hand up her thigh and eased his thumb into the slick center of the apex. Her eyes opened and she smiled at him, a smile of great sweetness. He stroked her and watched pleasure flare in her eyes before she closed them again.

He gauged her response to his caresses by the way she gasped and softly moaned, the way she arched her back, the way she moved against him with increasing speed and decreasing grace. In the same moment he felt the first clutch of her release, tears spilled from her eyes. Startled, he removed his thumb.

She opened her eyes and whispered, "Do not stop. Please."

He returned his thumb, resumed his caress, and let her climax draw on his own. Slow as honey, hot and sweet, it came on, an endless easy series of spasms. In the candlelight, sweat gleamed between Beatrice's breasts, along her full, swollen mouth; tears shone on her cheeks.

When the last shudder died away, she opened her eyes, drenched lashes glittering. She leaned down and kissed him, then nestled her forehead in the crook of his neck. He stroked her back. There had never been anything like this in his life; whatever he had imagined making love to Beatrice would be, he could never have imagined the reality.

"Sweetheart," he murmured. It seemed both strange and right to use the endearment. "Why did you weep?"

"Joy," she said, her mouth against his skin moving in a kiss. "Pleasure. It was too much."

His arms tightened around her. *Too much.* It had been too much; it had not been enough.

"I do not want to leave you," he said. Her hair was soft under his hand, waves rippling against his skin.

"I wish you would not go," she said, still speaking against his throat. "Must you?"

"As much as I wish otherwise, I think your father is right to bring me with him."

"Then you must go." She lifted her head and tried to smile, the effort plain in the trembling of her lips. "By going, you give us the sweetness of reunion."

"Oh, Bea."

Wisdom dictated that he should leave, lest they be discovered, but he could not be wise, he could not let her go. He would leave her all too soon, and when he left he would not see her again for far too long.

He held her all night while she drowsed, unwilling to sleep because morning would come all that much sooner if he did. Despite his effort and his prayer that the night might never end, dawn came quickly, filling the panes of Beatrice's windows. The light was still gray and dim when he eased Beatrice out of his arms and tucked the coverlet around her naked shoulders.

Her eyes fluttered open. "Is it dawn already?"

"Close enough that I must go, sweetheart."

Her mouth trembled until she clamped it shut. She nodded.

He touched her face. "If I can I will write to you."

"My father will send messengers to my mother once a week, sometimes twice," she said gruffly. "When my mother sends her replies, I will send letters to you."

The offer surprised him. As a girl, Beatrice would have done anything to avoid pen and paper. "Do you still dislike writing so much?"

She met his eyes, hers determined and steady. "I will write to you."

Chapter Sixteen

With an exasperated sigh, Beatrice kicked the coverlet off her body and sat up. She hesitated a moment, not thinking, aware only of the sharp tangle of frustration knotted in her belly. Sighing again, she jerked open the bedcurtains, wooden loops clacking, and slid off the bed. She padded across the floor to the windows as if she might find Sebastian in the small yard below.

She missed him, missed him so much she could not sleep nights, aching for his warmth and his passion. It had been a week since he had left; surely she had had time to grow used to his absence. But she still longed for him.

She leaned against the wall, resting her cheek on the window frame and staring out into the starlit night. Did Sebastian miss her as she missed him? Was he finding sleep as elusive? Or had he forgotten her as soon as he rode away?

She knew he desired her; that fear had been laid to rest. Yet if she had thought the knowledge would satisfy her, she had been wrong. Having gained the passion of his flesh, she now longed for the passion of his heart. She wanted to know he loved her.

Why?

Because, God help her, she loved him. Was this love new, or was it her girlhood love coming to life once more? Did it matter? Surely the ache in her breast, the fear of hurt and the longing for Sebastian's company would be the same, whatever its source.

She closed her eyes and pressed her forehead against the panes of glass, hard and cold against her skin. She did not want to love Sebastian. It could only mean pain and disappointment. Though Sebastian did not despise and hate her any longer, it did not follow that he would come to love her.

She opened her eyes and moved to the prie-dieu in the far corner of the room. She knelt, pressed her hands palm to palm and cleared her mind for prayer. But what to pray for?

Sebastian's love?

It smacked a little of blasphemy to ask for something as worldly, sensual and selfish as one man's love. Surely it could not do her soul any good to make such a request. If she was not to have Sebastian's love, what did she need, what did her soul require?

Strength. Strength and the patience to bear whatever fell upon her.

She bent her head and began to pray.

In the morning, she was still restless, as if the flesh beneath her skin itched. All through Mass, she fought herself and her body's reluctance to be still. She wanted Sebastian, and no amount of reminding herself that he was a day's ride away, too far to join, was enough to ease her longing.

As she left the chapel, wondering how she was going to endure a morning spent quietly stitching in the solar, John fell into step beside her.

"What ails you?" he asked.

"How now, John," she said. "Is that any way to greet me?"

"Do not be pert. I have not seen you fidget like that since we were children. What ails you?"

She sighed. John was as persistent as the tide and as unstoppable. "I miss Sebastian."

His eyes narrowed as if he understood what she meant, that her body missed Sebastian's. She held her breath, waiting for his accusation, or worse yet, his questions, but his expression cleared as if he had learned all he needed to in that one moment and would ask nothing more.

"What you need, Bea, is a good ride. Come, let us go."

"I must attend our mother," she said, though it was the last thing she wanted to do.

"You would rather ride with me than sit in the solar, I know it."

When they had been young, how much mischief had he coaxed her into by naming her secret wishes as if they were nothing to be denied or fought? He could have made a ride through hell sound reasonable. Yet, despite knowing that, she could not resist him, not when he named her need.

John had been right; the ride, across the fields and along the lanes around the castle, with her mare swift and strong beneath her, was what she had needed. She and her brother did not talk, but they rarely did when riding together. The pleasures of movement and wind, the changeable beauties of the country surrounding Wednesfield, consumed them both. They wandered for an hour, until the sky closed in. Turning toward home, they raced the rain to Wednesfield, winning but only just. The first fat drops plopped on the cobbles of the courtyard as they released the horses into the care of the stablemen.

In the screens passage, Beatrice stopped John before he could leave her. "Bless you, John. I did need that."

"It was my pleasure. I am yours to command."

She glanced at him in time to see him grin at her and she grinned in answer. "I am glad you are home. I missed you."

His grin disappeared. "Are you glad in truth?"

"How not?"

"You and Sebastian... Neither of you seemed best pleased to find yourselves betrothed."

His remark surprised her, enough that she frowned, hunting for the words that would speak the truth. "That is true, but you did no ill by either of us. You saved us from our folly. If we were not best pleased, it was no fault of yours."

"Then I am glad I am home, as well."

When she entered the hall, one of her mother's ushers met her with a message from her mother, bidding her attend the countess in her solar immediately.

"As I am?" she asked, indicating the dust clinging to the hem of her skirt and by extension the evidence that she had been riding.

"Yes, my lady. As soon as you return."

The usher's sober face as well as the fact that her mother wished to see her in all her dirt made her heart check for a moment before it resumed beating, quick and frightened. She left the usher without a word and hurried up the stairs to the solar.

Her mother was sitting in her chair with her eyes closed, her lone attendant reading from an open book. The peace of the scene halted Beatrice on the threshold. What had befallen that required her attendance in her riding clothes, yet left her mother able to listen to her woman reading to her?

Her mother opened her eyes. "You have returned."

"I came as soon as I arrived, as I was told you wished me to."

Her mother frowned and sighed, exasperated. "I did not intend that you should not refresh yourself beforehand. Margery, you may go."

"Yes, my lady."

The woman passed her as Beatrice stepped into the room. "I thought some great ill had befallen you."

"I am sorry if you were frightened, child. Come, sit beside me."

Her heart calming, Beatrice crossed the room to sit on the stool beside her mother's chair. She looked up into her mother's face. The afternoon light was bright enough to be unforgiving, exposing the web of lines at the corners of her eyes, the depth of the grooves beside her mouth. Yet her mother still had beauty in the shape of her bones, the penetrating clarity of her gaze. This was where her own beauty had come from, the mold from which she had been cast.

"Men have called me Helen of Troy," she said, still looking up into her mother's face. "Did they do the same when you were young?"

Her mother started as if surprised by the question. Did she not think Beatrice could see how lovely she must have been?

"No, but I was reckoned a beauty nevertheless."
Her gaze sharpened, moved over Beatrice's face as if
seeing it for the first time. "I do not think I was as
beautiful as you are, however."

"If I had not been so beautiful, my life would have
been much different."

"It would have been different, but perhaps not as
greatly different as you imagine."

There was no answer to that; her own remark had
been self-pitying and bootless.

"Why did you wish me to come to you?"

Her mother reached out and brushed her fingertips
along Beatrice's cheek, her touch tender for all its
lightness. "Can I not wish to see you?"

Beatrice caught her hand before it withdrew, unwilling to let her mother go. "I should have come to
you in any case. Surely you knew that."

"You have gone your own way since you were
hardly more than a child. I could not be sure."

"Have you wanted me to come to you? I always
thought you preferred Ceci."

Her mother's fingers tightened over her own. "Ceci
was always easier for me because she is so unlike me.
She favors her father in more than coloring, while you
and John are far too like me. I see things in myself
that madden me and also when I see them in you. But
I love you as much as I love Ceci. Never doubt that,
Beatrice."

Beatrice bent her head and rested her forehead
against her mother's knees. "Why did you not lock
me in my room and starve me into submission when
I said I would have Thomas as my husband? I know
you opposed the match." The words were spoken
without her volition, as if some other Beatrice said

them. Her mother's candor had called them, as if truth demanded truth.

"Your father would not let me, and I was not so sure of my judgment to fight him. If I had known how unkind he would be to you—"

Beatrice lifted her head. "How did you know Thomas was unkind?"

"You are my child. How could I not know of your unhappiness? If I had known before the marriage, I would not have stopped until I wore your father down. If I had known, you would not have married him."

"I did not ask my question as a reproach to you."

Her mother smiled gently. "Did you not?"

Beatrice stared up at her, weighing her heart, assaying it for the truth. Frankness for frankness. "Perhaps in part." She sighed. "If I reproach anyone, it is myself, for the folly was mine. Nevertheless, it is done and I will not spend another moment repining for what cannot be undone." She straightened. The kindness of her mother's smiles and words, the clasp of their hands, the way they spoke openly for once, gave her courage to ask a question that she would never have dared ask otherwise. "Does my father ever strike you?"

Her mother's grip tightened and relaxed as her smile faded and her gaze sharpened. "He never has, despite some provocation."

"Would my father ever strike you without provocation? Would he strike you because his cattle had murrain or the rain fell too heavily to hunt?"

Her mother's eyes were gray, full of light, her voice gentle. "Did Thomas beat you because his cattle were sick or he could not hunt?"

"I have asked Sebastian to wrest a casket of gauds

from Thomas's son. Every thing in that casket was given to me because Thomas lost his temper and beat me. I know my husband has the right to correct me, but if I have done no wrong—''

Her mother rubbed her hands, palms sliding softly over her skin. "Oh, child, child."

The grief in her voice surprised Beatrice. "He is dead, Mama. He cannot hurt me anymore."

"You are shaking, child."

So she was. She had not felt it until her mother spoke.

"He hurts you still, Beatrice."

"Not as much as he once did." And that was true, too, another thing she had not known until it was spoken. She was healing from the hurts of her marriage. Sebastian had had a hand in that, from the gentleness of his dealings with her, despite his anger, to his tenderness toward her in bed. The balm of that let her smile at her mother and turn the subject. "May I ask you again, did you send for me simply to see me?"

Her mother smiled in answer. "I will henceforth. Today, however, I sent for you because a letter has come for you."

"A letter? From Sebastian?"

"No, not from Sebastian. I believe it comes from Sir George Conyers."

She went cold, all the warmth in the room gone. *Why did you write...what if Sebastian finds out...? Why will you not leave me in peace?* She had known some evil would befall her, but she had never imagined this.

"Beatrice, you are pale. Does this Sir George threaten you? Shall I send for your father?"

"No!" She looked up into her mother's face. "I pray you, tell no one of this."

"Who is he?"

Beatrice bent her head and once again pressed her forehead against her mother's knees. "I am so ashamed. I cannot tell you." But she was going to tell her mother; she could feel it. It was why she had hidden her face.

"I will not condemn you, child. Was he your lover?"

Beatrice lifted her head, surprised once more by her mother's quickness. "Sebastian thought so."

"But no longer does." Her mother's eyes were fathomless, as if she had seen everything at least once before and had long ago left judgment to God.

"He knows better."

"Then Thomas never consummated your marriage."

The shock of that drove the breath from Beatrice. "How did you know?"

"Cecilia said something once about Thomas stabbing his foot to provide blood for the sheets. But I had wondered before that." A faint smile creased the corners of her mother's lips. "And Sebastian has done what Thomas could not."

Beatrice's ears burned. She had not wanted her mother to know... "How?"

"How else should Sebastian know you had not taken a lover than to lie with you and learn you were a virgin? I assume this has taken place since he arrived at Wednesfield."

"Yes." She could say nothing more, wishing the ground would swallow her. Was what she felt shame, or simple embarrassment? Only embarrassment; shame would not come, not for Sebastian.

"So, let us return to Sir George. If you did not lie with him, what was he to you?"

Beatrice sighed. After her priest and Sebastian, how difficult could it be to confess to her mother? Difficult enough that she had to reach for courage. "He wished to be my lover and I allowed him to kiss me and touch me where in honor I ought not to have done." She swallowed, her face growing hotter. "There are many things a man and woman may do without great risk. George and I did most of them."

"When did your dalliance with him end?"

"How do you know it was dalliance?"

"By the way you speak of it and of him."

She must be growing accustomed to the shrewdness of her mother's remarks; that one did not dismay her. "Sebastian found me with George." She frowned, remembering. "I told myself that I would not see George after that because it had shown me how easily Thomas might catch me and I would not risk that. But in truth, after seeing Sebastian, I did not want to see George."

"Do you know why not?"

"Are you not angry with me, Mama? I did not expect such forbearance."

"How not? You are no longer a child, Beatrice, and I do not think your mistakes have left you untouched. Shall I reproach you when you have reproached yourself? I said I should not condemn you."

"You did not know what I had done when you said that."

"But I knew your heart and my own. Tell me, if you will, why seeing Sebastian meant you no longer wished to see George."

Beatrice sighed. This she had never confessed; she had not seen it before. "Because I did not see my lewdness and shame until I saw the disgust in Sebastian's eyes. And after I saw, I could no longer behave so."

"Does Sebastian mean so much to you?"

Beatrice nodded. "I have not let myself know how much until now. Oh, Mama, I love him and I do not want to."

"Why not? There is no harm in loving your husband."

"He does not love me, not any longer. If he had never loved me, I might hope he would come to it, but a dead love cannot rise again."

"I pray you are wrong, child." Her mother's thumbs resumed rubbing the backs of Beatrice's hands, her touch firm and soothing at once. "Now, what are you going to do about that letter?"

"Return it unopened, as I have the others he has sent."

Her mother nodded, but a faint frown creased her forehead between her brows. "If that is what you wish, we will send it back with his messenger. However, it is not what I should do, if it were me."

Nothing she had done had driven George away, and her mother was the wisest woman she knew. "What would you do? Tell me."

"How many letters has he sent you?"

"Four or five. I have not kept count."

"You returned them all still sealed, if I understand you aright, yet he persists in writing to you. I think you must open his letter, read what he has written and then reply, telling him to desist."

"I do not want to contact him."

"You must tell him to stop or he will not. Does Sebastian know of this?"

"No!" She could not tell Sebastian, not ever.

"All the more reason to write to Sir George. Tell him you are betrothed and he must not trouble you any longer. Otherwise, it is very likely that one day one of his letters will be brought to Benbury. Not only will Sebastian find out about the correspondence, but I have no doubt he will realize you have concealed it from him."

"But I have done no wrong," Beatrice said, though she knew her innocence would not count with Sebastian in any matter touching George.

"Have you not? You have concealed these letters from your betrothed husband. If you have done no wrong, why have you hidden this?"

"Do you not believe me?"

"Of course I believe you. Have I not seen your dismay with my own eyes? I am only telling you what Sebastian is likely to think." Her mother released Beatrice's hands and stretched out her hand to pick up a square of paper, sealed with wax, that had been lying on the table. She held it out to Beatrice. "Here, read this letter so you may know what he wants, and then we will compose a reply."

Beatrice stared at the letter for a long moment before reaching out for it and then hesitated again before opening the seal. Was not opening the letter akin to letting George speak to her again? Refusing his letters had made her feel as if she was finally guarding her honor as she ought to have done from the beginning. Yet now her mother, whom she trusted with her soul, had advised her to do this. She broke the seal and opened the letter.

His handwriting was beautifully formed and very clear. She had not expected that; somehow, she had thought his fist would be hard to read. On the other hand, the passion of his words and the fervor of his pleas were as she had anticipated. He did not understand why she would not see him, did she not understand he loved her as a true knight, please let him come to her and he would prove how much he loved her. She held the letter out to her mother.

"He says nothing I wish to know," she said. "I pray you, read it and tell me what to do."

Her mother scanned the letter far more quickly than Beatrice had done. "He protests too much. I do not think he loves you nearly as well as he loves loving you." She looked up. "I do not mean that unkindly."

"And I do not understand it unkindly. I am glad he does not love me. I would not wish to hurt him."

Her mother snorted. "Some men, child," she said, "are not so easily hurt. Come, sit at the table and we will compose your reply."

"Can you not write it for me?" Beatrice said. She did not want to do this. If reading his letter made her feel as if she had given George leave to woo her, answering it felt as if she were encouraging him to continue.

"No, I cannot. This is your task to accomplish. Trust me. You will feel better when it is done."

Beatrice smiled tartly, a host of memories crowding her. "I am not a child."

"Do not act like one," her mother replied with a smile of equal tartness.

Beatrice's answer, composed with a great deal of help from her mother, was simple and straightforward. Whatever they had been to one another in the past was no more. She was betrothed to Sebastian Benbury and would marry him at Michaelmas. If George loved her as much as he claimed, he would only wish to please her, and it would please her if he would write her no more. Let him pray for her soul as she would pray for his.

Beatrice signed it with a shaking hand, her wrist aching from the unaccustomed effort. Her mother took the letter, read it again and then shook sand over it to dry the ink. "Well done, child. Do you have a seal?"

"The Manners seal, which I will not use," Beatrice said, watching her mother fold the paper.

"Very well. We will use the Wednesfield seal instead." She sealed the letter and returned it to Beatrice. "Give this to the boy without and tell him to bring it to Sir George's messenger."

Beatrice gave it to the boy and then watched him rush headlong down the solar stairs. As the turn concealed him, she had a sudden sense of foreboding, as if some harm would befall her for having sent the letter. She crossed herself to drive her fear away and turned back into the solar.

Pray God she had been wrong.

Chapter Seventeen

Sebastian and the earl turned into the short lane that led to Herron, road-worn, mud-splattered and weary. They had settled the quarrel that had brought them here within a day of their arrival and in the week since, the earl had kept his promise to guide Sebastian over the property. Together they had visited farms, seen fields and ridden through coppices, enough to show that Herron was still a jewel of a property. Sebastian had been pleased to see everything but his pleasure had been muted and halfhearted, as if incomplete. This was not how he had expected his return to Herron would unfold when the earl had mentioned it in London.

Returning now hardly seemed worth it. Even the house, that had loomed in his memory as a fine manor, was only a small stone building, sturdily built but no greater than one of the better houses of Wednesfield's tenants. And for all that he had dreamed of returning here, now that he was here, he found no comfort. At night, he could not sleep, his bed cold and too large. He knew he was a fool—how could he miss sleeping with Beatrice when he had only slept in her bed twice? Yet he did, fool or no.

Even more, he wanted to talk to her, to hear her voice and to watch the expressions pass over her face. God help him, how he missed her.

As he and the earl entered the house, the Herron steward came forward. "A messenger from Wednesfield brought these, my lord," he said, and handed letters to the earl.

The earl glanced through the letters and held one out to Sebastian. "This is for you."

His name was written legibly but gracelessly on the outside of the letter in the fist of someone who wrote only when she had to. As if he had conjured her, Beatrice was here with him. His memory of her was so vivid, he could almost smell her hair, feel the warmth of her skin against his. He opened the letter. Three lines, no more, crossed the page, thin on the white ground: her greeting, a line to say she was well and prayed the same for him, and her signature. So little for such a large sheet; the lines looked lonely. He read them three times, Beatrice in every wobble of the uncertain script. Before he could read the letter a fourth time, he folded it and tucked it in his doublet.

"If I may have your leave, sir, I should like to wash off the road." And answer this letter, though he had no notion what he might say in reply.

The earl, absorbed in his own letter, glanced up. "Very well. I will see you when we dine."

Sebastian bowed and left the hall.

When he had washed, he sent for paper and pen, but when he sat down to write, his mind was blank. What could he say to her? He wrote his greeting, hoping the act of setting pen to paper would prompt him.

It did not. The ink dried on the nib of his pen as he stared at his own writing, waiting for inspiration. She had said she prayed he was well. He could answer that. He dipped the pen and wrote. At the end of the sentence, inspiration dried, and so did the pen. Was she well? He dipped the pen again and wrote. This time, when he could think of nothing else, he put the pen in the ink so it would not dry a third time.

I do not wish to be here without you. I cannot sleep for longing for you. I lie awake and yet I dream of you. I will not be parted from you again.

He could not write any of those things. He would not risk putting his heart into her keeping again, no matter how she seemed to have changed.

He picked up the pen and signed his name.

Beatrice was with her mother in the solar, stitching a shirt for Sebastian, when the messenger came, bearing letters from Herron. One was for her, from Sebastian. Her mother handed it to her with a smile that warmed her cheeks; she was glad to have a reason to look away.

The letter was short, as short as her own had been. She had not known what to say, the letter to George weighing on her, her dislike of her pen constraining her. Was Sebastian short because she had been? And why was her heart in her stomach, as if she were disappointed? Had she expected a love letter from a man who did not love her?

"You do not look pleased, child. Is something amiss?"

Beatrice's eyes burned. She blinked hard and looked up. "No. I had hoped for a longer report, but he says no more than he is well and that he hopes you and I are also well.''

Her mother snorted. ''So your father would always write if I did not desire otherwise. He reports more fully. Would you like to hear what he has to say?''

Her heart lifted, rising as quickly as it had fallen. Love made her heart giddy, changeable and foolish, and she could no more contain its fits and starts than she could stop the tide. She met her mother's eyes and was eased by their wise warmth.

''I should like that very much.''

Her mother smiled, bent her head and began reading aloud.

They had resolved the dispute that had sent them to Herron; Sebastian had been most clever in handling the matter. Her father had done nothing but announce that the manor would be returned to the Benbury family come Michaelmas; that had been enough to restore good sense to the disputants. With the quarrel mended, Sebastian and her father had been spending their days visiting Herron's tenants and examining the farms, fields and forest that comprised Herron's acres. Sebastian had made a good showing to his tenants; her father had no doubt he would be a good master of the property.

Her mother folded the letter.

''Does he say when they will return?'' Beatrice asked.

''He does not.''

Beatrice nodded, unaccountably disappointed.

''You will wish to reply,'' her mother said gently, as if offering a hint.

''Yes, I shall,'' Beatrice said. She might dislike the pen, but if using it meant she reached out to Sebastian and perhaps provoked another, longer letter from him, she would write page after page without repining.

"It is too late to send the messenger back today. I will send him tomorrow. Sit at my table, use my pens and ink."

Beatrice went to the table, pulled a sheet of paper toward her, selected a pen, dipped it in the ink, and then sat for a moment, wondering where to begin. She had received his letter; she could tell him that. And she was well, as he prayed; she could tell him that, as well. She wrote carefully, trying not to make any blots. When she had finished, she stared at the letters, dark and crooked on the page.

I miss you.

She could not write that. Or could she? Her stomach turned over, a slow, hot roll. If she confessed this, might he confess the same? And if he did not?

Before she could let fear overwhelm her, she dipped the pen in the ink and wrote that she wished to see him. She stared at the words when they were on the page, her heart pattering against her ribs like the beat of a small, weak drum. She swallowed to calm her unease and added that she hoped he and her father were well.

When shall I look for your return?

Thomas would have ridden home just to strike her for daring to question him; somehow she did not think Sebastian would do the same. Taking her courage in her hands, she wrote the question and then signed the letter before she could add anything else. She rose from the table to give it to her mother. It was done. Let Sebastian make of it what he would.

The messenger sent to Wednesfield returned two days after he had gone, followed by another messenger from one of the earl's properties to the north of Herron. The earl took the letters from Wednesfield, sorted through them and handed one to Sebastian. Sebastian had it open before the earl finished examining the remaining letters.

It was from Beatrice, but he had known it would be. She had written a little more than before, saying she missed him and asking when he would return.

As soon as I may.

The words came from nowhere, from his heart. He stared at the letter though he no longer read it, one part of his mind noting the shakiness of her script, the gracelessness of her writing, while he listened to his heart pound. He wanted nothing more than to be at Wednesfield with Beatrice, not parted from her by a day's ride, their only connection the earl's messengers. The ache of wanting was sharp, persistent; it was why he could take no pleasure in the return to Herron. There could be no pleasure in anything when he was away from Beatrice.

Sweet Jesú.

He had not truly known until this moment how much he needed her. He could tell himself as much as he liked that he would not put his heart into her keeping but wishing changed nothing. If he needed her, what did it matter that he did not love or trust her? He was in her power nevertheless. With shaking hands he folded her letter, trying not to crumple it, and tucked it into the front of his doublet. He had feared that if he came close enough to Beatrice to win her love, he would also entrap himself. Did she love him? Or was he alone in his weakness, a fool for the culling? He did not know, had no way to know. Even her passion when she lay with him, the ardor that had delighted him, might only be her weaker woman's nature.

In the end, where did the truth lie? He no longer knew, and that was the most dangerous trap of all. He was fog-bound, lost, unable to move forward, unable to retreat. His only hope lay in stillness, waiting for the fog to lift so he might see his way clear.

"Whoreson!" the earl muttered furiously, his voice breaking Sebastian's thoughts.

Sebastian looked up. "Sir?"

"We will not be returning to Wednesfield as quickly as I had expected. I must go north and I wish you to come with me."

"What has befallen, if I may ask?"

"Idiocy," the earl said, folding the letter in his hands. "Arrant nonsense, yet I must ride north nevertheless." He looked up at Sebastian. "If you wish to reply to my daughter, you must do so tonight. We ride at dawn."

Sebastian's hand rose to his chest, to touch the place where the letter lay. It crackled underneath his doublet. In stillness lay his only hope. "No, sir. I make no reply."

"I cannot do this," Lucia said, sighing.

"No, you can. Let me show you again," Beatrice said. The idea to show her sister-in-law how to stitch blackwork had come when Lucia had seen the shirt Beatrice was making for Sebastian. The pattern was the same one she had used to make a shirt for him so long ago, black herons on white ground for Benbury. Lucia had taken the shirt from her and spread it across her knees, unfolding the linen so that the black stitches had shown up in all their intricacy against the white cloth. Her sigh and the way her fingers had barely grazed the cloth had been comment and inspiration enough.

"No, no more, please," Lucia said, sighing.

Beatrice looked at John's wife. Lucia was flushed and her eyes shone as if she might start crying at any moment. "Watch me. Perhaps that will help."

Once again, Beatrice moved her needle and silk through the linen, her stitches tiny and neat almost without effort. Lucia leaned her head close, watching.

"I will never be able to do that," she murmured.

"You will," Beatrice replied without lifting her eyes, imitating her mother at her most certain.

Someone scratched on the door to the solar. Beatrice's mother, reading her accounts, said, "Enter."

The door opened and one of the ushers entered. "An it please you, my lady, here is a letter from my lord the earl."

"Bring it here."

Beatrice looked up. Surely there was another letter. Sebastian must have answered her.

"Madam."

Her mother looked up, eyebrows raised. Had that voice been hers? It must have; why else would her mother be looking at her so?

"Is there no other letter?"

Her mother's look softened and she turned to the usher. "Go, you. See if there is anything else."

"My lady, there was nothing but that."

Her mother turned back to Beatrice. "You have your answer."

"Yes, my lady."

Sebastian's answer was silence, a void that gave nothing back. She could read whatever she pleased into that silence, save that no messenger had been sent. Sebastian was with her father…

"My lady, is Lord Benbury still with my father?"

Her mother looked first at her, then at the usher. "You may go. You may all go, save Lady Manners and Mistress Coleville."

When the door had shut behind the last of her mother's attendants, her mother put the letter down on the table. "Come here, Beatrice."

Beatrice rose and went to sit beside her mother.

"I do not know why Sebastian has not written you, but it does not become you to fret in this manner. He is a busy man, working with your father on your father's business. He may well not have time to write to you."

"My father writes to you." She did not want to say it, but the words, puling and weak, came out despite her will.

Her mother snorted and picked up the letter. "Here. Read what he writes to me." She handed the letter to Beatrice.

Her father wrote no more neatly than she did, so it was difficult to read the letter. Still, as she struggled through it, it seemed that every sentence began, "Do you do this…" or "I wish you to…" It was a series of instructions, involving food from the estate, money from their coffers, favors returned and favors granted. She handed the letter back to her mother, chastened yet dissatisfied.

"When your lives are as knit together as mine and the earl's, Sebastian will write to you as often and with as little love. Do not repine, child."

"I told him I missed him," Beatrice whispered.

"And because he does not answer, you fear he does not miss you."

Beatrice nodded; she could not speak it aloud.

"Perhaps he does not," her mother said, her voice gentle and pitched not to be overheard.

Oh, what a fool she had been, letting longing build up her hopes, letting her wishes become certainties. Did she not know that hope was stronger than knowledge, stronger than truth? Given its head, hope would let her forget everything wisdom bade her remember. She had known Sebastian did not love her but she had let hope persuade her otherwise.

"Beatrice."

She looked up at her mother. "I am well, Mama."

"Do not make too much of this. I have never known a man willing to put his heart on paper before he had spoken it."

"You said…"

"I know. What I ought to have said was that you cannot know why Sebastian has not written to you and you must not interpret it until you know more."

"He cannot love me," Beatrice murmured.

"How do you know?" her mother asked. "Has he told you so?"

Had he spoken those words? She could not remember hearing them, yet he had made himself plain. "I think he must have."

"When?"

"I do not know," Beatrice said. "I pray you, ask me no more. Does it matter if he said it or no if I am certain it is true? He cannot love me and if I love him, it is my penance for the ways I have hurt him. Have I your leave to go?"

Her mother frowned at her, the frown troubled rather

than angry. *Do not look at me so, I cannot bear it.* She wanted to go somewhere quiet, away from her mother, away from Lucia. There must be a place where she might ease her heart and find some form of peace—perhaps the chapel, which had become more of a sanctuary than she would have thought possible two months ago.

"Very well, child. You have my leave," her mother said slowly, the frown deepening.

She curtsied and left the room before her mother could stop her, Lucia's voice echoing behind her, "Madam?"

She closed the door and hurried to the chapel, tears burning her eyes.

Chapter Eighteen

The earl's business at the property north of Herron took longer to resolve than the quarrel at Herron had. The days, while the earl questioned, considered and berated his way to a decision, were long—Sebastian had little to do but attend the earl and listen to the tedious proceedings. But as slow as the days were, the nights, spent in a strange bed, were worse.

Sebastian lay awake in the darkness, unable to stop thinking of Beatrice no matter how he tried to focus his mind elsewhere, his longing for her aching like a wound. Messengers came every day from Wednesfield, but they carried letters from the countess alone. Beatrice did not write, keeping silence as if she wished to punish him and make him suffer. A little voice in the back of his head whispered that she did not write because he did not. He silenced the voice every time he heard it. Even if it spoke the truth, he still could not write her, not while he still needed her.

Finally, after an interminable sennight, the earl announced at dinner that he was satisfied with the resolution of his business and that they would ride back to Herron the next day, Wednesfield the day after. Sebastian's stomach clenched, whether from dread or excitement he could not tell. How would he face Beatrice after this parting? Matters between them had changed in the past few weeks—the long silence after those quick letters made that clear enough. Had they changed for the better—and if they had, what did it mean? He would only learn the truth when he saw her once more.

The journey to Herron and thence to Wednesfield was a journey from unfamiliarity to familiarity, and from anxiety to something akin to resignation as the land they rode became the hills and fields he knew. Whatever had happened between Beatrice and him in the past three weeks was done, the damage made and only repairs ahead of them. He had worn her down and won past the barriers of pain and distrust once already; surely he could do the same against a few weeks of distance. If he wanted to.

On the afternoon of the second day they came to the places he knew almost as well as he knew Benbury. Here were the woods he had hunted in company with his father and the earl; here were the hills he and Beatrice's brothers Jasper and John had ridden as soon as they were breeched. By the shape of the land, almost by the green of the hills and woods, he knew how close they drew to Wednesfield. And the closer they came, eagerness to see Beatrice grew. She was dangerous to him, he knew it, and yet he could not stop himself from wishing the horses would go faster.

Finally the towers and battlements of the castle appeared above the treetops, their stones silver-gilt in the gray light of a cloudy afternoon. The muscles in Sebastian's shoulders tightened. So close, so close, only a few minutes' ride, and then he would be face-to-face with Beatrice.

They turned into the lane that led through the gate in Wednesfield's walls. Passing under the gate, they rode through darkness that rang with hooves on stone before passing into the weak sunshine and crowded clamor of the great courtyard. The muddy yard was a hurly-burly of horses, dogs, stable boys and grooms; it looked and sounded as if the whole household had turned out to greet the earl. The din of shouting voices, clattering hooves, and yapping, snarling dogs beat against Sebastian's ears as the earl greeted grooms and ushers, signaled with his hand for largesse to be distributed and then leaped from his horse as lightly as a much younger man. Sebastian dismounted and followed the earl as he strode through the door of the great hall.

After the tumult of the courtyard, the hall was blessedly quiet, a world of calm and order. Informed by the man the earl had sent ahead to announce his return, the countess waited beneath the cloth of estate, women clustered around her. Sebastian looked for Beatrice in their midst and found her beside her mother, so close he wondered how he had failed to see her before. His heart lodged in his throat, hard as a green apple. Her hands were folded and her eyes downcast, and he could not tell if her aloofness was humility, pride or anger. She wore blue, the color he had said would please him, but if she did not look for him, what did it matter what color she wore?

Look at me. Please. Do not let me be the only eager one.

As if she heard him, she raised her eyes, her gaze meeting his for a long, tense moment. Her eyes were shadowed and sad, her mouth a soft, straight line. Neither pride, humility nor anger, then—what he saw was hurt. He wanted to cross the floor and fold her in his arms, soothing whatever ailed her. He could not do it, held back as much by a hardness within himself as by the forms of courtesy. Her eyelids swept down, veiling her gaze, and she did not look at him again as her mother turned to greet him.

"How now, Sebastian. Welcome to Wednesfield." The countess's smile was both kind and cool, as if she was displeased with him yet understood the cause of his trespass.

Had Beatrice said anything to her mother? And if so, what? "I thank you for your kind welcome, my lady. I am pleased to return."

The countess nodded and moved to greet another of the earl's attendants, a nobleman's stripling son fostered in the Wednesfield household. Freed, Sebastian stepped closer to Beatrice. She did not look up.

"How now, my lady."

"My lord." Her voice was hardly more than a whisper.

"Look at me."

She looked up, giving him obedience if nothing else. "My lord?"

"Why do you not use my name?"

She blushed, her whole face washed in pink. "It is not seemly that I should do so here," she said, and glanced at her parents.

"Will you speak my name if I command you?"

Her eyes dropped, avoiding his. "I am bound to obey you."

"Is that the only reason?"

"Is it not enough?"

No.

But he could not speak plainly to this withdrawn, wary woman. "Do as you list. I will not compel you."

Almost imperceptibly she stiffened and that tiny movement put distance between them as clearly as if she had taken a step away from him. He could think of nothing he might say or do to close the breach between them that did not also expose him and leave him vulnerable. He could not put himself in her power, but he wanted to draw her near, to have her smile at him as she had done before he had left. A pox on his confusion, on the desires that pulled against one another, depriving him of peace and an easy mind.

Thankfully, the dance of courtesy and welcome parted them a moment later, delivering him from temptation. As he followed the moves required of him, he watched Beatrice. She smiled when she ought, curtsied when she ought, used all who met her with the proper degree of hauteur or humility. She followed the steps of the dance with grace and ease—how not, when she had been raised an earl's daughter?

She glanced up and caught him staring, her eyes dark with distance. Color tinged her cheeks before she looked away, attending her mother with every appearance of interest. The countess glanced at him and then at Beatrice; she spoke and Beatrice left her side, moving toward him. She curtsied when she reached him.

"An it please you, my mother bids me take you to your chamber."

Left to her own wishes, would she do this? And why did the question even occur to him? He did not want to know the answer.

"It pleases me well. Lead on, my lady."

A quick glance flicked to his face as if to read it,

but she said nothing, turning toward the stairs that led to the chamber he had occupied before. Would he sleep there tonight? Or would she let him return to her bed? With a vividness he had denied himself before this, he remembered how warm and sweet she had been in those two nights he had spent with her, opening her body and, he had thought, her heart to his touch. Now he was sure only of her body.

And that was enough to release desire into his blood. Perhaps his need had only been that of the flesh, an answer to her responsive eagerness. And what if she had missed lying with him as much as he had missed lying with her? He climbed the stairs behind her, watching the sway of her hips beneath her full skirts, his wayward imagination picturing the white flesh moving under yards of blue brocade. At the top of the stairs, he took her by the upper arm, spun her around and pulled her against him.

"Seba—"

His mouth came down on hers, sealing his name on her lips. For an instant she stiffened as if she might resist him, then her body leaned into his as her mouth opened, yielding to him. He crushed her against him as the kiss deepened and grew hotter. He wanted to eat her alive; to judge by her soft, half-breathed moans and the heat of her kiss, she was as hungry for him. For an endless moment, he drowned in sensation, the kiss fusing them.

Bea, oh, Bea.

A door banged far away and voices echoed in the stairwell, recalling Sebastian to an awareness of where they were. This was no place to kiss her, not when they could be so easily found. He straightened and eased away from the kiss, the ache of wanting her sharper than ever.

"I missed you," he whispered, his mouth on her cheek. A chill passed over him. He had not meant to speak those words.

She pressed her face against his doublet, hiding from him. Her reaction dampened his ardor and his arms loosened. Did she not—

She spoke, her voice muffled by doublet and gown.

"What? I did not hear you." He put his hand under her chin and tried to tilt her face up. She jerked her chin free.

"I said I missed you, too." She sounded impatient and she had grown tense. He let her go.

"But you did not write to me." The words were out before he could stop them. If he was not careful, he would confess everything he meant to keep close.

She stepped back, distancing herself still further, and folded her hands before her waist; Beatrice armoring herself. "You did not write me when I confessed I missed you. How should I write you again?"

"You should have written."

For a moment she faced him without the bulwark of her reserve, anger burning in her gaze, in the color in her cheeks. She looked as if words trembled on her tongue, words sharp enough to cut if she spoke them. Then her lips folded tight and she swallowed. Her gaze dropped and the Beatrice who might have cried hard truth was gone.

"How should I? I thought you were displeased with me," she said.

No, you have pleased me too well, he thought, more words he could not say. Her plain refusal to be candid reinforced his determination not to speak. He would not expose himself if she remained hidden.

"I pray you, take me to my chamber as your mother bade you. I would not wish to displease her."

She curtsied, sinking so low it was either mockery or profound deference. Either way, it was another sign of the barriers that had risen between them in the weeks he was away. Without looking at him or speaking to him, she led him back to the chamber he had occupied earlier. At the door, she curtsied again as if, having delivered him, she intended to return to her mother. He put out his hand to stay her.

"Give me leave to come to you tonight." The words were out before he considered them, their demand naked of flattery. Surely she would say him nay; he would not blame her if she marched away without answering him at all. And yet it was not to lie with her that he spoke. Somehow he could not help thinking that if they came together in the bed where they had been close, nearly defenseless, Beatrice would drop her guard against him, releasing him from the need to guard himself against her.

She looked up at him, her eyes examining his face as if she had not truly looked at him before now.

"Do you wish to?"

"I would not ask if I did not." *Do not make me beg.* If she would not give him leave now, that would be the end of it. He could say nothing more.

She stepped nearer, still gazing at him, her movement closing more than the physical distance between them. "If you wish it, you have only to command me."

"I will not force you." He paused. "You know there is risk. I will not demand that you take it."

Her eyes dropped, color seeping into her face. "I should like it if you came," she whispered.

"Then I shall be there."

She curtsied a third time. "I must return to my mother."

Do not go, he thought, but he nodded. She had to leave; if she remained they would either talk or make love, each action carrying its own dangers.

She left without a backward glance. When he could no longer see even her shadow, he entered his chamber. It was unchanged—but why should it have been altered? He might feel as if he had been gone three years but his journey had only taken three weeks. Pushing his melancholy aside, he crossed to the window. It had begun to rain, drowning the greenery of the garden. The paths, endlessly curving upon themselves, reminded him of the times he had walked the garden in Beatrice's company, wooing her as best he could.

How could things have gone so awry in the short time they had been apart? Before he had left, Beatrice had been open to him, yielding herself to him in heart as well as body. He had enjoyed her company but he had not needed her, he not been in danger of losing his head again.

The only mercy in his precarious situation was that she did not seem to know her power over him. She used no arts to draw him, did not cozen him with smiles and coy looks. Instead she stood stiff in his company as if she expected curses or blows, as if the mere act of being in his presence discomfited her.

"Blessed saints, what a garboil," he muttered, and flung open the window. The roar and splatter of hard rain filled the room, echoes drumming against the ceiling. Cool, sweet air washed over him, streaming past his face; rain splashed on the sill, wetting his fingers. Calm, a kind of peace, washed over him, as well. He would have to win her back and find a way at the same time to kill his need. It was as simple as that. He thought of all the risks he had taken at his uncle's behest to refill the family coffers; surely he could risk his pride a little.

And in the end, if he was to live his whole life with Beatrice, what choice did he have?

Leaving Sebastian, Beatrice fled to her only sanctuary, the chapel. She had not expected that seeing him after his absence would hurt so much, had not prepared herself for the way pain would drag through her when he came around the screens at the bottom of the hall. It had been worse when he came to the dais. Instead of warmth and pleasure, there had been a kind of wary possessiveness in his eyes, as if she were something he owned but did not value. After that, she had barely heard a word he said.

Shoving the memory aside, she pushed open the chapel door and was surrounded by the smoky sweetness of incense, the fragrance enough to recall peace and a clean heart, but not enough to grant her either. She closed the door behind her, leaning against the panels as if she might bar her troubles from this place.

Of course she could not; wherever she went, whatever she did, her travails came with her. The latest one was her witless decision to admit Sebastian to her bed tonight despite the pain he caused her and the distance between them. Why had she done it? What madness had possessed her? On a wave of unexpected, unwanted heat, she felt his mouth on hers, his hard body pressed to hers, as if he kissed her now instead of moments ago. And in that surge of hunger she had her answer. Lust was the madness that possessed her. In its grip she could deny Sebastian nothing.

If she had any wit or will she would withdraw her consent—but she had neither. She went to kneel before the altar and with folded hands and bent head, she willed peace to come. Moments passed in tense stillness, but peace eluded her. In its place came an agitated fluttering, as if some panicked thing was trapped within her. Or was that panicked thing herself, frightened of what she had done and the pain it would cost her?

Her hands unfolded and covered her face. Why ask herself the question, when she already knew the answer? Oh, what a fool she was. She lowered her hands and lifted her head to stare at the quiet glow of the presence lamp. Loving Sebastian put her squarely in his power; with a word he could hurt her more than Thomas had ever done.

She sank down, her skirts rustling like wings in the quiet. What was she going to do? How could she protect herself against Sebastian and a broken heart?

You cannot.

The voice seemed to come from outside herself. Was it God? Or was it the devil, tempting her for his own ends? Reflexively, she crossed herself and her head cleared. How could the devil tempt her by reminding her that she could not guard herself from pain at Sebastian's hands? Where was the blandishment in that?

At least Sebastian did not seem to take pleasure in hurting her as Thomas had. That was a great mercy and reason to be grateful. If he hurt her, would he not be remorseful? He had even regretted the pain he had given in taking her maidenhead, a pain that could not have been avoided.

Have faith.

Again the voice seemed to come from without but this time she did not question its source. If Sebastian did not love her, neither did he hate her. Two months ago she would have been grateful for it. Had her pride and greed grown so great that she could not be satisfied by so much now? Or was her nature such that no matter how much she had, she must have more? Please God it was not so, but if it was, let her learn gratitude and humility enough to value the blessings she had been given instead of pining for the gifts she had not.

Abruptly she remembered her prayer while he was gone. She had told herself not to pray for his love—it was too worldly a thing to ask of God. Instead she had asked for the strength and patience to bear whatever befell her. And here she was at the first test, whining because she had not been given what she ought not to have wanted in the first place.

In Sebastian she would have a kind husband; from Sebastian, she would have children and honor. She rose to her knees and crossed herself again. It was her pride and her greedy desire that hurt, nothing more, and she would not give either her attention. What she would do was give thanks for the blessings she had; they were great and she must not forget that. If her fool heart whispered of love, she would not listen; her duty to Sebastian and their marriage would not be onerous. That was gift enough.

Strangely, Sebastian made it easy to keep her promise to herself that night. They sat together at dinner and Sebastian set the tone of the meal by offering her the kind of flattery she might have expected from a courtier who had no designs on her. His compliments were of the sort he might offer any woman he found himself sitting beside and if she longed for him to say sweet things that were for her alone, she did not pay heed to the craving. It must be enough that he gave her kind words instead of curses.

They danced a pavanne together and she spoke to him as he had spoken to her, dredging her mind for innocuous, meaningless things to say. Once she thought she saw disappointment in his eyes, but when she looked more sharply at him, he offered her a pleasant, impersonal smile and she knew she had been mistaken. When she danced with her brother, Sebastian danced with her brother's wife. After that, they danced a galliard, lively and fast-paced. At the end, she stumbled and fell against him. Heat slammed her and she heard the hiss of his indrawn breath. For a moment they rested against one another and then he set her on her feet, asking her pardon. He stepped out of the dance a moment later, leaving her bewildered and excited.

Shortly after that, he left the hall. She watched him go, her hurt no doubt plain for all to see. John crossed the room to her as quickly as if she had cried out and pulled her into the dance that was forming, his brows knotted over his nose in an irritated scowl.

"Do not look so," he said, squeezing her hand tightly enough to hurt.

She jerked her hand free. "That hurts."

"To look at you, that is not the only thing."

Blessedly, her temper ignited. "If I did not ask for your counsel, it is because I do not want it."

"You will have it nevertheless."

"And I will not heed it, so you might as well save your breath."

As if to give her the perfect parting shot for once, the dance separated them. Buoyed by annoyance, she smiled at her partner, a boy with down still on his cheeks. He flushed and stumbled. When he recovered himself, he would not look at her again. The dance brought her back to her brother.

"You are a fool and a shrew," he said as soon as they met.

"And you are proud and a braying ass."

Laughter sparkled in his eyes and he grinned. "Your tongue is as sharp as ever. I feared time had dulled it."

"Be careful lest it cut you," she said, her anger crumbling a little under the force of his delight.

"I can guard myself."

That was the worst of it—he could protect himself against anything she might do. The dance separated them again, leaving her with another partner, an older man who had long been part of her father's household. He was used to her face; if he had ever found her beautiful it no longer affected him. He danced neatly and without flaw, returning her to her brother with her feathers smoothed, her anger almost dissipated.

"Has Sebastian hurt you?" John said without preamble.

It was her turn to stumble. "What makes you ask?" she said, buying time to think.

"Your face during dinner, the way you looked when he left."

She looked at John and found both concern and a little belligerence in his gaze. What would he do to

Sebastian if she said yes? Whatever it was, Sebastian would not deserve it. His only sin lay in not loving her.

"If he has hurt me, it is because I have wanted too much of him," she said as calmly as she could. "He has done me no deliberate harm and if he knew he had done me accidental harm, he would be sorry for it."

"What could you want that would be too much for him to give?"

His heart.

She could not say it; if she did, she would start crying, the composure granted by her temper crumbled to dust.

"Do not ask, John."

He looked at her with narrowed eyes as if to gauge her conviction. She could almost hear him wondering if he should push her. Abruptly he nodded.

"I will not press you, chuck. But know that if you need an ear to speak into, mine is always available."

Her throat ached. "Like confession?" she asked, striving for lightness.

He grinned. "Yes, but without the vow of celibacy or the need to set penance."

They danced on in silence and amity until the music ended. John took her by the hand and began to draw her toward his wife, sitting beside their mother. She stopped, pulling him to a halt. He turned to look at her, his eyebrows raised in a question.

"I am weary and wish to retire. If you will, distract our mother. I do not wish to ask for leave and I do not wish her to see me go."

"She will give you leave. She is not so unkind as that."

"I know. It is asking... Please, John, help me in this."

He frowned. "Very well. Sleep well. It will be better in the morning."

"I pray so."

Chapter Nineteen

Sebastian was waiting for her in her chamber, dressed in shirt, hose and nothing more. The glow of a single candle spilled gold light and black shadows over his face, rendering it unreadable. She closed the door and stared at him, her breath shallow and quick. Without a word, he crossed to her and cupped her face in his hands. She had only a moment to see the bright light in his eyes before he bent his head and kissed her, the kiss hot and hungry.

A flood of desire spilled over her, swamping her fear and pain, and she groaned. Nothing else mattered but his mouth on hers, his hands on her body. She thrust her hands into his shirt, to feel his warm skin under her palms. He pushed her against the door, pressing her against its panels with his hips and thighs. Her head spun and sweat prickled along her scalp. The weeks without him reared up, sharpening the edge of her lust. Through her skirts, he insinuated his legs between hers, setting his groin against hers and thrusting against her. Pleasure licked through her and she cried out against his mouth.

He lifted his head enough to whisper harshly, "I cannot wait."

"Do not," she replied, blinded by the need to feel him against her, inside her.

He lifted her up and carried her to the bed where he set her down crosswise, her hips on the edge of the bed.

A voice inside her head said, *You are behaving like a wanton.*

I do not care.

She wanted him too much to deny him, too much to insist on being wooed, on caresses and kisses and all the persuasion he could muster. If she could not have his love, his lust must suffice. When he pushed her skirts up, she helped him, their hands touching and clinging. He freed himself, gripped her hips and thrust into her.

The sweetness of it, for all its speed, was like a feast after a long fast. There was no tenderness, but she would not hold out for tenderness. She would take what he gave her, the furor of his need, the force of his movement. She moved in answer, her legs around his waist, her hands clutching his shoulders as he moved within her, driving her relentlessly toward release. She felt him pulse and the throb of it freed a cascade of pleasure that swept her under, drowning her. The room echoed with groans; she was dimly aware that they both cried out. Sebastian collapsed against her, his face buried in her neck.

The room was quiet with the kind of charged stillness that followed a great storm or terrible quarrel. She said nothing, afraid of what would be released if she spoke, of what she might start by speaking. Her headdress poked her scalp, her busk stabbed her, the pressure of Sebastian's weight made her hip joints ache. She lay still, uncomplaining, unexpectedly desolate. They had come together as gracelessly as this before, but then there had been something like joy. There was nothing like that now.

Tension rose in Sebastian's body; in another moment he would lift himself from her. Though the intimacy of their bodies only seemed to deepen her loneliness, she did not want him to go.

"You bewitch me," he said quietly. There was no pleasure, no dalliance in his voice. He spoke as a man who had been cursed.

"Not by my will," she whispered. She heard the despair in her own voice and wished she could unsay the words.

He grunted, the sound perhaps a laugh. "God help us both."

"Why did you not write to me?"

She had not intended to ask the question, had not even known it lingered in her mind. Sebastian sighed and lifted himself, easing from her gently. She watched him push her skirts down and set his clothing to rights, all without looking her in the face. She wanted to unsay the words, to tell him not to answer, but something, some stubbornness, stayed her.

"Does it matter?" he asked, arranging his clothing.

"Yes."

He tied the laces of his shirt and crossed the room to the chest where he had put his doublet. Standing in the shadows, he was only a gleam of white linen, a sheen of bright hair, his movements flinging darkness on the wall behind him. "You did not write to me, either."

"Will you not answer me?"

He came forward into the flickering light. "No."

She rose from the bed, smoothing her skirts as if he had never lifted them.

"Then go. I do not wish you here."

He looked at her for a long moment, as if to gauge her sincerity or her resolve. She lifted her chin, afraid that he would see how weak her will truly was. If he remained, she would end by pleading with him, begging for his love. It could only disgust him and shame her.

"As you will it," he said, and turned away.

Do not go! She bit her lips to keep from crying out, pushed her nails into her palms to keep from reaching for him. He did not look back, closing the door behind him with a soft, final thud.

She stared at the door's panels for a long, long time, unable to believe that he was gone and that she had sent him away. The stillness had returned to the room, the kind of stillness that fell when someone had said something unforgivable. What had she done?

Nothing she could undo without chasing him through Wednesfield's corridors. Numbly, she readied herself for bed as best she could without Nan. Plaiting her hair, she remembered the night in London when Ceci had said she was going back to her Court post.

I loved a man. I thought he loved me. I need to know the truth. I need to know how he feels. Beatrice heard her sister's voice as clearly as if Ceci were in the room. How had she found the courage? Even now, the thought of it took Beatrice's breath away. Where had the daring come from, that allowed Ceci to risk the pain of learning the man she loved did not love her?

If he does not love me, I must know.

With sudden, piercing clarity, she saw the answer.

Without knowing how the man she loved felt, Ceci remained in limbo, unable to move forward with her life. With knowledge, however painful, she could move on, making decisions and ordering her life as best she could. Perhaps that was true for Beatrice, too. Was it not better to build her life on the truth? She thought of distant past, of the pride and doubt that had kept her from asking Sebastian if he intended to marry her when Thomas had made plain his interest in her. If either of them had spoken the truth then, how much might have been different.

I am sore afraid.

She had been afraid of Thomas and had survived him. She had been afraid of Sebastian's anger and disgust and had overcome both. Pain passed as surely as happiness. The only thing that endured was the truth.

She finished plaiting her hair, put on her nightcap and tied its strings. In the morning, when there was daylight to fire her audacity, she would ask Sebastian if he loved her or not.

At dawn Sebastian rose from his bed, still dressed in his shirt and hose from the night before. He had not slept a minute of the long, slow night, his thoughts turning 'round and 'round like a mill wheel, moving and going nowhere. Last night had given him physical release but nothing more. His hope that somehow physical intimacy with Beatrice might lead to openness had been in vain—the act that had once shown promise of bringing them together had only driven them apart. Now he did not know what to do.

He picked up his doublet from the floor, where he had flung it the night before. While he pulled it on, he stared at the wall, trying to think of nothing. If he thought at all, he inevitably thought of last night and what was the point of that? He had worn a rut in his mind, going back and forth, and had come to no conclusion. Sighing, he crossed the room and opened his chamber door. On the floor, curled up like a hound on the hearth, his man Ned slept. Sebastian had dismissed him on his return from Beatrice's chamber, too wound up for company. Evidently Ned had not wished to go far. Sebastian stepped over him; even less than he had last night did he want Ned's company now.

In the distance he heard voices, the early noise of a rising household. The doors would have been unbarred; he could escape the castle without occasioning remark. In the great hall, menservants were setting out trestle tables for the first meal, working with speed and certainty. Sebastian acknowledged them with a nod as he passed through to the garden.

Dew silvered the shrubbery, the damp glinting in the early sunlight. Standing outside the door at the place where the paths converged, Sebastian took a deep breath, held it and released it slowly. A little of the tension in his shoulders lifted, but how long would he have to stand here breathing to ease it all? The way he felt now, he would be in the same place come Judgment Day.

He moved onto one of the paths and as he walked, memories of Beatrice flooded him as if his mind had only been waiting for the opportunity to consider her. He had commenced his wooing here, certain that he could win her without being won himself. How wrong he had been—in trying to breach her defenses he had left himself undefended and she, who was to be overthrown, had overthrown him. What was he going to do?

The garden brought him no peace. He returned to his room and let Ned dress him, went to the chapel to hear Mass and to the hall afterward to break his fast. Beatrice did not appear and he did not know whether to be relieved or disappointed. At the very least, her absence put off their next meeting, at least for a little while.

Shortly after breakfast, a rider from his uncle arrived to announce that Master Isham would be at Wednesfield within the hour. Why was he here? Sebastian considered and then dismissed the question as pointless. What did it matter why Henry was here? Whatever his business, surely his arrival would distract Sebastian from all the things he did not want to think about. Most of all, his uncle would make it possible to stop thinking about Beatrice.

Beatrice opened her eyes and looked at the tester above her, faintly visible in the thin line of light threading through a gap in the bedcurtains. Her sleep had been dreamless and now she floated on the mattresses of her bed, the coverlet enclosing her in a soft warmth. She listened for Nan's breathing but heard nothing; the room was still. Where was Nan? Frowning, she sat up and tugged at the bedcurtain. It opened, revealing the sunlight spilling in a stream of gold through the windows. Beatrice stared, shocked. She had thought it early, not much past dawn. To gauge by the sun's height, it was at least the middle of the morning.

She swung her legs out of the bed and slid to the floor. The sun had warmed the boards; her feet relaxed in the heat. She padded to the table by the windows. A bowl and a ewer had been laid out on its top with a towel folded beside them. Beatrice poured water from the ewer into the bowl and washed her face and mouth, the water cool against her skin. The door creaked as she was drying herself. She turned to see who it was.

Only Nan. Her heart sank into her belly as if she had hoped for Sebastian. She turned away to hide her disappointment.

"Why did you let me sleep so late? It is nearly noon." An exaggeration—it was only midmorning.

"An it please you, my lady, when I tried to wake you, you bade me leave you be." The door closed quietly.

She frowned at the bowl of water. "I do not remember."

"No, my lady. I did not think you had wakened, but I did not wish to disobey you."

Swallowing, she faced her maid. "It does not matter. I am awake now. Help me dress. I must find Lord Benbury."

Nan came forward and pulled Beatrice's night rail over her head. "He is in his chamber, my lady."

"Hurry, Nan."

Why rush? Because she wanted to take the risk before her courage failed her. Her eagerness infected Nan, who hurried through all the steps necessary to turn her out as befit her station. Sooner than she would have thought possible, Beatrice was gowned and hooded as if they had lingered for hours.

"Bless you, Nan!" she said, staring at herself in the little silver mirror Nan held up.

Nan turned pink. "Shall I attend you?"

And hear Beatrice ask and Sebastian reply? "I shall be well enough alone. Attend me when I return."

"Yes, my lady."

Beatrice stepped into the corridor outside her chamber, her heart pounding in her throat, her ears hot, her stomach queasy. She had missed Mass and breakfast both and would have to act with neither to bolster her.

This can wait. Do it tonight, dread and doubt murmured in the depths of her mind.

She took two slow steps and stopped.

If you do not do it now, you will never do it. The voice was Ceci's, the tone gentle. A wave of longing for her sister swept over her, followed by a wave of courage. *If Ceci can do this, so can I.*

Her resolution renewed, she moved through the castle toward Sebastian's chamber, going quickly as if to outrun cowardice, her skirts swinging like a bell against her ankles. Her steps slowed again as she approached Sebastian's door, her courage cooling. The door was half open and through it she heard a male voice she did not recognize, murmuring something she could not hear clearly.

For a moment she wanted nothing more than to flee. The force of that longing frightened her, as if it might carry her away before she could prevent it. She took three steps that brought her just outside the door and stopped, halted to collect herself.

She heard Sebastian. "It does well enough, Uncle." He sounded annoyed, as if his uncle had asked a question he did not wish to answer. Caught by the sound of his voice, Beatrice moved closer to the door.

The other voice said, "Do you love your wife?"

In the depths of her mind, a tiny voice whispered, *Say yes,* and her heart stood still, waiting.

"No," Sebastian said. "I do not love her."

Her heart started beating again, the beat uncertain,

stumbling, and when she took a breath, when she remembered to breathe, it hurt, as if she had been stabbed. She had not hoped, she had been sure she knew this—why, then, did it hurt so much to hear it?

She turned and went blindly down the corridor to the stairs.

By the time she regained the haven of her chamber she had mastered the worst of her pain, though her heart lay heavy and sore against her ribs. She felt as if she dared not think, as if thinking could only jostle and reopen an agonizing wound.

As if waiting for her, Nan stood by the bed, small body and small face tense. "My lady, Sir George Conyers is here to see you."

What?

For a moment she did not understand what the words she heard meant, as if Nan had spoken the language of Muscovy or Cathay. And then understanding came and with it dismay, crowding out heartbreak.

Blessed Jesú. George, here? What other disasters would befall her today? She did not have the strength to face him yet she must somehow find it—after his persistence in sending her letters she did not answer, she suspected he would not be driven away by anything less than her insistence. Or Sebastian's. The thought chilled her; the chill cleared her head and numbed her heart.

"Where is he, Nan?"

"He is below in the hall, my lady."

"Go to him and bid him wait for me in the garden."

"Yes, my lady."

While she waited for Nan to return, Beatrice paced her chamber floor, skirts and petticoats whispering softly as they swirled around her ankles. Her thoughts moved with the same to-and-fro rhythm, a fretting voice crying, *Why is he here? Go away.*

Too quickly, Nan returned, her eyes bright with speculation. Wisely, she asked no questions. "It is done, my lady."

"Very well."

The finery she had donned for Sebastian's eyes now mocked her, too fair for a man she no longer wished to seduce, but there was no time to change. She must see George and send him on his way before Sebastian discovered his arrival. She hurried down to the hall and through it into the garden.

George waited perhaps a dozen yards from the hall door on one of the branching paths, staring into the middle distance, his hands on his hips. He was as pleasing to the eye as he had been in her memory: broad-shouldered in his dust-covered doublet, his legs strong in his hose and boots. She remembered suddenly that it had not only been his pursuit of her that had led her to dally with him. Once the sight of that hard profile had been enough to make her stomach flutter. Now she was unmoved, her appreciation of his comeliness akin to the admiration she felt for a fine piece of horseflesh or a lovely length of cloth. She noticed something else with a jolt of surprise. He was not as tall as Sebastian, not as tall as she had remembered.

The path crunched underfoot when she stepped onto it. George spun on one heel, his quick movement betraying some nervousness. That calmed an apprehension she had not been aware of—no matter how coolly he behaved, she would know he was as unsettled by this meeting as she. Recovering himself, he came forward with his hands outstretched, dark eyes bright, mouth curved in the mocking, confident smile that had once excited her. She did not take his hands; his smile faltered and his hands dropped to his sides.

"How now, Beatrice," he said softly.

"How now, my lord."

His brows lifted. "How is this? You have called me George before now."

She had forgotten his audacity, the way he could bend and twist her words and ideas until he had tied her in knots. If she let him deflect her from her purpose, she would be lost.

"Why are you here?"

"Are you not pleased to see me?"

"That does not answer my question. Why are you here?"

He stepped closer and raised his hand as if to touch her cheek. She stepped out of reach. He frowned.

"Tell me what constrains you, Beatrice."

"Honor constrains me."

"Your betrothal?"

"Yes."

"That was fast work," he said.

The edge in his tone sent heat into her cheeks. She lifted her chin, armoring herself in pride. "I will not discuss it with you. Tell me why you wished to see me or I shall leave."

"I came to find out why you answered none of my letters before the last and why, after all we have been to one another, you bid me leave you be."

"I have promised to marry Lord Benbury, that is why I bid you leave me in peace," she said sharply. Tension was pinching her back, her neck; she could feel herself listening for Sebastian's step, waiting for discovery. *If he finds me in a garden with George again...*

"You loved me."

"I was your leman."

"You were more than that."

"No, I was not."

"I love you."

"I do not believe you."

He stepped forward and grabbed her hands, moving so quickly that he had her before she realized he intended to seize her. His grip was hard; she would have bruises by nightfall. She would not look at him, refusing to encourage him.

"I do not blame you for not believing me, Beatrice." His hands loosened and slid to her wrists. "Look at me."

"Say what you must and go," she said. His doublet was a little worn, threads fraying along the shoulder.

"Beatrice, I will not go until you look at me."

Reluctantly she raised her eyes to his. They were gray, so dark with emotion that they looked black.

"I want to marry you."

"I am promised to Lord Benbury. The betrothal cannot be broken."

"I do not believe it." His hands moved to her shoulders. His grip was not hard but she did not doubt it would tighten if she tried to break free. She stared at him, fascinated and frozen by his expression, a rabbit bewitched by a snake, and all the while, she listened for Sebastian. "I love you, Beatrice, and I believe you love me."

"No."

His hands were on her shoulders, his thumbs warm against the skin of her collarbone. His eyes had softened and there was something about the set of his mouth that made her think of how vulnerable she felt, faced with the knowledge that she loved Sebastian who did not love her. Unexpectedly, unwillingly, sympathy eased into her.

"Does Benbury love you?" George's voice was gentler than it had ever been, but the question broke the spell he had cast. His hands loosened, nearly releasing her. She stepped out from under them and walked a few steps away from him.

He followed her. "He does not, does he?"

The wound was too raw to conceal. She could not compose herself nor make a mask of her face to hide her feelings. She heard him come closer.

"If he does not love you, why will you marry him?"

I have promised...marriages are not made for love...I have lain with him... Her thoughts tumbled, confused. "I must."

"Why?" His murmur was soft, pleading.

She thought of Sebastian and his uncle.

Do you love her?

No, I do not.

"I will not be forsworn."

"You can say you promised to marry me. He does not love you and your betrothal has not been announced. None need be the wiser."

"I would know."

"I will make you happy, I swear it."

She stepped away. "You cannot." Sighing, she turned to face him. "I do not love you, George. I will not marry you."

Color darkened his face as if he were ashamed. "Is

it because I am a knight and he is a baron? Do you disdain me because of my station?''

She spread her hands helplessly. ''I had no thought of that. I am promised to Lord Benbury. That he does not love me means nothing. We do not marry to satisfy our passions, you know that as well as I. Even as we dallied, did you not pursue heiresses and widows to make a good marriage? I did not fault you for it then and I do not fault you for it now.''

''Please, Beatrice, I pray you…''

''No, George.''

''I need you, Beatrice,'' he whispered. ''Please, I beg you, marry me.''

''No,'' she said, her voice as low as his. ''I will not marry a man who loves me if I do not also love him. That is unkindness.''

''You will come to love me.''

She bent her head. She could not look at him when she spoke. ''No. I love Sebastian. I have always loved Sebastian.''

''He will break your heart.''

''I know. I do not think that means I should break yours instead. And I will break it, George.''

''You will not.''

She turned to look at him, trying to put all that she knew and felt in her eyes for him to read. ''I will. How can I not? You will grow tired of loving a woman who loves someone else and you will become angry because no matter what you do or how you try, she does not return your love. And then that love will turn to hate. I would not wish that on anyone.''

''What of you? Will you not feel the same?''

''It is not the same. You know I love Sebastian. I

know that if Sebastian does not love me, he does not love anyone else.''

"For the last time, Beatrice, marry me."

"For the last time, George, I will not." She saw the hurt bloom in his eyes, saw it set his mouth in a hard line. "I will pray for your contentment," she said, a small sop but all she had to offer.

"A pox on contentment." He lunged and before she had time to read his intent, his mouth was on hers, hard and begging for response. Horrified and repelled, she jerked her mouth from his and pushed him away, freeing herself by dint of surprise. Glaring at him, she scrubbed her hand across her lips.

"Go and do not return. I will have none of you."

She backed away from him, waiting for another leap to capture her. It did not come and she turned to hurry up the path toward the hall door. Sharp, unpleasant emotion roiled in her chest, pulled tight across her shoulders; with a start, she realized she was furious.

The doorway was dark and she blundered into someone standing in the passage. Hands grabbed her arms to steady her. She recognized the touch in the same instant she recognized the scent.

Sebastian.

All at once, her anger was gone. How much had he seen? What did he think? The center of her stomach was cold, as if she had swallowed ice.

"Is that who I think it is?" Sebastian said very softly. Her eyes had not yet adjusted to the dim of the hallway; she could not read his expression.

"Sebastian—"

"Answer me. Is that Conyers?"

"I can explain—"

"I have no doubt you can. I do not wish to hear it from you. I would rather hear it from Sir George."

"What will you do?"

Her vision had cleared enough to see that his mouth was a tight line. "For whom do you fear?" he asked, looking down at her. "Me? Or Conyers?" He let her go. "Go within. I will find you when I have finished with Conyers."

"Do not—" Do not what? She did not know what she feared, except the look in Sebastian's eyes.

"Go, Beatrice. I will not ask again."

"No."

"Very well, then. Watch me. But do not interfere."

She would not unless she thought he endangered himself. She did not care what he did to George so long as it did not cause him harm. He pushed past her and walked out into the sunlight. With one part of her mind she noticed the sun gleaming on his fair head, while another thought that if she had not seen his face and heard his voice, she would have known how angry he was just by the set of his shoulders, the stiffness of his neck. She followed him to the door, stopping when she could see George, hoping she could not be seen.

Sebastian stalked toward George, his hands half curled as if they wanted to make fists. George folded his arms across his chest, his eyes narrowing and an unpleasant smile curling his mouth. He was afraid and she could not blame him. To judge by the tension in Sebastian's body, he must look ready to do murder.

Do not hurt him, she thought. *He is not worth it. He is not worth any of it. Make him go and I will do whatever you ask of me.*

Chapter Twenty

Beatrice and Conyers, conversing in a garden. Beatrice and Conyers, kissing.

Sebastian stepped into the garden, his head empty and light, his thoughts silent, a great tension coiled in his limbs. He was so angry he felt nothing. The tiny stones covering the path moved under his shoes; the birds in the trees sang in the sunshine, their music sweet.

"How now, Sir George," he said with careful calm. "How do you come to Wednesfield? Was it at my lady's invitation?"

Conyers, clever and dangerous, narrowed his eyes and folded his arms across his chest. Weighing his answer? Or gauging Sebastian's temper? A moment too late, he bowed, his obeisance shallow and mocking.

"I do not betray confidences, my lord."

"What business do you have with my wife?"

"Your wife? I had not heard you married her."

"I have."

"She did not tell me so. She said you were betrothed."

Why had she not told Conyers they were married? Doubt welled up, cracking the edifice of his anger. With an effort, he shored up his fury; he would need it.

"She misspoke. We are married."

Conyers stared at him for a long moment, calculation in his eyes. Sebastian, goaded, held his gaze. Whatever Conyers saw, he seemed to come to some decision. His shoulders straightened and relaxed and the calculation left his eyes, leaving frankness. Sebastian could not tell if it was genuine.

"Beatrice did not send for me. In truth, when she wrote to me, she bade me leave her be." He sounded truthful enough, but a good liar would.

Sebastian did not relax. "When did she write to you?"

"I received the letter five days ago."

While she had disdained to write to him, she had been writing to Conyers. Sebastian's anger renewed itself.

"Why should I believe you?"

Conyers reached into his doublet and took out a square of paper. He held it out to Sebastian. "Read her letter yourself."

Reluctantly, Sebastian took the letter and unfolded it. It was her hand, graceless and messy, but the language she used was more harmonious than the language she had used in her brief letters to him. The past was dead, she was betrothed to be married at Michaelmas. If Conyers loved her, he would write her no more. She would say prayers for his soul. Her signature was shaky, as if it pained her to write.

Though it confirmed Conyers's word that she had repudiated him, Sebastian had no comfort from the letter. Beatrice, reluctant to write to him, had shown no such reluctance to write to her erstwhile lover. He tucked the letter into his doublet.

"That is my letter, my lord."

"Not any longer."

"My lord—"

"If Beatrice did not send for you, why are you here?"

"I love Beatrice. I want to marry her." His eyes sharpened, watching Sebastian. "If you do not love her, release her to me."

"Who says I do not love her?"

"She does."

Why would she say such a thing? He thought of his conversation with his uncle, of the question that had startled him so much that he had taken refuge in a lie. Could Beatrice have heard them? How, when he had had no sign of her presence?

"Do you love her?" Conyers's voice interrupted his thoughts.

"That is not your affair."

"By the love I bear her, it is my affair. Release her to me. Surely there are other women you might have."

There was only one woman and he would not release her, least of all to this caitiff.

"No. She is my wife."

"I will be kinder to her than you."

"It does not matter. We are married."

Conyers frowned and sighed, and it was as if he had clouded, clear water turned muddy. "Surely you do not want her when she has lain with me."

Sebastian smiled, half angered and half pleased by Conyers's lie. "Since she did not lie with you, that has no weight."

"She was my mistress."

"I will concede that she behaved as she should not have, but I know how far she went with you. You did not lie with her."

"She has cozened you. I can tell you the shape of her breasts, the color of her—"

Sebastian interrupted. "She was a virgin when I lay with her the first time. That with our betrothal makes our marriage. She is my wife and nothing you say, no pleading you can offer, will change that. Now get you gone from this place before I have the dogs set on you."

Conyers reddened. "But I love her."

Sebastian stepped close to him. "So do I and I will not let her go. Get you gone, Conyers. My patience is wearing thin."

"She loves me." It had the desperate ring of a lie, but even if he spoke truly, Sebastian did not care. Beatrice was his.

"Then she will spend her life eating her heart out for you. Go, Conyers. You are not welcome here."

He turned on his heel and walked back to the hall. Beatrice waited in the passage, a shadow in the dimness. He passed her without speaking, his anger still too great to be contained. If he spoke to her, he feared he might strike her. He kept going until he found an usher. He bade the man find a few others to go to the garden and remove an unwelcome guest, and then he went on, looking for John. He needed sword practice to blunt the edge of his anger before he faced Beatrice.

Men from the hall trotted past Beatrice and went into the garden. They surrounded George, one of their number speaking softly to him. George's face darkened and he scowled at them. When he replied, she could hear the anger in his tone. The ushers crowded close to him, the threat implicit in their movements. Would George heed them? If he did not, what would he do? And what would she be forced to do to ease the situation?

George spoke again. The apparent leader of the ushers shook his head and nodded toward the house. All at once George's shoulders sagged, emotion draining from his face, leaving it worn and defeated. He had given up, whatever thought he had had of resistance gone. *Thank God.* She stepped backward until she could no longer see George and then turned to enter the hall.

Once there she did not know what to do with herself. She ought to go in search of Sebastian, to see what damage this had done to their already battered marriage, but she did not want to. She dreaded to hear what he had to say and feared what she might do or say in response. Anger simmered at the edge of awareness and if Sebastian so much as looked at her crosswise, her temper would surely erupt in an unseemly and dangerous display.

A man entered the hall from the solar stairs, tall, broad-shouldered, his clothes rich if road-worn. She watched him with a kind of weary curiosity as he crossed the hall toward her, stopping when he was within a few feet of her. In his weathered face, his eyes shone bright blue, as full of light as a June sky, and by that color alone, she knew him for Sebastian's kin. His height and the grace of his bow to her only emphasized the resemblance. It was as if she had been given a glimpse of Sebastian in middle age.

"How now, mistress," he said, eyeing her carefully as if to gauge her response to his address.

"How now, sir. You must be Master Henry Isham."

"So I am. And who might you be, mistress?"

"Lady Manners, your niece by marriage."

He bowed again, the bow deeper than before. "I am honored to meet you." His words and actions were courteous, but his blue eyes were watchful and cold, weighing her, noting everything. Despite their physical resemblance, he and Sebastian were not much alike. Sebastian could conceal nothing; this man, everything.

"And I am pleased to meet you, though I am curious. What brings you to Wednesfield, sir? Our wedding is not for another month."

"I have discharged a commission Lord Benbury gave to me, one that touches you. I have recovered your jewels, my lady."

"I am afraid I do not understand."

"Did you not ask my nephew to recover your property from your late husband's son?"

For a moment she stared at him, the gears of her mind refusing to mesh. Then in a burst she remembered the letter from Thomas's son, refusing to return the things Thomas had given her. How long ago that seemed, especially after this morning's turmoil—it was no wonder that she had forgotten about it.

"I beg your pardon. I did ask it of him. It was good of you to aid him. I have no doubt he is greatly pleased."

"Do you not wish to see them?"

She frowned at him, puzzled. All she had wanted was to keep Thomas's son from holding that which was not his. Yet Master Isham's expectation that she would wish to examine the casket was so clear that she could not disappoint him.

"Where are they?"

"I have come from putting them in the solar."

"Sebastian did not keep them?"

"He has not seen them. Before I could show them to him, he left me to find you. Did he not?"

Her blush was sudden and hot. "He found me."

His brows rose, a question in the gesture. If she did not distract him, he would begin probing and she did not think she had the cleverness or strength of will to hold him at bay.

"If you will, bring me to them."

His eyes narrowed briefly, as if he could not quite get her measure, but rather than question her, he nodded pleasantly and offered his arm. She took it and prayed his forbearance would continue after they arrived in the solar.

There was no one in the solar when they entered, as if her mother had withdrawn to give Beatrice this chance to meet with Isham without witnesses. The iron-bound casket she had left behind in Norfolk stood in the center of the big table, its paint as bright as the last time she had seen it. Her hand tightened on Isham's arm. It was almost as if she could hear Thomas's tread on the stairs outside, as if she could hear his rasping breath as his temper grew hotter and more dangerous. Her shoulders tensed, waiting for the blows that would never come again.

"What is it, my lady?" Isham asked gently.

She took a deep breath that caught in her throat when she let it go. "Nothing. It is nothing."

Isham's hand closed over hers. "I do not believe you. Let me help you. Tell me what ails you."

"Memories," she whispered. "Nothing but memories."

"Ah-hh," he said as if he understood. But how could he? How could anyone?

She let go of his arm and crossed the solar to the table. For a long moment she stared at the casket, a little box of wood and iron, paint and gilt. Slowly, she reached out and lifted the lid, revealing the rich gauds and bejeweled baubles her wealthy husband had given her to soothe the bruises and welts he had inflicted on her. Cloth rustled and then Isham was beside her.

"That is a fortune," he said in a matter-of-fact voice that was more soothing than pity would have been.

"So it is," she said, her voice rough.

"I knew your late husband for many years. If you will forgive me saying so, he was not a shrewd or kind man. In my opinion, it would be very like him to offer such a fortune in payment for his cruelties."

Her throat closed. How had he seen so much? She wanted to tell him he had guessed aright, but she did not trust him. He might be testing her on Sebastian's behalf, to see how she misspoke her late husband to strangers.

"It is not good to speak ill of the dead. And surely a man may use his wife as he pleases." She glanced at him as she finished, trying to read his countenance. He looked thoughtful, nodding as if he considered her words.

"There is truth in that, but a wise man does not beat his wife unless it is needful. If I am angry because a storm claims one of my ships, it is not needful that I strike my wife. She has not raised the wind that sank the ship. She does not need correction. I have no respect for a man who takes out his anger on his wife, his horse or his dog.''

''I would rather be struck and have done than live with resentment all my days.'' The words caught in her throat, coming out in a jerky rasp.

''Do you think my nephew resents you?''

She nodded, unable to speak, growing used to Isham's sharp eyes and bluntness in speaking of what he saw.

''Perhaps he does. Do you not think he has reason?''

She nodded again.

He reached out and pulled the casket closer. From atop the pile of pearls, gold and glittering gems, he removed two items. He brought the two pieces close so she might see them. She recognized them instantly, a wave of relief passing over her. They had been in the casket. Thomas's son had not found them, not held them back. More than anything else in the casket, these were things that she would not willingly give up.

On Master Isham's palm lay a sapphire and diamond *B* and a small gold heron embellished with diamonds and jet. Thomas had had them made for her without ever knowing what they meant, her reasons carefully concealed from him. She had told him she wanted a *B* for Beatrice when in truth it was a *B* for Benbury, and the heron was a Benbury heron. It had been her talisman, a reminder that Sebastian had once loved her, before she had been a fool and thrown it away. She took the heron from Master Isham and closed her fingers around it.

''What do these things mean, my lady?''

She held the heron against her stomach as if she feared he might take it from her. ''Sebastian.''

"You love him, do you not?" His voice was very gentle, kindness itself.

She nodded and then gathered the courage to whisper, "But he does not love me."

"How do you know that, my lady?"

"I heard him speak to you earlier today. I heard what he said to you."

"Ah-hh." He closed the lid of the casket, lowering it carefully so that it made no noise when it touched the box. "Do you not think your love will win him to you?"

"No. I have been a great fool and it is too late."

"What have you done that is so terrible?"

"I cannot tell you. Please believe me when I tell you Sebastian does not forgive me for it, nor will he ever."

"If you will give me leave, I think you are wrong."

Hope flared up, so intense and unexpected it hurt. She closed her eyes to contain it. "Do not, I pray you. I cannot bear to hear it."

"I had not thought you so fearful a woman, my lady."

That opened her eyes. "Fearful? You think me fearful?"

"Timid as a nun," he said, no bite in his tone. "Everything I have, I gained by daring. Everything Sebastian has, he gained by taking risks."

She frowned at him, disturbed by his words. "Everything Sebastian has he inherited from his father."

"What Sebastian inherited from his father was debt. He has worked hard these five years to clear it, to make something of his estate."

Sebastian had been in debt? Whatever she had concealed from him, she had thought Sebastian had hidden nothing from her, from anyone. For a moment anger flickered like lightning. How dare Sebastian condemn her for withholding things when he had done the same? Understanding followed quickly, dissipating the anger—he had not been frank with her for the same reason she had not been frank with him. He had dared not when he could not trust her.

"I did not know…" she said.

"He did not wish any to know."

"Then why do you tell me this?" she asked, raising her chin. If Sebastian wanted his secrets kept, who was Isham to reveal them?

"I am not sure why," he said, as blunt about himself as everything else. She had not thought him the kind of man to admit such weakness. "Perhaps to encourage you to pursue that which you desire, my nephew's love. Perhaps to show you that he is a man capable of daring. He might well dare to love you, my lady. How will you know if you do not try?"

"I betrayed my first husband and Sebastian knows it. This morning he discovered me in Wednesfield's garden with the man I dallied with before. At this moment he believes me untrustworthy and wanton. I know it."

Isham whistled softly. Her stomach fell with the sound. "Are you untrustworthy and wanton?"

She shook her head. "I am not."

"Then why did you meet this man?"

"To bid him go."

"You could have written him."

"It was a letter that brought him here in the first place. If I sent him another, no doubt I should find him in my bedchamber next," she snapped, and then closed her mouth tightly, lest worse escape her.

Isham's eyes gleamed as if he appreciated her display. "Why you wish to conceal your mettle is a mystery to me, my lady. Put that fire to good use. Win my nephew."

"Why do you wish it, Master Isham? What good will I do Sebastian?"

"Since his father died, Sebastian has been dogged by a faint melancholy. I had thought it was his father's death and the discovery of his father's debts that ailed him. Now I am not so sure. Tell me, my lady, when did you marry Lord Manners?"

"In May, five years ago. Six weeks after Sebastian's father died."

"Ah-hh. And when did Sebastian learn you were to marry Lord Manners?"

"Two weeks before his father died," she said. "Do you mean to suggest his melancholy was for me? I doubt me that." She doubted it because she wanted so much to believe it. Let this maddening, hurtful conversation end. She did not want to hope, not when it was bootless.

"I do not doubt it all. That melancholy has lifted, my lady. I think it is because he has married you. For that alone I would urge you to win him."

"But there is more."

"There is. I will be frank with you, my lady."

"Have you not been?" she asked, lifting her eyebrows. "I fear to hear you if you have been dissembling before this."

His grin, surprisingly boyish, lit his face for a moment before he replied. "With the contents of that casket, I can make Sebastian a wealthy man, wealthy enough to go to Court and provide me with the information and aid I need to make us both still wealthier. I would not wish him to pass up such a fortune.''

"It is his to do with as he likes.''

"And if he wishes to include that carcanet and the pin you hold in the fortune he invests with me?''

Her hand tightened on the heron. She could not give it up; there had been days when it had been all she had had to hold on to. She had clutched it when Thomas cursed her and struck her, remembering the days when she had been the light of Sebastian's eyes, days of happiness long vanished. But if Sebastian asked her to give up the pin and the carcanet and she refused, what good would either piece do her? Both would remind her of all the ways she had failed him.

"I will do whatever he asks of me.''

Isham nodded, his face softening in a look of unexpected, compelling warmth. She took a step nearer to him, as if she might find shelter with him.

"And I will do what I can to win him to you.''

"Do you think he can be won?'' The pitiful question forced its way out and she flinched, afraid of what it revealed and afraid of what Isham would do with the revelation.

"I never invest in anything I do not think will succeed. Trust me.''

She looked up into his eyes, so like Sebastian's. "I do.''

Chapter Twenty-One

By the time Sebastian found John his anger had splintered into frustration, fury and hurt. He could not face Beatrice while his emotions threatened to burst their bounds, yet he needed to confront her, to find out what she had thought she would accomplish in bringing Conyers to Wednesfield. Did she think he would not find out? He strode through corridors and chambers, aware of ushers and henchmen flattening themselves against walls to get out of his way. If he had been less consumed by the tangled knot of emotion in his chest, he would have been amused by their alacrity.

He found John in the place he should have looked first, by the pool on the river. Dressed in shirt and trunk hose, he stood in the shallows of the pool, fishing, an extra rod on the ground under the trees as if he had expected company. Sebastian stared at the fishing rod for a long moment. He had not gone in search of something as calm and quiet as fishing; he wanted hard physical activity to blunt the edge of his temper. As it was, he would no doubt scare away all the fish if he so much as put a foot in the water. Restless, unable to think of what else to do with himself, he sat under the tree. His fingers pulled little stones out of the ground, stones he threw, one by one, into the long grass waving in the breeze.

He ticked over his grievances. Beatrice had written to Conyers, not him. Beatrice had met Conyers in Wednesfield's garden though she must have known how angry it would make him. Beatrice did not love him. Did she love Conyers? Should he have released her? He dropped the remaining stones and pressed his fingers to his eyes. It did not matter whether he should have released Beatrice or not. They were married, bound by words and deeds, and nothing could undo that binding. She was his wife, did she desire it or no, just as he was her husband. He believed Conyers when Conyers said he loved Beatrice; how could he not?

If he and Beatrice had not been securely bound, would he let her go? No, never. She was his, had always been his, despite anything she did. He had never willingly let her go, had always believed that the bond they had forged when very young was strong enough to eventually pull them back together. He had denied it to Ceci over the years, pretended that Beatrice did not matter to him, but every time he had spoken, he had been lying to protect his pride. And he would do it again now, because pride was all he had.

"A pox on it!" John cried. Water splashed and splashed again, as if he had struck the surface of the pond with his rod.

Sebastian lifted his head. John waded to the shore, his lips moving as if he cursed under his breath. Turning, he hurled his rod to the center of the pool. It spun, turning like a whirligig in midair before plunging into the pool, sinking out of sight as soon as it struck.

It seemed John was in no better humor than he.

Turning back to the shore, he looked up, saw Sebastian and scowled fiercely.

"Why are you here?" he asked rudely. "I do not want company."

"If you are as foul-tempered as you seem, you are exactly the company I want."

"Go away, Sebastian."

"I need sword practice."

John crossed the narrow shore to the path that led to the trees. "Find someone else."

"No."

"Curse you, Sebastian." He climbed the path.

"Fight me first."

"Stand up and I will."

Sebastian rose to his feet. John lunged and slammed the flats of his hands against Sebastian's shoulders. Sebastian staggered backward a step or two, then surged against John, shoving him. They pushed and scuffled, slipping on the grass, falling down and rising, in the kind of undignified fool's battle they had not fought since they were boys. John was cursing in a language he did not understand; he was muttering "whoreson," over and over again as if he knew no other slur.

John slung an arm around Sebastian's neck as if he meant to pull him down. Sebastian bent and hurled his shoulder against John's ribs, bearing them both to the ground. John wriggled half free and tried to wrestle him flat; he let go and surged over John. John got a handful of Sebastian's doublet and gripped it like a hound, using it to keep them together as if it might mitigate the advantage Sebastian, taller and heavier, had in this contest. Slowly, patiently, Sebastian gained the upper hand; slowly, patiently, he bore down on

John until John was facedown with his shoulders pressed to the ground.

"Cry mercy," he said, his mouth next to John's ear.

"No," John said, the ghost of a laugh escaping him.

Sebastian put his knee in the small of John's back and leaned his weight on it. John grunted.

"Cry mercy, my boy."

No, John mouthed.

Sebastian pressed his forearm across John's shoulders.

"Cry mercy."

"Mercy."

Sebastian gathered himself and leaped out of John's reach, lest he find himself with his face in the turf and John crushing him down. But John made no move to catch him, only rolling onto his back, breathing in gulps broken by snatches of laughter. Sebastian, equally winded, lay on his stomach, his face in the crook of his elbow. It had not been sword practice, but it had more than blunted the edge of his anger. Weariness lent him a kind of peace.

"If it had been swordplay you would not have won," John said.

Sebastian raised his head. "If you recall, I asked for swords. It was you who would have none of it."

John wiped his forehead on his sleeve. "True, true. But you still would not have won."

"I know."

He heaved himself over onto his back and stared at the sky. Clouds, fat as feather pillows, glided across its surface. He thought of ships on the Thames sailing downstream to the Channel and all the ports of the world, ships that had rebuilt his fortune, such as it was. He tried not to think what he might have had by now if he had not been faced with that mountain of debt; it did him no good, put no gold in his coffers, gave him no rest at night. But sometimes, especially at moments like these when body and mind were tired, regret slipped through.

"So," John said, "why the sudden need for sword practice?"

Sebastian watched one cloud, shaped like a rabbit and out of place in the fleet of clouds, cross the blue. He would rather tell John nothing, but he could not think of anything to put him off. "I was angry and wished to wear it down."

"What made you so angry?"

Sebastian hesitated. He did not think John would take kindly to hearing his sister disparaged, but how else to answer the question?

"Sebastian?" John rolled up on his elbow.

"Beatrice." He put his arm over his eyes so he would not have to see his friend's face. "Beatrice made me angry."

"Is that all? I thought it was something serious."

Sebastian lifted his arm to stare at John. "What do you mean, you thought it was something serious?"

"God has ordained it that wives will anger their husbands and husbands their wives," John said, grinning. "And you quarreling with Beatrice is nothing new."

"I did not quarrel with her."

"That is new. Why not?"

Sebastian sat up. "I was too angry too quarrel."

"Ah."

"What do you mean, 'ah'?" Sebastian snapped. "Did they make a priest of you?"

"Do not quarrel with me because you are wroth with my sister," John said.

"I am not."

"As you will. Why were you angry?"

"George Conyers is here." He waited for John to say something, anything. He turned his head to see why he did not speak and found him waiting. "George Conyers."

"Sebastian, I do not know who George Conyers is."

"Beatrice was his—" He could not say leman; she had never lain with him. But what other word was there to describe what Beatrice had been to him? "When Beatrice was married, she—" She what? "Conyers would have been her lover if she had let him."

"I see."

"Do you?"

"You are jealous."

"Jealous? I?"

"Yes, you, my friend. Why else be wroth with Beatrice for this man's actions? Unless it is by her will that he is here, and that I will not believe."

"No, he comes despite her wish that he stay away. But he is here and she has allowed him liberties—"

"Here and now?" John said.

"No," Sebastian said impatiently. "Before Manners died. Do not interrupt me. He has made free with her body and her mouth and he will do it again unless I prevent it. But I am so angry I fear that if I speak to her I will only strike her. Manners did that for less cause and I will not use her so."

"So you came to me to blunt your anger."

"Am I not clear?" Had John not been listening?

"I wish to be sure I understand. What do you want from me, Sebastian?"

Sebastian sighed. What did he want from John? "Tell me what to do."

"Have you spoken to Beatrice at all since you learned Conyers is here? And how did you learn of it?"

"I found him with Beatrice in the garden."

"What? Why did you not say this before?"

"I told you he was here."

"But not that he was with Beatrice. What happened?"

"They spoke and then Conyers kissed her."

"Did she go to him willingly?"

He forced himself to remember, to look past the wall of hurt and see Conyers seize Beatrice again. In his mind's eye, he watched Beatrice shove Conyers away, wipe her mouth and hurry up the path toward the house. Her face was white except for two slashes of red across her cheekbones, her mouth set hard. Conyers's kiss had not pleased her.

"No, she did not."

"I am relieved to hear it. For a moment you had made me think my sister a wanton." He sat up and rested his forearms on his upraised knees, clasped hands dangling. "So the land lies thus. You spied Beatrice in the garden with her former swain, who stole a kiss. That made you so angry that you dared not speak to Beatrice and find out what had brought this braggart to our doors. Is that it?"

"I sound like a fool."

"Not quite. I should be angry, too, if I had been in your place, though I do not know that I would be so angry I could not trust myself. Still, there is something

I do not understand. If you did not speak to Beatrice, how do you know she bade this Conyers stay away?"

"I saw the letter she wrote him," he said, and his banked anger flared. "She wrote to him when she would not write to me. And she wrote more kindly to him than she did to me."

"Ah."

"Will you stop saying 'ah'!"

"What did her letter to him say?"

Sebastian pulled the letter from his doublet and tossed it to John. "Read it yourself."

John unfolded the letter, read it and chuckled.

"What?"

"My mother wrote this."

"That is Beatrice's hand."

"I know. Her fist has not improved. But the language is my mother. I have no doubt she told Beatrice what to write."

"Are you sure?"

"Why do you ask me? Why not ask Beatrice?" John tossed the letter back. "In fact, why not ask Beatrice about all of this? It seems to me that you have spent too much time looking for reasons to condemn her without taking the time to hear what she has to say. I should start there before making any decisions."

"What decisions?"

"If you did not have to make any decisions, why did you want me to tell you what to do?" John stood and grinned. "I will tell you something that has not changed. Beatrice still makes you lose what sense you possess."

"She does not."

John laughed and shook his head before bending to

lift his remaining rod. "I will not quarrel with you. I am for home and my wife."

"Wait. I will come with you."

They were halfway to the house when Sebastian said, "Thank you."

"It was my pleasure."

When Sebastian entered his chamber he found his uncle still there, the casket he had brought with him open on the table. Sunlight gleamed on pearls, glittered on gold and gems, dazzling him.

"Where did that come from?" Sebastian asked, closing the door behind him.

His uncle sat with his arms folded on the table as if he had been contemplating the wealth before him for some time. "Lord Manners's gifts to his wife, now yours. Or at least this will be yours once you marry the widow."

"Are you sure this is hers?"

"As sure as I am of anything," his uncle said, looking up. "She did not seem discomposed to see this, so I believe there is nothing amiss. Did you know it was so much?"

"No," Sebastian said, crossing the room to examine the treasure more closely. This alone made him a wealthy man. He thought of the earl, urging him to return to Court. With this in his coffers, he could well afford London expenses. "She said she did not care for the gauds, but Manners's son should not take what was hers." He poked a finger into the gold and pearls, hearing rings clink softly against chains as his finger moved them. "This makes that hard to believe."

"Believe her. She has no love for this hoard." He paused, eyeing Sebastian.

"What is it, Uncle?"

"If you will entrust this to me, I can invest it and make it grow."

"It is not mine to give," Sebastian said without thinking.

His uncle's eyebrows lifted. "Whose is it, if not yours?"

Sebastian closed the lid. "This belongs to Beatrice."

"She has nothing in law."

"I know. But I will not give this into your hands without her leave. Whether or not she loves these things, she wanted them back. I will not snatch them from her in the same moment they are returned to her."

"Strange scruples, Sebastian. I thought you did not love the lady."

Sebastian sank down onto the nearest bench, put his elbows on the table and covered his face, rubbing it as if he might also rub away the memory of what he had said earlier. "I lied, Uncle," he said from behind his hands.

"I see."

Sebastian dropped his hands. "Do you? I have fallen into the trap I swore would not catch me."

"But are you alone in its toils?"

"Of course I am. Beatrice does not love me."

"How do you know? Have you asked her?"

He stared at his uncle as if a stranger lived behind that familiar face. Ask Beatrice if she loved him? Let her know the question mattered to him?

"I gather from the look on your face that you have not. Why not? Do you fear to give up the advantage in your negotiations? Let us consider it. If you ask her if she loves you, you will reveal your interest in her answer, that is true. At the same time, what answer can she give you that will leave you at a disadvantage? If she says yes and you believe her to speak the truth, then you know you are not alone. If she says yes and you disbelieve her, you know she attempts to cozen you.'' Pausing for a moment, he looked intently at Sebastian. ''If she says no and you believe her, you may guard yourself. And if she says no and you disbelieve her, then you know she fears to speak the truth, and you have another battle in front of you. It is very simple, Sebastian.''

Sebastian continued to stare at him. It was not that simple, it could not be. If it was, why was his heart pounding?

''Or is it this, Sebastian—you fear to learn the lady does not love you.''

Sebastian stood and realized he did not know where he meant to go.

''You feared you would lose all you had when your father died, but you did not. Do you remember why?''

''You took risks.''

''No, you did. I admit I guided you, but if you had let your fears rule you, I would not have been able to help you. Take a risk now, Sebastian. Find out where you stand with the woman you love.''

Chapter Twenty-Two

Though her heart fluttered in her throat and her hands would not stop trembling, Beatrice was so fired by Master Isham's faith in her that she left the solar almost eager to find Sebastian. As she searched for him, she tried to think of how she would open the conversation, but every opening she considered faltered and died. Until she saw him, she would not know what to say to him that would encourage him to hear her out.

Sebastian was nowhere she looked, not even the old tower, the last place she hunted. When she called his name, echoes answered her, her own voice whispering over and over again. She was not going to find him before it was time to go to the solar to dine. God willing, she would be able to make an arrangement to speak to him alone after the meal—she could do nothing else. In the meantime she must go to her chamber and put the carcanet and pin in her jewel coffer for safekeeping.

And then, when she had given up the search, she found him. He was in her chamber, placing the coffer from Manners on the table in the corner, when she entered.

"You are here," she said stupidly.

"So I am," he replied. He put his hand on the casket. "I came to bring you this. It contains the jewels you wanted from Lord Manners."

Whatever she had been expecting, however she had anticipated this conversation would unfold, she had not imagined this.

"I know what it contains. I do not want it," she said, her hands tightening on the heron and the carcanet, sharp edges biting her palms.

He frowned. "My uncle rode to Norfolk to collect this for you. It is a little late to say you do not want it."

She sighed and gathered the wits that had scattered on finding him. "I am glad he did so. But, Sebastian, we are married. Anything I possessed is now yours, including the things in that coffer. It does not matter if I want it or not."

"I know what is mine. But my uncle retrieved those baubles for you, not me, and I did not expect you to be ungrateful."

"I do not think your uncle found me ungrateful."

"You spoke to my uncle?" He did not sound pleased.

"He wished to show me what he had brought. I did not know I was forbidden to speak to him."

"You are not forbidden to speak to him," he said impatiently. "Is that where you have been? I have been looking for you."

"And I have been looking for you," she said. She leaned against the door to close it, unwilling to set down the treasure in her hands. "I wished to speak to you."

"Did you tell my uncle you did not wish for this casket? Did you throw his effort in his face?"

Apparently he was no longer angry about George Conyers. Now he was angry about Master Isham. "I did tell him how I felt about the casket and why. He was not displeased." She stepped closer to him, hoping she might be able to read his face if she were nearer. "He said that if you gave him the jewels to invest for you, he could make you rich enough to return to Court and aid him. He wishes to increase your fortune." She hesitated, wondering how far she must take the risk of speaking truthfully. "So do I."

"I do not wish to go to Court."

She looked down at her hands, curled in fists around her treasures. He would not dare go to Court if he believed she could not be trusted. "If it will ease your mind, I will stay with my parents while you are gone. If you ask it, they will keep me close so you will know I will not dishonor you."

"I do not need that to know you will not dishonor me, Bea," he said gruffly.

She lifted her head. "But after Sir George came—"

"He showed me the letter you wrote." He cleared his throat. "John says you wrote it at your mother's bidding."

Her face warmed. "I did."

"Did you not wish to write it?" he asked softly, and as she had once before, she heard the pain in his voice.

The warmth in her face turned to heat as she took another step closer to him. "I wanted him to leave me in peace. He wrote before and I sent his letters back unopened. I thought if I did it often enough he would understand I wanted nothing more to do with him. My mother said he would not understand anything I did not tell him.'' Believe me, Sebastian. *Believe me because I speak the truth.*

''I was angry when I found you with him the garden.''

The more she spoke frankly, the easier it grew. ''It was wrong to meet him but I did not know what else to do. All I could think was you must not find out. I did not think you would believe I did not send for him.''

''I did not believe it until I saw the letter,'' he said in the same soft voice he had once used to remind her that she had lain with George. He frowned when he had finished, his gaze turned inward.

''Then I must be grateful that he brought it with him. If he did not, you would still think I had sent for him.''

His frown deepened. ''That is not true,'' he said slowly. ''I did not realize that until now.'' His gaze sharpened as it met hers. She felt as if he could see into her soul, could see everything. ''I always knew he was not here by your will or leave.''

Then you trusted me. She dared not say it aloud, lest he deny it, but her heart ached as she had once imagined saplings must ache as they burst into leaf. ''Oh, Sebastian.''

''You said you wished to speak to me. Was it of this?'' he asked.

''No,'' she said. She was not ready to say she loved him, not yet. ''It was for another matter.'' He watched her intently, as if he saw nothing else. ''Your uncle gave me something from the casket. I should like to keep them but if you wish to invest them…''

He relaxed as if he had expected her to say something else. "What are they, Bea?"

She stepped closer and held out her open hands, the carcanet and the heron on her palms. "Those."

He stared at her hands without speaking. His throat moved as if he swallowed.

"Where did you get these?" he asked quietly.

"I asked Thomas to have them made for me."

He stretched out a fingertip and touched the heron. "For Benbury?"

"Yes."

"Why, Bea?"

And now it was easy to speak, easy to answer the plea she heard in his question. "Because they made me feel as if you were with me through all my troubles. It was foolishness, I know, but… But I did it nevertheless." Every word she spoke lightened her heart, as if she shed a burden, piece by piece.

"I love you," he said abruptly, still looking at the bright jewels in her palms. "I think I never stopped."

For a moment she thought she had misheard, but then he lifted his eyes. His heart was in their depths, unguarded. She wanted to speak, but words were gone; she hurt, but the ache was sweet.

"Do you think you can love me?" he asked softly.

She sighed and the tightness in her chest loosened. "I do, I already do," she whispered. "That is why I wished to keep these things. So I would have something of you."

He lifted both her precious talismans from her palms, laid them on the table, then took her hands, lifting them to kiss the places the jewels had lain. "You have all of me," he said, and put his arms around her, pulling her close.

She clung to him, a little dizzy and uncertain. "Do you mean it?"

"Let me show you."

He bent and kissed her, his mouth wandering over her lips, cheeks, brows and throat, his fingertips following his mouth as if he was learning the taste and touch of her all over again. He lifted her hood from her hair and combed out her plaits with his fingers, caressing her ears and scalp and neck as he did so. He touched her as if he could not stop.

When he had spread her hair across her shoulders he paused to look at her, his eyes blazing, before kissing her again, tightening his hold so she felt him all along her length. Between kisses, she murmured, "I cannot believe this is true."

He stopped and looked down into her face. "Why?"

"You told your uncle you did not love me."

Surprisingly he reddened. "It was a lie, Bea. I said that because I did not know what else to do. Did he tell you?"

"I was outside your chamber. I heard you."

He closed his eyes, his head dropping back. "Saints protect me," he said. He raised his head to look at her. "Will you forgive me?"

"If you love me, I already have."

"I do, I do."

Heat built and his kisses grew fierce. And now it was she who could not stop touching him, shoulders, arms, throat and hair, all under her hands while he caressed and fondled her. She clung to him, whispering his name, pleading with him, pressing herself against him, their clothing a barrier she wanted to surmount. Need blinded her, the hunger to lie with him in love freely given and freely received gnawed her. As if he read her wishes, he bore her to the bed and lay with her upon it, mouth and hands everywhere.

"We must go to the solar to dine," he said at one point, his mouth against her throat, his hand on her thigh, her belly.

"No," she said. "I cannot, I cannot."

"No, nor I."

He got up and bolted the door, stripping off his shirt as he returned to the bed. The last thing he wanted now was an interruption and not simply because he wanted release. He did not want this to end; he wanted to go on touching her and tasting her until dark and beyond. It did not matter that they had the rest of their lives for this. He wanted to make love to her now, make love to her for the first time knowing that she loved him, for the first time without fearing that he loved her.

He unlaced her bodice for her and eased her out of it, revealing more Beatrice to caress and kiss and madden. Her skirts came next, dropping to the floor in a heap. Taking his lead, she unlaced his points and helped him out of his hose, laughing and kissing him as she did. When he was free of them, she reached down to caress him. He gasped at the pleasure and felt the thread of his control thinning.

"Not so fast," he said. "Let me make it last."

She grinned at him, shameless and glowing. The look moved him as much as her touch had and in much the same way. He grabbed her and threw her onto the bed, falling with her. She smothered her laughter—in truth she giggled, the sound sweet as rain—against his shoulder while her hands touched him, inflaming him.

"I will not be able to wait," he growled.

At that moment someone scratched on the door and

the latch rattled. "My lady, are you within? The door is bolted," a maid's voice said.

Beatrice stiffened beneath him. He looked down at her, into her eyes, where shame had begun to dim the laughter. He held his breath, willing her to send the girl away but only if she could do it with a clean heart. She must not feel regret for what they did; she had known too much of it. He kissed her forehead, hoping she knew he would follow her lead in this.

She took a deep breath and closed her eyes. "I am here, Nan. I have a headache and wish to be undisturbed."

"Very well, my lady. Her Grace the Countess wished to know if you had seen my lord Benbury, as well."

"No, Nan. I could not find him."

"Yes, my lady. Shall I return in an hour?"

"Three hours, Nan. I wish to sleep deeply."

"Yes, my lady."

She opened her eyes. Mischief and heat glinted in their depths while her hands began their wicked work once more. He moved against her to hear her gasp, touching her everywhere he had learned gave her delight. Her pleasure deepened his, became his; he kept teasing, caressing and easing back, to see how far they could both go before it was too much.

Beatrice was shaking, panting, her hair darkened by damp and clinging to his skin and hers. At last, too soon, he eased into her—and had to stop, gritting his teeth until he had brought himself under some kind of control. Then and only then did he begin to move, moving slowly, savoring all of it. Beatrice arched against him, openmouthed and blind. "Sebastian," she whispered, "please."

"Hold on, hold on," he said against her throat. "Not too fast."

"Soon, Sebastian, please."

"Soon, yes, but wait a little."

"I cannot," she gasped, and then she clenched him as her climax overtook her.

It broke his control over himself. He drove into her as if he must give everything he had, everything he was, to her now, in this moment. She strained against him, sobbing; he sealed her mouth with his, to take her cries into himself. If he could have, he would have taken her whole body into himself. The pressure of his need built and built until at last it burst, white-hot and shuddering. He gave himself over to it, thought gone, consumed by joy and fierce pleasure. When it subsided, he sank down against her, spent and at peace.

For a long time they lay joined together. He lifted himself onto his elbows to relieve her of his weight and to look at her, softly smiling and sated. Fine tendrils along her hairline had wound into springy curls clinging to her skin; her mouth was swollen and red, tempting. He yielded to the temptation and kissed her and then eased from her, rolling onto his side and carrying her with him. He stroked her hair as he looked at the blue sky through her windows. She was warm and soft against him, turning her head to kiss his shoulders, little nibbling kisses that tickled.

"Is this what you meant when you said you wished us to live in harmony?" she asked suddenly, resting her chin on his chest.

This? He would not have been able to imagine this. "I was not so ambitious," he said.

"Do you think we can live in harmony?"

"As the saints and angels do, in perfect accord?" he asked.

She grinned at him. "I am not so ambitious. No, I meant do you think we can make a good marriage from this moment?"

Her question was not idle, despite her grin. "Do you?"

"Yes," she said simply. "I think it for two reasons. The first is that we have learned the hard way that we must be truthful with one another. Think how our lives would have been if we had spoken frankly to one another five years ago, if I had asked you if you wanted me and you had said yes. I know I will speak my mind to you from this moment and I trust you will do the same."

"I will." His arms tightened. He did not want to think of what might have been—what he had was so sweet he could not repine. "And the second reason?"

"This moment, here. Having known this sweetness, I will not settle for less. I have learned that some risks are worth taking."

He rolled so that she was beneath him again, her hair spread across the mattress. Her eyes shone up at him trustfully; he thought he could see into the depths of her soul, see everything. Perhaps he could. And if not, did he not now have a lifetime to learn her depths?

"So they are," he said, "if the reward is great enough."

* * * * *

From Regency Ballrooms to Medieval Castles, fall in love with these stirring tales from Harlequin Historicals

On sale March 2003

THE SILVER LORD by Miranda Jarrett

Don't miss the first of **The Lordly Claremonts** trilogy!
Despite their being on opposite sides of the law,
a spinster with a secret smuggling habit can't resist
a handsome navy captain!

FALCON'S DESIRE by Denise Lynn

A woman bent on revenge holds captive the man
accused of killing her intended—and discovers
a love beyond her wildest dreams!

On sale April 2003

LADY ALLERTON'S WAGER by Nicola Cornick

A woman masquerading as a cyprian challenges a
dashing earl to a wager—with the stake being an island
he owns against her favors!

HIGHLAND SWORD by Ruth Langan

Be sure to read this first installment in the
Mystical Highlands series about three sisters
and the handsome Highlanders they bewitch!

Harlequin Historicals®
Historical Romantic Adventure!

Visit us at www.eHarlequin.com

HHMED29

SAVOR THE BREATHTAKING ROMANCES
AND THRILLING ADVENTURES
OF THE OLD WEST
WITH HARLEQUIN HISTORICALS

On sale March 2003

TEMPTING A TEXAN by Carolyn Davidson

A wealthy Texas businessman is ambitious, demanding
and in no rush to get to the altar. But when a beautiful
woman arrives with a child she claims is his niece,
he must decide between wealth and love....

THE ANGEL OF DEVIL'S CAMP by Lynna Banning

When a Southern belle goes to Oregon to start a new
life, the last thing she expects is to have her heart
captured by a stubborn Yankee!

On sale April 2003

McKINNON'S BRIDE by Sharon Harlow

While traveling with her children, a young widow falls
in love with the kind rancher who opens his home and
his heart to her family....

ADAM'S PROMISE by Julianne MacLean

A ruggedly handsome Canadian finds unexpected love
when his fiancée arrives and he discovers she's not the
woman he thought he was marrying!

Harlequin Historicals®
Historical Romantic Adventure!

Visit us at www.eHarlequin.com   HHWEST24

These are the stories you've been waiting for!

Based on the Harlequin Books miniseries
The Carradignes: American Royalty comes

HEIR TO THE THRONE

Brand-new stories from

KASEY MICHAELS

CAROLYN DAVIDSON

Travel to the opulent world of royalty with these two stories that bring to readers the concluding chapters in the quest for a ruler for the fictional country of Korosol.

Available in December 2002 at your favorite retail outlet.

HARLEQUIN®
Makes any time special®

Visit us at www.eHarlequin.com

PHHTTT

Steeple Hill Books is proud to present
a beautiful and contemporary new look
for Love Inspired!

HEARTWARMING INSPIRATIONAL ROMANCE

Love Inspired.

As always, Love Inspired delivers
endearing romances full of hope, faith and love.

Beginning January 2003
look for these titles
and three more each month
at your favorite retail outlet.

Steeple
Hill®

Visit us at www.steeplehill.com

LINEW03

magazine

♥————————————————————— **quizzes**

Is he the one? What kind of lover are you? Visit the **Quizzes** area to find out!

♥————————————— **recipes for romance**

Get scrumptious meal ideas with our **Recipes for Romance**.

♥————————————— **romantic movies**

Peek at the **Romantic Movies** area to find Top 10 Flicks about First Love, ten Supersexy Movies, and more.

♥————————————————— **royal romance**

Get the latest scoop on your favorite royals in **Royal Romance**.

♥————————————————————————— **games**

Check out the **Games** pages to find a ton of interactive romantic fun!

♥————————————————— **romantic travel**

In need of a romantic rendezvous? Visit the **Romantic Travel** section for articles and guides.

♥————————————————————— **lovescopes**

Are you two compatible? Click your way to the **Lovescopes** area to find out now!

HARLEQUIN® ♥♥

makes any time special—online...

Visit us online at
www.eHarlequin.com

Corruption, power and commitment...

TAKING THE HEAT

A gritty story in which single mom and prison guard Gabrielle Hadley becomes involved with prison inmate Randall Tucker. When Randall escapes, she follows him—and soon the guard becomes the prisoner's captive... and more.

"Talented, versatile Brenda Novak dishes up a new treat with every page!"

—*USA TODAY* bestselling author Merline Lovelace

brenda novak

Available wherever books are sold in February 2003.

HARLEQUIN®
Makes any time special®

Visit us at www.eHarlequin.com

PHTTH

On the lookout for captivating courtships
set on the American frontier?
Then behold these rollicking romances
from Harlequin Historicals.

On sale January 2003

THE FORBIDDEN BRIDE
by Cheryl Reavis
*Will a well-to-do young woman defy
her father and give her heart to
a wild and daring gold miner?*

HALLIE'S HERO
by Nicole Foster
*A beautiful rancher joins forces
with a gun-toting gambler to save her spread!*

On sale February 2003

THE MIDWIFE'S SECRET
by Kate Bridges
*Can a wary midwife finally find love and acceptance
in the arms of a ruggedly handsome sawmill owner?*

THE LAW AND KATE MALONE
by Charlene Sands
*A stubborn sheriff and a spirited saloon owner
share a stormy reunion!*

 Harlequin Historicals®
Historical Romantic Adventure!

Visit us at www.eHarlequin.com

HHWEST23